Copyright © 2026 by Kat Mellon

All rights reserved.

No part of this publication may be reproduced, distributed, or transmitted in any form or by any means, including photocopying, recording, or other electronic or mechanical methods, without the prior written permission of the publisher, except as permitted by U.S. copyright law. For permission requests, contact kat@katmellon.com.

The story, all names, characters, and incidents portrayed in this production are fictitious. No identification with actual persons (living or deceased), places, buildings, and products is intended or should be inferred.

ISBN-13: 9780984947379
Book Cover Design by Kat Mellon of Bad Kat Studio
Interior Formatting by Kat Mellon of Bad Kat Studio
Editing by English Proper Editing Services
First edition 2026

DEDICATION

To my therapists, my medications, and to glorious caffeine. I couldn't have written this book without you.

So Far Away addresses sensitive topics such as addiction and the death of a young sibling. The story also includes mentions of suicide and infant loss. For a full, up-to-date list of content warnings, please visit katmellon.com.

CHAPTER ONE
Elizatine

When I saw the ads online for Thera Quest Inc.'s experimental group therapy service, I was hooked.

The idea of going on a simulated quest for self-discovery with fellow sufferers? Incredible. I'm a bitch with a shopping addiction, so I've been suffering in style. Ever since I was old enough to hold a quarter, I was destined to consume. I was also destined to be a nervous wreck that only the siren call of a clearance rack could soothe, and the pair have worked their dark magic to fuck up my life ever since.

Two months after I signed up for TQI's treatment lottery, my long-time boyfriend called it quits. He blamed our incompatibility on my lifestyle, which I couldn't argue with. How does a minimalist deal with a packrat who loves a good bargain, the thrill of the hunt? Who'd rather browse the racks during a sale than have vanilla sex with the lights turned down? I got it, truly, I did, but the breakup still stung nonetheless. It was clear to me that my way of life had become unsustainable, and I begged the overlords above to please, *please* make me one of the lucky few who made it into the program.

TQI made some bold claims, but the best one of all—that you'll emerge from your Quest a fundamentally changed person—was what stood out to me the most. They claimed they could cure urges. Gambling, drinking, even shopping. And I'm no Slim Jim either; my consumption kink has me packing on the pounds, although they're mercifully distributed in an hourglass shape along my average-height body. Men would describe me as "buxom;" I would describe myself as a problem.

My parents named me Elizatine, of all things. They couldn't decide between my grandmother's names, Elizabeth and Christine, so they decided to *Renesmee* the thing and call it a day. Eliza, like Elizabeth, plus tine, like the tines of a fork. I like to think they forgot how Christine is pronounced.

Coincidentally, my work involves forks and spoons. I take antique silver cutlery and turn it into custom jewelry. Rings, necklaces, bracelets, you name it. Between my hair—orange on the left half, platinum on the right—and my spoon-ring-adorned hands, I'm hard to miss at craft shows. Kids call me the Spoon Lady.

Well, kids, the Spoon Lady has been in group therapy for two whole months and is about to embark on the biggest, most experimental quest of her life.

There are six of us in the program. Three women, three men. The youngest is a girl named Amara. She's Middle Eastern as far as I can tell, with a big beautiful smile and rounded glasses. She uses a wheelchair due to having POTS, a syndrome that causes her to pass out from standing too quickly. She always shows up to group with her hair in a low ponytail that looks slept in. She's the type to spout off facts about the most obscure shit you've ever heard of, which I appreciate, but it's not always at the most appropriate times.

The other woman, Lana, is an alcoholic who won't admit she's an alcoholic. She's a dark-skinned Mexican lady with short, wavy, graying hair pulled back in a low, messy bun. She, too, boasts a wide white smile. Lana clearly exercises and takes care of herself; I couldn't believe it when she told us she was in her fifties.

Next is Tanner, a gentle guy in his forties with a heavy-lidded, Leonardo DiCaprio-level squint and navy-blue eyes. He runs his hands through his dark-blond hair whenever he's anxious, and he's quick to comfort us whenever anyone gets too worked up over the subject matter. Religious, big drinker.

Felix is a short and incredibly attractive thirty-something like me. White mixed with something I'm not quite sure of, a smolder that could melt steel, and the most perfectly tousled brown hair, just long enough to tuck back behind his ears. He's depressed, but doesn't know why because his life is "so great."

In contrast to Felix is the final guy, Rowan, who looks a bit like Felix if you stretched his features out horizontally in Photoshop. Wide-set eyes, a broad Roman nose, and an attitude more insufferable than a no-return policy. I don't know how he made it so far in this program when he clearly doesn't give a damn. He's snarky, rude, and a general mood-killer among a group of otherwise charming people. I keep holding out hope that TQI will drop him, but alas—he's still here, getting hooked up to the same bucketload of nodes as the rest of us.

We're in a sterile, white room, lined up against the wall in beds attached to the most futuristic-looking control board I've ever seen. I glance over at Amara to my left, who looks reasonably terrified. To my right, Tanner stares stoically at the ceiling as a nurse places various needles in his skin. I'm not the best with needles, so I imagine myself in my happy place—the thrift store on a sale day—as the prodding and poking begins.

The ins and outs were explained to us in a way we could understand. We'll be placed in a virtual simulation, where we will most likely become detached from our memories of the real world. Our vices and struggles, alas, will remain, so I'll probably still be grabbing at virtual shit and trying to buy it. I wonder how Lana and Tanner will do, knowing they can get away with drinking without affecting their mortal bodies. I can't help but think how counterproductive that aspect of the simulation might be. In addition to a group quest, we'll have a quest of our own to tackle—something unknown to us, but that will remove us from the simulation once it's been completed regardless of the group quest's status.

The amount of time that will pass in real life should be negligible, a matter of minutes, but the experiences in the simulation could potentially last a lifetime. The prospect of spending a lifetime in a simulation terrifies me, but at least I won't remember it; no conscious memories are formed during the simulation, although the deeper, more meaningful lessons learned are retained forever, hence TQI's bold claims of lasting change.

"You ready?" a voice asks me. It's not one of the techs; it's Tanner from the bed over. It's just like him to check on everyone.

"Yeah," I say, closing my eyes as another apparatus pokes into the skin of my temples. "I don't know about you, but I'm ready for the elf ears."

The forms we filled out before the simulation were extensive, exhaustive, all-around time consuming, but my favorite part was that we had the option to select if we wanted elf ears. "Just a fun little extra," they said, as TQI is preparing to add more fantasy character options to their offerings in the future. How could I say no?

"Same," Tanner says to me with a chuckle.

"What elf ears?" Rowan asks from the bed beyond Tanner's.

"There was a place to check it off on the form," I hear Felix say in his usual chipper tone. "You didn't do it?"

"No, I didn't fuckin' do it," Rowan grumbles. "Didn't see *elf ears* anywhere on there."

Rowan would be better suited to some little devil horns in my opinion, but I digress.

"You good, ladies?" Tanner asks, gesturing at Amara and Lana beyond me. Amara nods and gives a thumbs up, clearly scared but putting on a brave face. Lana looks relaxed and unbothered as the nodes clamp down around her temples. Based on our time in the group together, I'd guess that she probably showed up to this procedure drunk. And why wouldn't she? I nearly did the same myself. I've never been great with medical settings, plus the experimental aspect of this has me shitting my pants a little.

I'm glad I'm next to Tanner. I'd turn scarlet next to the smoking-hot presence that is Felix, and Rowan would make me irrationally irritated with his sourpuss attitude.

"What about you, Tanner?" I ask, and he seems surprised by my question. As if he didn't expect anyone to ask him the same in return. "Calm, cool, collected?"

"Not really," he says, although his countenance suggests otherwise. "Never done anything like this before."

As if *any* of us have, but I nod my head and smile anyway.

"I did shrooms a couple of times," Felix supplies, raising his voice a little to reach the rest of us. "I bet the simulation will be similar. The trips were *incredible*. You guys ever do magic mushrooms?"

I highly doubt any of the rest of us boring-ass people have tried magic mushrooms, but before anyone can answer, our therapist claps her hands together from beyond Lana's bed.

"It's time, guys!" she shouts in her thick Boston accent. She's a short, spritely woman with spikey-layered black hair and big brown eyes. "Remember, you'll find me almost right away. I'll look a little different, but I'll be there with you nearly every step of the way."

Our lucky therapist gets to keep all of her memories during the whole process. What a dream job that must be—like getting to watch a movie unfold in real time with characters who are stranger than fiction, bitching while fighting their inner demons.

If I can ever get my act together, maybe I'd like to work here someday.

The lights dim, leaving a sea of glowing lights from the control panels and the nodes in our heads. Fear bubbles up in my chest, but I try to hold it down. Next to me, Amara lets out a soft sob. She's a sensitive girl, but she's holding herself together better than I thought she would.

I can't believe I'm doing this.

"Your TheraQuesting session is about to begin," a voice says from the room's speakers. "Please count down from 10…9…8…"

I take a deep breath and count down with the voice, my words shaky. A sudden coldness fills the room, along with a wooziness that feels thicker to wade through than an overstuffed clothing rack. It's getting harder to count along.

5…4…3…

There's no use fighting it. I'm done for. I let my eyes close as the simulation sweeps my mind up in its strange, unknowable embrace.

When I open my eyes, I'm standing in a lightly wooded clearing. The world around me doesn't appear cartoonish like I feared it would—it looks legitimate, taken straight out of reality. The rest of the group stands around me. Lana and Rowan's eyes are open, and the rest soon follow. We're all wearing the same thing: a basic black t-shirt, gray pants, and black sneakers.

"Yeah!" Felix shouts as he reaches up to his ears, which are now comedically elongated to elf-like proportions. "Legolas *who*, bitch?"

I thought the dude couldn't get any hotter, but I was clearly wrong.

"Urgh," Amara groans from beside me. "Still have the wheelchair. Figures I'd still have POTS in here. You guys couldn't let me walk?!"

"They made you just as annoying, too," Rowan mutters under his breath. Stuff like this is why I find him so irritating. Here's someone trying to get help, and he insults them at every turn? Amara's barely an adult, sure, but you're in your damn *thirties*, dude—act like it.

The smell of the ocean hits me, and I turn around to look at what's behind us. We're high on a cliff, and the ocean laps gently at the shoreline below, stretching as far as the eye can see. Ahead is a well-defined, snaking path leading to an indeterminable location.

I look at my fellow group members and reach for my own ears. Everyone but Rowan is sporting sexy, long elf ears, which gives me a feeling of satisfaction. Good. Let him feel left out.

"You guys look great," I start to say, but I'm interrupted by a small scream from something behind me.

"*Huuuuumaaaaaaans!*" screeches a tiny voice. Perched upright on a rock at the edge of the cliff is the tiny, unholy matrimony of a frog and a dachshund, its body long and hairy with a generously plump stomach. Its eyes bulge aggressively, and an array of sticky frog toes smattered with patchy hair splay across the rock face.

"The fuck kind of AI shit is this?" Rowan mutters as the creature continues to scream, and for once, I have to agree with him. The creature's eyes bulge even wider as it stares at us, snarling with dog-like teeth and flaring its frog nostrils wide.

Jeez, I've seen less scary stuff in my *nightmares*. Is this what the simulation is going to be like? Just abomination after abomination? No wonder they make us forget everything afterwards.

"*Dissguuustiing!*" another voice, slightly higher-pitched than the last, shrieks back.

"You know, we *just* got here," Felix says, crouching down to examine the creatures more closely. "Can you give us a chance, please? We're not going to hurt you."

The creatures gaze at him, then look up at his ears in unison.

"*The eeaaarss! Oh, they are the looong-ears! We has nothing to feeeaar!*" the first creature exclaims. The flared nostrils and vicious snarl disappear, leaving an oddly charming and warted creature with a happy dog smile and floppy ears in its place. "*'Tis the shoooort-ears we cannot staaand!*"

As much as the guy grates me, I move my body in front of Rowan to block him from view—the only one of us not sporting long ears.

"Can you tell us if there are any other humans around here?" I ask the first creature. I feel slightly ridiculous. I don't know what I was expecting to see in the simulation, but it wasn't tiny, shrieking dog-frogs. "Any safe places to go?"

"*The wiiiiiitch,*" says the second creature. "*Down the roooaad.*"

I don't know if I like the sound of visiting a witch down the road. I've heard the story of Hansel and Gretel, thank you. I'm no kid anymore, but there's a lot of meat on me and I'm not sure I want to take any chances.

"Do we even have any supplies?" Rowan grumbles. "Are we just going in there blind, or what?"

He has a point. None of us have stopped to check if we have anything on us that could be useful. Weapons, food, clothing. To my absolute dismay, I only have the clothes on my back and my favorite silver spoon jewelry on my fingers. No one else has anything either, save for Amara's wheelchair and a facsimile of the overstuffed planner she carries everywhere. It isn't even the motorized wheelchair she normally wrangles; it's a basic one, the kind that requires a lot of upper body strength to use.

"Guess we're gonna go see a witch," Tanner says with a shrug.

"Hope she doesn't bake us all into a pie," Lana chimes in jokingly. "God, I could use a drink right now. She'd better splash us with some cooking wine."

The dog-frog creatures hop away as we start down the path before us. Tanner offers to push Amara's wheelchair, Felix sidles up beside me, and Rowan lurks behind the rest of us.

It's wild that I can feel a light breeze right now. Frankly, the depth of detail in this simulation blows my mind. I would absolutely believe this was real life if I didn't know better. Even the rocks below our feet are unique and textured. I can't imagine how much resources it's taking for us to be in here, how many hundreds of thousands of gallons of water this quest must be consuming.

I hope it's worth it.

"I kind of want one of those things as a pet," Felix tells me with a grin, gesturing back to where we came from. "Can you imagine hearing that voice all of the time? *Feeeeeed ussss! Take usss for waaaaaalkiiiesss!*"

"Oh, *hell* no," I say. "It's like Jar Jar Binks and a gremlin rolled into one. I couldn't handle that."

The witch's house appears as we turn a corner in the path. It's exactly the kind of house I'd expect a witch to live in—cozy, backing an enormous tree that seems to be growing out of the house itself. Two cobblestone steps lead to a large, arched wooden door, surrounded by little white and pink flowers growing wildly from the ground and the window boxes. The house is an A-frame, the sides bowing slightly as if the inside is overstuffed. Moss and berries climb the shingles of the roof and into the tree branches above. The windows are aglow with a warm orange light, suggesting someone is indeed home and ready to receive us. I can't help but think that I'd love to have a studio like this. My current setup is a folding table from Walmart in my studio apartment, but a cottage like this out in the woods where I could tinker with my silverware all day?

Pure heaven.

Felix confidently strides forward and knocks on the door, humming an unfamiliar tune under his breath. As if she were expecting us, the witch unlocks the giant door and beckons for us to come inside.

"Come, come, you lot. Get in here," she says.

But her voice isn't witch-like at all—no cackling, sinister tone, or high-pitched snickering. If anything, she has a thick Boston accent.

The first thing I notice about the witch is that she has three eyes. Two where they'd usually be, but the third is all pupil and blinks out of sync on her forehead. She's relatively young, maybe Tanner's age, with pale skin, stern eyebrows, long, pointed ears, and waist-length black hair tied into two messy braids. She wears a black gown with lacy sleeves and an upside-down triangle of lace beneath her chest traveling down to her navel, and dons a stylish witch's hat with a full, wide brim.

In other words, she's a hot-ass witch and everything I aspire to be.

The witch retreats as the six of us spill into her kitchen. Behind me, the cobblestone steps flatten themselves into a ramp for Amara's wheelchair; it's nice to see they're taking accommodations seriously in here.

"I'm Airthsept," the witch announces in her thick accent. "Welcome to my humble home. Well, it's not really so humble in my opinion, but you know what they say."

Airthsept's home is beautiful. Everything is wooden, of course, and the back wall is interrupted by the base of the tree visible from the outside of her house. In front of the tree is a work desk with a variety of tools and jars scattered around. The kitchen counter overlooks a large arched window on the left, and open shelves with an assortment of jars overtake the walls. To the right, a crackling fireplace burns near a few small floor cushions. Lana sits on one of the cushions with her back to the fire, but the rest of us remain standing.

"Thank you for having us," Felix begins, charming as ever. "Some little creatures told us to come this way—that you might be able to help us?"

"Oh, the Grokes?" the witch asks. "Big eyes, floppy ears? They'd be right. I'm a helper, that's what I do. Here, you," she says, pointing to Felix, "you first. Come here."

She gestures for him to sit down with her at her work table, and he obliges.

"My, what a handsome one," she says, running a long-nailed hand across his sunken cheekbones with curiosity. "A charmer. I know what you need."

She quickly gets to work chopping strange items and adding them to a jar; a couple of shakes later, the ingredients turn into a dark purple liquid.

"Drink," she tells him, eyeing me next. "You, come here."

While Felix eyes the concoction with trepidation, he rises from the seat and I take his place.

"Hold my hands," she instructs, and I comply. Her hands are ice cold against mine. "Hmm. You are large, beautiful. You crave…more."

She kicks at a trunk beneath the desk and pulls out a small crossbody purse. Brown, leather, and otherwise nondescript.

"For you," she says, handing it to me. This thing won't hold shit, but I thank her anyway and move so the next person can have their turn.

"You," she says, pointing to Amara. She wheels herself across the floor to Airthsept. "You resent this contraption and wish to be free of it. Well, then, be free!"

The witch rubs her hands together, mutters something low, then claps her hands against Amara's chest. Amara lunges forward and screams as a pair of enormous black wings shoot from her back, fanning out to catch her fall from her wheelchair.

Felix takes one look before chugging his drink.

"Can I be next?" Lana asks from beside the fireplace. "That shit was *cool*."

"Ah, yes," Airthsept says to Lana. "You. You desire control, power. Drink this," she says, gesturing to a jar that's already on her shelf. "Just a little bit," she warns.

Lana leaps up and unscrews the lid of the jar, not hesitating even a second before taking a large swig.

"So, what's this do?" Lana asks, wiping her mouth with the back of her hand.

"Look into the fire and command it as you wish."

"Well, I wish for it to pour me a stiff one," Lana says, but nothing happens.

"I'm not a fire, but *I* can do that," the witch says with a smirk. She opens a cabinet door and pulls out what looks to be a bottle of booze. "Ask the flames to do that which only a fire can do."

"I want you to grow bigger," Lana says jokingly, staring at the fire. She and I let out a scream as the fire surges past the fireplace, scalding the floor before it with hot ash. Tanner runs over to check on us, but no one is hurt—just freaked the hell out.

"And you two," she says, looking between Tanner and Rowan. "Your gifts are to be kept to yourselves. Come."

Airthsept shoos the rest of us back outside. Amara is struggling to stay in her wheelchair due to the bulk of her wings, and I help her push them out behind the wheelchair so she can rest against the backrest again. It occurs to me that my purse is probably more than meets the eye, so I stick a hand in. Strange—I can't feel the bottom no matter how far I stuff my hand down.

"Do you feel any different?" I ask Felix, and he shakes his head.

"Not really," he says with a lopsided smile. "Just a little sleepy."

"I'm great," Lana says, sipping the *stiff one* the witch poured for her inside the cottage. "Never felt better. Just a little headache from the screamin', that's all."

Tanner and Rowan join us outside soon after, and neither say a word about what the witch did for them. Tanner looks content, whereas Rowan is glowering. Guess he doesn't like whatever it was she thought would befit an asshole.

"By the way," Airthsept says from her doorway, "there's a village not far from here. Real small, just a couple of buildings. Has everything you need for your first night here. A tavern, a clothing shop, places to stay. And your gifts will carry you far—but as with all magic, there's a cost. You four,"—she points to everyone but Tanner and Rowan—"you'll learn that cost soon enough."

Oh, great. So it's going to be like having a hotel mini fridge; tempting to use, but unjustifiably expensive. What's the point of giving us powers and magical items, then? To torture us a little?

"Well, I wish you luck!" the witch says, and then she slams her door shut in our faces. The locks click shut quite loudly and emphatically.

Well, damn. Did something happen to me when I stuck my hand in the bag? Is it going to curse me? Should I throw it away and forget I ever got it? Then again, the other women received something helpful; maybe there will be times when its usefulness outweighs the price the witch was talking about.

I'm starting to notice that the details I remembered about my life outside the simulation are fading. I was upset about something, someone; but who? I know I worked as a jeweler. I still remember how to make a spoon ring. But family, friends, that kind of thing? The memories of them, the pain feels so out of reach now. I suppose that's fine. I have five people with me right now who need me here and present, and I certainly need them, too. I wonder if everyone else is forgetting right along with me.

"Are we sure this bitch didn't just curse us?" Rowan asks. "Maybe we shouldn't listen to those frog things anymore."

"The Grokes," Amara interjects proudly. She opens up her planner, and stickers fall to the wayside as she leafs through for an empty page.

"Whoa," I say, glancing at the pages. "Your handwriting. It's gibberish."

Sure enough, her journal entries and notes look like they were turned into AI slop, like text in a dream that you're desperately trying to make sense of, but the letters keep changing. Her cute, slightly messy writing has been replaced, no doubt due to the loss of her memories and the strict protocols around the simulation itself.

"Oh. I hope I can still write in here," she says, sounding agitated. She takes out her pen and tries to write down *The Grokes*, and her attempt works. She closes the planner and reopens it to the same page, and the words remain.

"Write down *Rowan's brother*," Rowan offers in an uncharacteristically helpful manner. I can't remember why his brother is important—guess that's the memories from our group sessions fucking off—but she gives it a try. Within seconds, her handwriting warps into the same unreadable slop as the rest of her earlier notes.

"I guess I can only record new memories," Amara says, disappointment filling her voice. I remember she's scared of forgetting things. "And I'm sure they'll disappear once we're out of the simulation. I'll do what I can."

It seems Amara is taking it upon herself to be our note-taker, which is great because fantasy terms don't stick in my brain. Airthsept? Grokes? You bet I need that absolute *nonsense* written down for me.

"Let's keep going," Felix offers helpfully. Lana sets her empty glass down on a tree trunk, and I sling my new bag across my body, not quite ready to chuck it into the woods just yet in case it comes in handy for something fabulous. "We'll find the village, come up with a plan, maybe even get our group quest."

As we set off toward what is hopefully the village, we chat about what we still remember of our pre-simulation lives.

"I remember pain," Tanner says. "And that I'm a man of faith. *God Bless America*, that kind of guy. Drank too much. Can't remember what my job was, though."

"I remember my faith, too!" Amara interjects. "Alhamdulillah! Plus the POTS, of course. I wish I could forget it."

"I remember my family's band," Felix says, which surprises me. "Touring with them. Singing and playing sax. Weird thing is that I can't picture what my family looks like anymore, just that they were…*there*. All together in a circle, playing shows. They're faceless now."

"I remember my good-for-nothing husband," Lana chimes in. "Well, sort of. Just that I'm angry at him and that he's good-for-nothing. Couldn't tell you why or how, though."

"Elizatine?" Felix asks. "What about you? You remember anything?"

"I remember how to make my jewelry, at least," I say. "And that I have a big fat shopping addiction. Nothing else is sticking out anymore."

A couple of us turn to look at Rowan.

"Pass," he says. "None of your business."

No one wants to press him for more details, so the conversation ends in silence. Soon, it's the six of us walking toward a big unknown, bracing ourselves for the beginning of our self-discovery. It's scary not to remember the details of who I am, to feel like I have an incomplete picture of myself. I suppose I still have my essence, the things that fundamentally make me, *me*. I still have empathy. I still want the best for the people around me, even Rowan. I want to see them smile, to feel fulfilled. Maybe that can be enough.

Maybe *I'll* be enough.

CHAPTER TWO
Elizatine

After a little over half an hour of walking, the village comes into view. It's as small as the witch made it out to be—if you could even call it a village. I suspect it's just a collection of buildings tailored to our interests and nothing more. A clothing store? In this setting? *Please.* That has *Elizatine* written all over it. I'll be in there putting together the most killer questing outfit you've ever seen. And then you've got the tavern, which every single one of us has a reason to enjoy—some more than others, of course. Felix will want to perform; me, Grumpy, and Happy might want to drink; and may Lana and Tanner find the will to abstain altogether.

Tanner has the better chance of success from the simulation, in my opinion. Lana has done nothing but drink since we got here. I don't need to drink; I'd rather spend all of my time with the clothes, my personal canvas. I'll get the same kind of high, plus I can finally see what this leather purse is really capable of holding.

If what I suspect about this purse is true, then I can pack a whole wardrobe in here. I suppose the real question is if I can afford whatever they're charging.

The unquestionably coolest part about this little village is the inn. It's a mixture of little Hobbit cottages built into a hillside and treehouses in the trees growing directly above them. If given the choice, I'm down for a treehouse—I love being perched up high with a view. It might even help us get a sense of where we're headed next.

"Tell you what," Felix says to the group as we take in our surroundings. "Let's start at the tavern, get our bearings, and then split up from there. We'll regroup when the sun goes down and then head to the inn for the night. That sound like a plan to everyone?"

No one has anything better to suggest, so we all agree; never mind that Tanner and Lana have no business setting foot in a tavern. Part of me is tempted to babysit them and keep them from entertaining their inner demons, but the other part of me is drawn to the clothing store like a cartoon duck to a fragrant, simmering soup.

The inside of the tavern is interesting. It's medieval-style, with washed brick flooring, pale gray stone walls, arched windows, and high ceilings with wooden beams stretching overhead. There's also a chandelier and hanging pendant lights that would clearly need to run on electricity. The bar itself sits under a second floor balcony, the perfect place to deliver a dramatic speech before swinging down on the chandelier to start a bar fight. In the same type of wood as the bar are a smattering of rectangular tables and bar chairs gathered beneath arched windows.

I've never seen anything quite like it before. It's anachronistic, but why wouldn't it be? We're in a simulation with witches and dog-frog creatures. It's only going to get crazier from here.

The five of us pile into one of the tables, and Amara pulls herself up along one of the free table edges. There are several other patrons in the bar, including a shadowy figure with their hood pulled up.

Definitely not ominous whatsoever.

"It's occurring to me that we don't have any money…" Felix says, glancing around nervously.

"Money?" a deep voice asks from beside us. "I can help with that."

I glance up expecting to see a large man standing before us, but my eyes are met with yet another unholy abomination. The lower body of this creature is human, sure, but wrapped around its neck are four pimply toad appendages leading up to a squashed, Gollum-like green head covered in scaly-toad skin. The creature's toad fingers strum together from beneath its chin, and its large, sunken eyes survey each of us in turn. Its nose and ears are pink and rounded, in a drunkard sort of way.

"Name's Lisft," the creature says, its voice gravelly. "Are you adventurers? I've been waiting for someone to take me up on my quest."

All of us perk up at the sound of a quest. Of course! That's one of the things we're here for; the group project that will help heal our festering emotional wounds.

"We're down for a quest," Felix says, sticking his hand out high for a handshake. The creature frowns and swats his hand away.

"Disgusting," the creature says. "Anyway, I have a proposition for you. My brother, the absolute fool, has left me with this…this *terrible* book of his that I never wanted. It's cursed, you see. No one should dare touch it. They would meet a terrible fate that only a great deal of magic could undo. I would like you to return it to him. He lives on the other side of The Trembling Forest and the Beasteous Bog. I will pay you handsomely for completing this task—half now, and half upon delivery."

We have no money and no quest, so the proposition is a no-brainer—of course, transporting a cursed book doesn't sound like the safest option, but I suppose that's why he's paying so handsomely.

"Sir," Felix begins, "we—"

"Ma'am," the creature corrects with a look of displeasure. "Continue."

"Ma'am," Felix says, flustered. "We accept your quest."

"Well, *that* was simple," the creature says. "I expected more resistance. After all, this is a book of great power. Anyone who touches it shall—"

"Yeah, yeah, they'll be cursed, whatever," Rowan interjects. "So, we'll take the book and the payment now. A few of us could *really* use a drink," he says, patting Lana and Tanner on their shoulders. Tanner chuckles uncomfortably.

The creature smiles.

"A short-eared human," she says. "Ah, yes. Lisft likes this one."

The creature places a satchel on our table and lifts out an object wrapped thickly in animal skins—no doubt the cursed book. She drops it with a loud *thunk*, followed by the delicate tinkling of coins from a small leather coin pouch.

"Here," the creature says, and she disperses ten gold coins to each of us. "This is more than enough to tide you over for your quest. Spend it wisely. I will give you no more until your quest is complete. Get this book as far away from Lisft as you can! Disgusting, vile book! Lisft hates books, but Lisft especially hates *this* book!"

"What does your brother look like?" I ask, since no one else has thought to ask yet. If this is what the females look like, I can't even begin to imagine how fearsome a male must be.

"Glaks is hideous," the creature says. "The opposite of me! Ey, look for a fellow with the body of a frog and the head of a short-ear human. He is a collector of rare books! He will stop at nothing to add a new book to his collection! Except for *this* book, that rotten, ungrateful little spawn…"

I'm pretty sure someone smashed a bunch of keys on a keyboard to come up with these creature's names, but I keep my thoughts to myself.

"Have a good evening," the creature says. She slings her satchel back over her shoulders with her human arms and straightens out its placement with one of her toad appendages. "And do *not* touch the book!"

"Yeah, we got it," Rowan says as the toad creature whose name I already forgot exits the tavern. "I don't know about you guys, but I'm getting a drink."

"Right behind ya," Lana says. She grabs Rowan by the upper arm, and the two head over to the bartender while the rest of us sit and contemplate our next move. Felix is eyeing a guitar propped conspicuously by the small stage on the opposite side of the bar, Amara is rifling through her distorted notes, and Tanner is looking back and forth between the bar and the cursed book.

I reach out and put my hand over Tanner's and shake my head. Lana has yet to acknowledge she has a problem, but Tanner has been sober for a month. I'm not letting him ruin that if I can help it.

"I'll go scout out the inn," Tanner says, clearing his throat in what I assume is embarrassment. "See how much it costs, what we're working with."

Felix is already picking up the guitar and tuning it. You can't take the performer out of the guy. I respect it. Part of me is tempted to wait around and listen to him sing, but the siren call of the clothing store is getting louder and louder by the minute.

"Amara, where do you want to go?" I ask, hoping she's a bit of a girly-girl like me. "Please say it's the clothing store. We need to put something killer together."

"You read my mind!" she exclaims. Somewhere along the way, the giant wings protruding from Amara's back disappeared; it seems she's able to summon and hide them at will. "I need something backless in case *those things* come back out again," she adds with a shudder. "It feels like a charlie horse in my back when they come out. Just awful."

The three of us leave the tavern. Tanner heads for the inn, and I help push Amara toward the store. A quick peek inside makes it clear that this is another anachronistic abomination, although one I very much approve of; it's the equivalent of a contemporary resale store inside of a medieval building, complete with stone and wood hangers and surfaces.

What catches my attention are the sprawl of open wooden trunks to the side of the building with a *70% Off!* sign taped to each. While Amara browses the inside of the store, I crouch down and begin digging through what's peeking out of the chests. It's the coolest stuff I've ever seen—sequined corsets, medieval bodices with floofy sleeves, all manner of intricately decorated leggings, even the most adorable, old-timey stuffed animals. It isn't lost on me that just about everything is a size 3X; there was no doubt in anyone's mind that I would be the only one drawn to this stuff. I pile it high in my arms, the familiar thrill washing over me tenfold.

This feels better than my best thrift hauls; it feels like a dream come to life, the kind of dream where you find an absolute treasure trove of the thing you love. I can see the potential in it all; the combinations, the outfits, how nice it would be to have it. I grab as much as I can carry before bringing it into the store and dropping it on an empty, wooden counter set atop pale gray stones, before going back outside for another round of digging.

A creature turns to look at me as I return, looking rather judgmental as they survey my damage. It's yet another frog-hybrid, this time with a deer body and a frog face with sweet little deer ears poking out of the side of its head. It strikes me as funny that the creature is entirely nude save for an elaborate necklace made of metal zippers.

What is the deal with all of these frogs? Someone in the group must have mentioned them on their intake form. I'm no fantasy buff, but shouldn't there be dragons and hot centaurs roaming around instead?

The pile is massive now, and I'm feeling a little ashamed as the creature rises to its hind-legs to start counting up my total. I add a large water bottle, a pack each of underwear and socks, and a hat to the pile since I figure I'll need those.

"Five credits," the creature rasps quietly. "No refunds."

At seventy percent off, I don't particularly care. I pass half of my coins over, and the creature uses its hoof to push them into a large glass jar below the counter. I hear the bell on the door jingle, and a slightly drunk Rowan strides in.

"What the *fuck*, Elizatine?" he asks, eyeing my pile of loot. "You're seriously getting *all* of that? Why?"

"It's cute," I say lamely, but the truth is that I couldn't really stop myself. There were too many decisions to make at once, and too much potential to leave behind. Plus, I've got a secret up my sleeve that will shut him right up.

I open the flap of my purse and begin to stuff things inside.

"How's that supposed to work?" Rowan asks with a laugh, but then he pauses as the pile continues to disappear into my tiny little crossbody bag. As I suspected, it's something akin to bottomless; I can tote around as much shit as I want. It's not even getting heavier.

As I push more of the clothing into my bag, I notice that my forearm looks a little bigger than before. Am I allergic to something I touched in those chests? Maybe I was bitten by something. I'll look myself over later.

I continue to load up my bag. My sweatpants are suddenly feeling tight.

A few more shirts later, and the shirt I'm wearing pops some stitches.

What the fuck is going on?

"Oh, that's *brutal*," Rowan says, stifling a laugh. "You'd better look in a mirror."

The doorbell chimes again, and the rest of the group walks through the door just in time for my shirt and bra to rip completely off of my body. I grab at my chest to cover it up, but there's too much of me. Tanner immediately grabs a large cardigan to drape over my exposed body while Rowan cackles in the background.

"Holy shit," Lana mumbles. "Girl, what the hell *happened* to you?"

It's a good question. Rowan pulls a mirror on wheels forward from the back wall, and that's when I'm able to see for myself what everyone else is ogling at.

I weigh at least six hundred pounds.

So, *that's* the price of my magic, then—whatever I carry in this bag gets added to my physical weight. I'm already pretty thick to begin with. I'll only be able to carry the bare essentials if I want to feel comfortable in my own skin, plus maybe a backpack for good measure.

Feeling defeated, I pin the cardigan under my armpits and begin to pull things back out of the bag. I can feel the rolls rapidly shrinking, my body returning to its usual size. As I do this, the creature's quiet words repeat in my mind.

"No refunds."

What in the hell am I supposed to do with all of this clothing? Now that I can't carry it with me anymore, I have to leave it behind and let those credits go to waste. I'm much bigger than Amara and Lana; they're not going to want this stuff.

I can't believe I wasted half of my money this early on, and for what? Nothing.

"The inn is six credits a person," Tanner adds, trying to change the subject. I immediately burst into tears because I only have five.

"You're too much, Elizatine," Rowan says from across the room. "You're telling us you can't even afford a room tonight? You really *do* need help."

Tanner puts a hand on my shoulder sympathetically, and the gesture makes me feel like a weight has been lifted. At least *someone* here is showing me kindness. Even Amara, who normally chimes in at the first sign of injustice, has been stunned to silence by my greediness.

Tanner excuses himself as I sit on the floor, stunned by what just happened. Although the burning hot embarrassment has already faded, I can't help but wish everyone would quit staring. But wouldn't *I* stare at such a thing myself, seeing someone stretch out by hundreds of pounds in under a minute? I can't exactly blame them; I know I would have done the same out of sheer human curiosity.

"Well, girl, good luck with that," Lana says with a mix of sincerity and sarcasm. "I'm heading to the inn."

Rowan and Felix follow after her, leaving me and Amara to face my predicament.

"I think I can use this," Amara says, reaching down for a loose-fitting top with white, billowing sleeves. "I don't like stuff to be tight anyway. I'll just wear a belt to cinch it in. Do you maybe want to try some things on, see what works the best?" she asks. "I can give you my opinion."

"I appreciate it, Amara, but I'd better do this by myself," I say. She looks visibly disappointed. "But please, take that top. Take this belt too," I say, handing her one of the three I had added to my pile. "Do what you can with them. I'll meet you guys at the inn a little later."

She pays for her own modest purchases—two credits for a backpack and a pair of brown pants—and takes off, leaving me covering myself with a cardigan on the floor and surrounded by my shame.

I sort through everything as calmly and as carefully as I can. I set aside a henley-collared, off-white baby doll dress to wear as a nightgown, along with a golden, sequined corset that's too cool to leave behind. I play with a couple of options and eventually settle on a low-shouldered, long sleeved corset top in a dark-moss color with gold trim layered beneath a pine-green skirt and brown, embroidered tights. I cinch one brown belt tightly across my waist and let the other sit loosely at my hips. I wrap a long necklace around my neck that dives down into my cleavage like a scared hamster, and I complete the look with the most comfortable pair of shoes in the lot, a pair of brown leather boots that hit my mid-calf area.

For all that embarrassment, I feel pretty gorgeous and vaguely period-appropriate. My boobs look great, too, not that I'm trying to impress anyone.

Well, maybe a little. I shouldn't lie to myself.

I keep the socks and underwear, a light-weight blanket, and the backpack. I allow myself about fifteen pounds worth of stuff in the crossbody bag because anything more starts to make the clothes I'm wearing feel too uncomfortable, and the rest of what I keep will have to fit in the backpack without breaking my stupid back from the weight.

I finally distribute things to my liking, then wave down the frog-deer shopkeeper.

"You're sure you can't take returns?" I ask.

"No returns," the creature repeats emphatically.

"Alright," I say, placing what's left of my haul back on the counter. "It's all yours again, then. I can't take it with me."

As I leave, I see the creature carry the pile outside and dump it right back into the *70% Off!* chest. If this weren't a simulation, I'd be a little offended.

I walk up to the inn feeling heavier and pulled down by the weight of my overstuffed backpack. I wanted to stay in one of the treehouses, but I get the feeling I'll be sleeping outside tonight. Maybe I can crash with Lana or Amara and pay for half of their room.

I sit down on a tree stump and listen to all of the strange sounds around me. In addition to croaking and wheezing, there's birdsong; some kind of intermittent animal noise that sounds like a sob, and the faint strumming of a guitar, no doubt Felix perched high in the trees serenading the wildlife.

"Well, don't you look nice?" asks a voice from beside me. It's Lana, whose complexion looks flushed through her dark skin tone. "Maybe I should get me some fancy clothes. Sweats and a t-shirt don't look right next to all *that*, you know? Wouldn't want you to get all of the attention. Never know when you might have to seduce a frog-man. Man-frog?"

"That's a mean way to talk about Tanner," I joke, and she laughs. Although they're within a decade of each other's ages, and are both attractive and active people, I can't really picture the two of them together. Their auras are so different. Tanner is calm, while Lara is unpredictable— raging like the baited flames in the witch's fireplace.

"Tanner would have to drop all the God shit, and I don't think he'll be doing that anytime soon," Lana says. I don't know what to say to that, so I say nothing at all. "You think God fucks around with simulations?"

I'm a reasonably spiritual person, and I'd never discount someone's religion. It is an interesting question, though, how spirituality would work within the confines of a simulation.

"I guess that would depend on whether or not we're considered *real* in here," I say.

"Ah, not you, too," Lana says. "Great."

I try to change the subject.

"Can I crash with you tonight?" I ask. "I burned through half of my credits on useless shit."

"Oh, and I *didn't*?" she asks, laughing. "Child. I have two credits left to my name, and I only remember *half* of my name now. You still remember your last name?"

Come to think of it, I don't.

"We could pool our money together and get a room," I suggest.

"Oh, didn't you hear?" Lana says. "One person per room. I guess the frog-person running this joint is a prude, thinks we're all going to start sleeping together and pop out thousands of babies overnight or something."

Great. There's no way I'm getting a room tonight, then. There are lots of dried leaves at the bases of the trees; hopefully they'll provide enough cushion for me to sleep comfortably.

"Hey," Tanner says from the distance; hopefully he didn't hear our awkward exchange about God a few minutes ago. "You guys sleeping outside tonight?"

"Not you, too," Lana groans. "You blew through your money already? On *what*?"

"I didn't. I bought a couple of supplies, that's all," he says. He's wearing a coat with a big fur collar and dark, thick pants full of pockets. He gestures to the backpack and rope on his back. "Six coins for one night in a room is *outrageous* compared to what this stuff cost. We'll be fine out here."

We settle down in the leaves. It's actually not half bad. I pass out a couple of my longer clothing items, including a cape, to use as blankets. I'm surprised we need to sleep. Then again, maybe TQI is trying to keep things feeling as authentic as possible. Nothing would surprise me anymore, not even a little frog-caterpillar licking me awake via my ear in the morning. This place is so much like a lucid dream; a place where you're somewhat in control, but the overall framework is batshit crazy.

I'm in the middle of Lana and Tanner. Lana turns her back on us immediately, but Tanner and I talk for a few minutes while laying on our sides.

"Thanks for saving my dignity back there in the store," I say sheepishly. "That whole thing was…humiliating, to say the least."

"Eh, don't mention it," Tanner says. "I'm just glad you're okay."

"And I'm glad you didn't drink tonight," I say.

"Me too," he admits. "The temptation was there, believe me."

We look at each other for a few long seconds.

"Well, good night," I say, rolling on to my back. "Don't let the bed-frogs bite."

Tanner chuckles, and in the high distance, Felix's singing and strumming lulls us to sleep.

CHAPTER THREE
Felix

It feels nice to pick up a guitar. My brother usually handles guitar on everything we play. Pops and I do the vocals, and my sister's on drums. Cousin plays bass. It's been a nice family affair, the five of us touring around. We started pretty young, filming YouTube videos and building a following from our cover albums. Mom and my aunt are our managers. They book the gigs, make the travel arrangements, all that kind of stuff. We just show up and play.

I used to love my life. I craved traveling around and documenting everything. We'd see some of the coolest shit—stuff the average person has no chance of experiencing. I'm grateful for it, truly, I am. But something's been brewing in me for a couple of years, this deep sadness I can't explain because everything in my life is objectively great. I've always wanted to be an entertainer, to have fans—and I *have* them.

So why isn't that enough? Is it that I crave *more*? Surely that can't be the answer. I didn't think TQI would be the answer, either, but I had to try. I owe it to my family to be the best version of myself again, one that doesn't have panic attacks offstage and nearly ruin tours.

I convinced the bartender to let me buy the guitar sitting in the tavern for one credit. After the deal was done, something came over me—I felt like I was about to fall asleep then and there. I'm still a bit groggy, but I've decided to perch myself up on the windowsill in my treehouse room and do a little singing and playing, calm my soul a bit. Then I'll get some sleep.

I re-tune the guitar as best as I can without a tuner, humming to myself as I go along. I suddenly remember playing the saxophone in fifth grade, right when band started up for us little kids. At that age, I wanted to be a rock star. Solo act, me and me alone up there on the big stage. I'd enter all the talent shows—playing sax, singing, dancing, whatever spoke to me that year. I won sometimes.

I loved it.

I don't really shine like that anymore. I'm part of a whole now. Just a piece in a bigger machine. There's no getting off of that train now that I'm on it, though. I don't think my family would ever forgive me.

The last time I saw my cousin, he looked so angry with me. I'd fucked up the sax solo, twisted the head joint at the last second and brought the whole instrument out of alignment. Easily one of the most embarrassing flubs of my career, but I thought he'd get it. Nope. He screamed at me like I was hell-bent on ruining the experience for people on purpose. That I should be embarrassed and "get my shit together." I practice for hours a day when we're not touring—how is that me *not* getting my shit together?

I strum a little louder and start to sing softly. My voice has been shaky lately, although it still sounds pretty good. I've lost that confidence I used to have where I could sing anything, hit those Freddie Mercury highs. Now I have to be careful, shrink back behind my dad. He's a powerhouse. It's easy to fade into the background when I need to hide what a shit job I'm doing.

I'm not sure why I haven't forgotten my real-world life yet. It seems like everyone else has lost theirs, yet mine's still here in mostly-clear detail. It's making it hard to get immersed. I want to enjoy all the little creatures, the quest, the people, but I keep going over my family stuff over and over in my head.

I glance down at the ground. Tanner, Lana, and Elizatine are getting settled under a tree for the night. Smart of them. This room is cool and all, but it was expensive. Would've been wiser to save the credits, probably, but I couldn't turn down the idea of staying in a treehouse. At least I've got an audience. Elizatine kept saying how much she wanted to hear me sing, so I guess this is her chance.

I should have done something to help her in that store, but in that moment, I was just…frozen. Couldn't understand what I was seeing with her there, half-naked and bulging out like someone from *My 600-lb Life*. If it weren't for her distinctive hair, I wouldn't have even recognized her.

She's a nice person. She reminds me of my sister a little. They both smile a lot and like clothes. I guess girls just need a lot of shit to wear sometimes. Do *we* do that to them? Us guys? I hope they don't feel like they need all of that just to impress us. Some of the most beautiful women I've seen are the most plain and understated, just letting their natural beauty shine through. We don't care about sequins and capes. I don't know why they think we do.

I've noticed Elizatine's face turns a little red when she looks at me sometimes. Maybe she's got a crush. I'm not sure she's my type, really, but she is pretty. Just bigger than the other girls I've dated. Maybe I should give her a chance. It's not like she's 600 pounds anymore, and even people *that* big find love. She's just a little overweight, that's all. I'm not perfect, either. I'm shorter than the average guy, got teeth going in different directions, and gas that can clear a room in thirty seconds flat.

But don't they say you shouldn't date people you're doing therapy with? I feel like that's something people must say. Same with dating coworkers.

I couldn't date *my* coworkers even if I wanted to. I think that might be illegal.

I strum a little louder to match my singing. My mind is going a million miles a minute like it always does. Hard to keep my thoughts together. They tend to wander everywhere, and not always to the most helpful places.

I beat myself up a lot over having depression. They tell me it's chemical, that anyone can get it, but why *me*? I've got a great life. A supportive family. They'd do anything for me, absolutely *anything*. They rib on me sometimes, sure, but that's just our dynamic. I don't mind.

And yeah, touring can be a lot, but I wouldn't trade it for anything else. I love living life on the road. Staying put to do this group therapy while a stranger fills in for me has been torture. I just want to get back out there.

I remember the look on Elizatine's face, the moment she realized she fucked up with all those clothes in her bag. That *oh shit* moment.

I think I'm having one of those right now.

Maybe it's not the touring. Maybe it's not my family.

Maybe I just don't like *touring with my family*.

Maybe I'm craving that old feeling of stardom, of individuality. Where people are there for what *I've* made.

Maybe I'm not feeling fulfilled, and maybe I hate what that's doing to me.

But I could never walk away. How could my parents ever forgive me? We're a family band. That's our whole deal, our selling point. My cousin would be *pissed*, I know that much. If he blew up that much over a sax solo, I can't imagine what he'd do if I told him I was leaving the band, leaving *him* after all of these years. We gave up so much of our childhoods for this. It doesn't feel fair to back out now.

I realize I'm singing too damn loud and soulfully now, but I don't care. Maybe I need to let it out, let myself take center stage for once.

I have my own songs. They're there, under my bed in a box. I'm always meaning to record a demo, but it never happens. It's more of a pipe dream at this point. What would it even look like, touring by myself? Taking control of everything? Not falling back on my pops when the decisions get tough? Frankly, I fall back on Pops anytime there's a decision, *period*. I can't remember the last time I got to pick the fast food stop or the catering. Always his decision or my brother's. They never think to ask me.

Maybe I need to be the one making decisions. I had the tiniest taste of that today with people following my lead, and it felt great.

Maybe I need to take the step that feels so impossible. Sit my family down, tell them how I'm *really* feeling. Then again, they'll probably tell me to pop some pills and get over it, to *get back out there*. No, I'd have to straight-up *quit*. Leave no room for negotiation.

What if I can't make it on my own? Would they take me back? Would I be making the stupidest mistake of my life? See, that's what I get hung up on. Not knowing the right thing to do. Well, I know the right thing to do for my *family*. But more and more, the depression is eating at me, and this could be why. Maybe I'm outgrowing the band.

Maybe I need to be someone new—a Felix 2.0.

Post-simulation Felix won't put up with this shit anymore. Felix 2.0 picks the restaurant, plans the tour, writes the songs, greets the fans, does the intro. No answering to anyone else.

Just myself.

"*Noooo moooooooreeee!*" a creature screams from one of the windows. Even from this far away, I can see its eyes bugging out at me. I know it's talking about my singing, but it's bang on about what I'm *thinking* too.

No more family band. No more putting myself second.

I've got to sit them down and tell them I'm fucking done.

CHAPTER FOUR
Elizatine

The morning arrives uneventfully. No wet willies from strange frog creatures. I'm almost disappointed—it would have been exciting, waking up to another artificially-generated creation with more eyes than brains all up in my face.

I can't wait to see what we encounter today.

"Mornin'," Lana says from beside me. She shakes out her hair and pulls it back in a claw-toothed clip. "That's me getting ready. Do we still have to piss in this simulation? I feel like I have to take a piss."

"I don't think so, but I saw bathrooms around the back," Tanner says from beside me, and Lana quickly dashes away.

"You've got a little something in your hair," I tell Tanner, eyeing the leaves sticking out of his disheveled, dark blond mane.

He smirks lightly.

"So do you," he admits.

We take a moment to delicately pick leaves out of each other's hair like monkeys, and then it's time for me to gather up all of the things I loaned out overnight and put them back in my bags. Lana made a good point—do we need to use the bathroom in here? Do we even need to eat or drink, or would it just be for the taste?

"Nothin'," Lana says as she stumbles back to me. Tanner is long gone by now. "Felt like I was about to piss myself, but a whole lot of *nothin'* came out. Just like real life, that fuckin' irritable bladder bullshit. You ever get that? Can't believe I still have it. Thought it'd be like a vacation in here from all my, you know, *ailments*."

She's right. My back *still* hurts from the weight of my blouse clowns. I should have booked that reduction while I still had a chance. It's one of those things that seemed too overwhelming to pursue even though it'd give me a better quality of life. Hunching over my spoons all day, every day has done a number on me.

I'd give anything to have someone just crack my back in half. It might kill me or it might fix me, but I'd win either way.

We meet everyone else outside of the inn as the light peeks over the massive mountain range. I have no idea where we're going from here. Rowan volunteered to take the cursed book with him last night, and he's cradling it like a baby this morning.

"I made a map," Amara announces, opening up her planner to a page near the middle. Some stickers fall out again, and I pick them up and hand them to her. The sticker designs look like pixelated nonsense here in the simulation. "I couldn't make out much from my room, but I drew what I could see. The curves of the road, buildings, stuff leading up to the big forest."

We gather around and look at her sketch. It's confusing, and she has to explain a lot of her notations to us, but it gives us an overview of what's coming up on our quest to deliver this book to the human-frog brother with the gibberish name.

"What's past the forest?" Felix asks.

"Darkness," she says. "It was too hard to make out."

We decide to follow the path that leads out of the town. It seems straightforward enough. As we do, Felix walks up beside me again. God, I hate that everyone saw me at such a low point last night. I felt like a pig at the trough with a spotlight on my bare ass.

"Morning, Elizatine," he says with a lopsided grin that could melt a thousand hearts. "You look beautiful today."

A flurry of butterflies begin rustling in my stomach.

I'm about to thank him when his eyes suddenly close. Felix collapses to the ground, and I'm just barely able to catch his upper body and keep him from thunking his head. I lay him down gently, and everyone gathers around in concern.

I crouch down next to him. He's still breathing; quite evenly, in fact, the way someone would if they were sleeping.

"Did he just…fall asleep?" I ask out loud. I shake his shoulders, but he lets out a snort and continues to lay motionless aside from the rise and fall of his chest.

"Hey, well, being Prince Charming is hard work," Rowan says.

But maybe Rowan's on to something. When I asked everyone if they felt different after the witch had her way with us, Felix said he felt sleepy. Is this the cost of his magic gift? Falling asleep at the most inopportune times?

He did call me beautiful and flash that charming smile of his. Maybe that has something to do with it.

"Wake up, Felix," I say again, shaking him harder. After about a minute, he stirs and squints up at us, the simulated sunlight striking his face.

"Did something happen?" he asks.

"Yeah," I say. "You hit on me, and then you had the audacity to *fall asleep*. You're lucky I was there to catch you."

"Fell asleep, huh?" he asks. He stands up and dusts himself off. "You know, after I haggled this guitar down to one credit, I felt like I was about to fall asleep. Both then and now, I was trying to be…"

He pauses.

"...trying to be charming, I suppose."

"Looks like you'd better stop that," Tanner says.

"Sleeping Beauty. Got it," Rowan chimes in from the back of the group.

"So, it seems your charm is effective," I say, outing myself, "but it comes at a price. Just like my sack of junk."

"I guess so," he says, looking forlorn. I get the feeling his charm is something he relies on heavily.

"So what's *my* cost?" Lana asks. "Never figured that one out."

"Me neither," Amara chimes in. "I'm too scared to bring the wings back out. As cool as flying sounds, I don't need to pass out way above the ground."

"If only you *would*," Rowan says to himself, loud enough for her to hear.

"What's your problem with me?" Amara asks, snapping her head to the side to look at Rowan. "Why can't you just leave me alone?"

"Relax," Rowan says, bored. "I'm an ass to *everyone*, not just you. You're not special."

Amara huffs in frustration.

"Let's just carry on," Felix says, holding his hands up. "I'll lay off the charm. We'd better keep going. This book isn't going to deliver itself."

We start walking again, Felix still at my side.

"I realized something last night," he says. "About my family."

"You still remember them?" I ask. "I can't remember mine at all. I can't even remember my last name."

"Yeah," he says. "I remember everything for some reason. Dad, my brother and sister, my cousin. The whole band."

"You sounded great last night," I say, and it's true—he has a raw, gritty voice with a lot of emotion behind it. I enjoyed listening to him last night underneath the stars. It was quite peaceful. "Thank you for sharing that with us."

"Thank you," he says, suddenly looking a little emotional. "It means a lot. Especially because I—well, I think I figured out why I'm so depressed."

We trudge along a little more before he elaborates. Behind us, Amara and Tanner are chatting about politics—or what little they can remember about politics, anyway.

"I need to quit the band," he finally says. "God, I can't believe I just said that out loud. I need to quit the band and do my own thing. I'm creatively fucked right now. I have so many ideas that go to waste, and it's time for me to bring them into the world. Man, I wish I'd done it sooner."

I wrap my arm around his shoulders sympathetically.

"Hey, I get it," I say. "You've been in that band since you were a kid, right? It's time to let your own talents shine. Charm them all on your own."

"Yeah," Felix says with a wide smile, nodding his head. "I'd like that."

And then Felix disappears.

"The fuck?" Rowan asks, and the rest of us freeze in place. Felix's guitar clatters to the ground along with the rest of his things.

"Is this a joke?" I ask nervously, waving a hand in the space where he just stood. Surely he didn't just complete the simulation. We still have an entire group quest to do. "Felix? Felix, can you hear me?"

"Well, they did say our individual quests outweigh the group quest," Tanner reminds us. "So maybe he's done. Maybe he figured his shit out already."

"He just told me he wants to quit his band," I say. "Go out on his own."

"Good for him," Lana says. "Quick and easy. Me, I'll be stuck in this simulation until the end of time."

I know it's crazy to feel this way, but I'm oddly gutted. We were just starting to talk a little. I wanted to get to know him. He was so ridiculously *hot*. I thought he'd be here longer. I thought all of us as a *group* would be here longer. Who knows how long we'll be living here together? I wasn't ready for things to change, for a big dynamic shift.

And who's supposed to be the leader now?

"Sorry, boys—*I'm* taking charge," Lana announces with a grin. "I say we head back to the tavern!"

She chuckles as we stare back at her.

"I'm kidding," she says. "As good as that may sound. Elizatine? Lead the way."

Me, the leader? I don't love it. From what little I can

remember about my real life, I get the feeling I keep to myself. Work on my little spoon crafts, keep my circle tight, don't take any leadership positions outside of my own person.

But if no one else is stepping up, maybe I should give it a try.

"Tanner?" I ask, because he seems like the kind of guy who could lead an army into battle.

"Nah, Elizatine, you've got this," he says from behind Amara's wheelchair, giving me a reassuring nod. "Take us away."

I glance down at Felix's guitar, lamenting the loss of that deep, husky voice and the charmer attached to it.

"Alright," I say. "Unless you guys want to ransack Felix's belongings, we're moving on. Like he said, this book isn't going to deliver itself."

"Speaking of which, anyone else want to carry this thing?" Rowan asks, holding the book out. "Anyone? I need a ransacking break."

"Put it here," Amara says, patting her legs. "I'll hold on to it."

Without so much as a *thank you*, Rowan dumps it unceremoniously on Amara's lap.

We walk in relative silence lest someone else ascends our simulated coil too early. I haven't had any big revelations aside from learning the cost of my gluttony, so I'm probably safe for now.

Eventually, the trail leads to a cluster of six small houses just off of the trail, their bases round with shingled roofs shaped like pointy hats. The path connecting the houses is made of loose stones, weaving past a low stick fence. They look stunning next to the billowing clouds and light-blue sky in the distance. They're human-sized dwellings, sure, but I suspect they house the strangest creatures imaginable.

"Do we knock on one of the doors, or do we keep going?" Lana asks.

Seeing as we don't seem to need to eat, drink, or relieve ourselves, there's not much aside from information that the creatures could offer us. Information about the Trembling Forest could be helpful, though, so I point this out to the group.

"And maybe they have a map we could copy," I continue. "Something that gives us the full picture. I don't like that we don't know what's beyond the forest."

We travel up the stone path to the first arched doorway, and I take the initiative and knock. The door opens quickly, as if whoever is there has been expecting us.

"Hello there," says a booming voice, and out steps a large man. He's wearing a massive fur coat, leather gloves the size of dinner plates, and comically large boots with way too much toe room. I guess fashion works a little differently in here.

"I take it you are travelers on a quest?" he asks.

"We've been tasked with delivering a book to someone's brother," I say, and the man frowns.

"Best keep your quests to yourself, Miss," he says.

"You never know who might be listening."

He gestures for us to come inside his house, and when we do, it becomes clear this is an office of some sort—maybe a book-binding operation. There's specialized equipment all around, plus a small collection of bound books along the wall.

"There's a man out there who's feverish about collecting books," he warns. "Be careful. He'll do anything to get his hands on a book that catches his eye."

He rubs his enormous black gloves together and stares at me.

"What can I help you with?"

"We're looking for a map," I say. "Or any information, really. We're trying to get past the Trembling Forest and the Beasteous Bog in order to make our delivery. We don't know what we're up against."

"This is my map," Amara interjects, pulling out her planner. The man's eyes grow wide as she raises it up, and a few stickers spill out from the bottom. She opens it to the correct page and hands it to him. "This is what I could see from my room at the inn. What's the darkness just beyond the forest?"

But the man is too busy inspecting the construction of the planner itself to notice the map. He runs his gloved hands awkwardly over the cover, admiring the finer details. It's a nice planner, I'll give him that, but he's looking at it like it's a Wagyu steak.

"Tell you what," he says. "I'll trade you my finest map for this wonderful book. The map is hand-drawn, incredibly detailed. Did it myself. Has all sorts of notes in the margin about the creatures around here and when they're most active, how to avoid them, that sort of thing. I don't think you'd find a better map anywhere else, in fact. Do we have ourselves a deal?"

Amara gasps.

"No, we don't!" she shouts. "That's mine! All of my notes are in there!"

Never mind that almost all of her notes and drawings are illegible here in the simulation. It's a source of comfort and regulation for her, and I knew the second he made his offer that there was no way we were getting that map. She's too attached.

"I see," says the man. "Well, then, we have no deal. You may go now. I'll leave you with one tidbit, though," he adds. "Don't touch the flowers in the Trembling Forest. It trembles…for a reason."

He shoos us out of his office and slams the door closed.

"It's just a notebook full of gibberish, Amara!" Rowan yells. "Use your fucking brain—if you even *have* one!"

Amara begins to sob. Tanner places a hand on her shoulder as he tends to do, and she starts to collect herself again.

"Cool it, Rowan," I say, shooting him a warning glance. I'm frustrated, too, but I understand her refusal. I'd have the same reaction over giving away some of my clothes and jewelry—especially the fork ring on my index finger, although I can't quite remember *why*—so I can't judge her for not being able to hand it over.

"We're just going to have to figure things out for ourselves," I say. "We're adults here. We can do this."

I take a deep breath. From what I understood of Amara's map, the Trembling Forest is only a couple of hours away. With a name like that, it's got to have some pretty fearsome creatures in it. Then again, the point of this whole experience is to heal us of some deeper wounds—letting us get deep-throated by a giant monster probably wouldn't achieve that effect.

"Well, we're going in blind," I say. "Hands off the flowers, and speak up if you see anything weird."

As we walk forward with me in the lead, I can't help but feel kind of badass. Here I am, in the coolest outfit I've ever worn, leading a group of people into a scary forest. I'm pretty sure I haven't done anything this dope in my *real* life. It's a shame I won't remember it. I'd love to hold on to this feeling of confidence. It's not an out-of-control sort of confidence, but a quiet one; like I have enough faith in myself to know I can do a good job, even if I'd rather be trailing in the back. I'm capable. I can lead this group to safety.

We're going to get this book where it's supposed to go, *and* we're going to fix ourselves.

"Oh, *Great Leader*," Rowan blurts. "You've got a little something on your boot."

Sure enough, I look down and see an inexplicably tiny creature clinging to my boot with sticky trunk feet. It's a miniature elephant with frog eyes and green, warted skin. It looks more like an insect you'd spot trying to blend into a tree branch. The creature is trying to jab its trunk into my boot, thinking it's about to meet skin.

"Yep," I say. "That's definitely what I was expecting to see."

I swat it off of my leg, and it runs off on the path in a hurry. Alarmingly fast for a little elephant.

"Check yourselves for whatever that was," I say. "I think it tried to suck my blood. And I've been meaning to ask this, but who the fuck put *frogs* on their form?!"

"I did," Amara admits awkwardly, and I immediately regret posing my question so aggressively. I thought for sure it would have been Rowan or Tanner. "I've been going through a bit of a frog phase lately. Reptiles, too. I'm sorry."

"Don't be," I say. "There have just been a *lot* of…well, frog-creatures around here. Didn't know what was up with that."

The forest begins to thicken and darken, and we soon find ourselves entering what I assume is the Trembling Forest. The trees are tall and thin, but heavily leafed; at their bases are scattered patches of vaguely creepy, purple flowers. The forest is dark, but not overly so. Bits of sunlight still manage to make their way through the overgrowth of trees.

The path remains reasonably wide, allowing us to walk side-by-side as needed. The air feels cool, crisp. I think I hear the little pitter-patters of feet and rustling through the leaves, but that might just be my imagination talking. As we pass a tree more closely, I see a small herd of those little elephant frog creatures stampeding vertically toward the sunlight along the tree bark.

I wonder what kinds of weird shit we'll see next.

CHAPTER FIVE
Amara

I don't understand why everyone in the group hates me.

Well, hate might be a strong word, and it's not *everyone*. I just get the feeling they don't like me very much. Elizatine, she wanted nothing to do with me last night at the clothing store even though I offered to help her. Then she completely looked past me this morning after Felix left and didn't even suggest me as a leader—just Tanner. Is it the wheelchair? Why does she think I'd be any less capable of leading the group? And the whole frog thing has me so mad, too. I used to bring my Build-A-Bear frogs to the group every single day.

Surely she remembers that. Of *course* it was me who talked about frogs on their form, yet she had to go and be so rude about it. I don't understand what I did to make her not like me. I've been nothing but nice to everyone. I'm not a mean person.

Don't even get me started on Rowan. He's never had a nice thing to say. He's made me cry more than once, and I just don't understand why. How can someone be so cruel? Lana doesn't help me or stand up for me, either. She just watches and laughs. The only person who's looked out for me is Tanner, and he's cute, but he's old enough to be my dad. I'm barely twenty. He probably just feels sorry for me, being in this wheelchair that I don't even fucking *want* to be in. My mom insisted I use it because I kept passing out from the POTS. I hit my head pretty bad one time and got a concussion and a black eye. I think that was the last straw for her. I live at home, from what I remember, and the wheelchair just makes life a hundred times harder. People don't look at me the same way anymore. More than anything, I just wish life could be the way it used to be, back when I could run around and play and do whatever I wanted without having to worry about fainting. To have my own place, my own boyfriend or girlfriend or *theyfriend*. A place where no one judges me for being sensitive or having my little hyper-fixations.

I can't believe TQI put me in a wheelchair for this. They couldn't let me walk? In a *simulation*? What, were they worried I was going to run off or something? Why limit me, embarrass me like this? Life has been embarrassing enough already with all of my medical stuff. I thought this would be an escape. I thought there'd be more people like me.

Maybe TQI wasn't the right place to go. I don't think the people here understand me. Maybe this isn't going to work. My therapists keep telling me I need to work on *self-acceptance*, but it's all a bunch of bullshit. I *don't* accept this. My loss of independence is offensive and unacceptable.

I'm stewing on all of this as we enter the Trembling Forest. It doesn't seem like a very scary forest. It's a bit dark, and there are some creepy-looking flowers along the path, but nothing like in the Disney movies with talking trees and stuff. I think a talking tree would make me pee my pants in real life.

I used to look at the stickers in my planner all the time. I can't do that now. They look like a jumbled mess of colors in the simulation, but I remember what they were. I had a frog holding the pansexual flag, a book that said "books are better than people," and a bunch of cats. My mom ordered them for me online once, in a big pack. I'll never forget opening up that pack of stickers and picking out my favorites. It was so calming. I like to stack them in order and rotate through them. It makes me feel better, plus I like the texture of the gloss against my thumb. At least I still have that. Plus the shapes are still the same.

The wheelchair hits a big bump, and the book sitting

in my lap goes flying toward the ground. I stand up to get it out of habit, but I forgot how bad the POTS hits me now. Within a few seconds, I have to sit back down. Even sitting in a wheelchair isn't perfect—I still have to lay down every couple of hours. I'll never forgive TQI for making me use a wheelchair in what's supposed to be a cool action fantasy. I *love* fantasy. I even told them how much I love Tolkien and all of the *Lord of the Rings* movies.

This feels like torture, being pushed around. I'm not an active participant. Elizatine, she gets to walk up there and strut around and get the guys' attention. Me, well, no one's looking at poor little Amara in her wheelchair.

Amara, who can't even give up her planner for a map.

They just don't understand how important it is to me. Even if I can't read it right now, it has all of my journal entries from this year. Notes from my friends. My dog's paw print before she had to be put to sleep. So many things that bring me comfort. I don't know what I would do to calm myself down without it. Probably cry all of the time. I like having lots of information. I miss my phone too. I was always looking up YouTube tutorials, learning how to do new things. I asked Elizatine about her rings, and she told me about the tutorials she posted online. It made me sad that she didn't want to show me in person. That's one of the many reasons I think she doesn't like me that much.

My eyes start to water, and I try to blink the tears away. None of this feels fair. I couldn't even stay in a treehouse last night. No one offered to help me up, so I couldn't go. I had to stay in one of the rooms on the ground. I could have drawn a better map if I was up in one of the treehouses with a wider view.

I have talents I can use, but I don't think everyone else sees or appreciate that. They just see a silly girl in a wheelchair.

Tanner pats me on the shoulder as Rowan picks up the book and puts it back on my lap.

"You don't need to feel ashamed," Tanner says. His words make me feel better. He does seem to see me, know when I'm hurting. It makes me want my dad, but my dad's been gone a long time. He used to be supportive like that, when he was sober. My mom is stressed out all of the time, and isn't always the nicest. I'm surprised I can remember all of this in the simulation because I thought we were supposed to forget. I guess that's something I have that Elizatine doesn't.

Suddenly, I spot something furry lying between two trees off of the path. It's breathing slowly. Maybe it's hurt.

"Wait!" I say, trying to be quiet. "There's something over there."

Tanner stops pushing me, and I begin wheeling myself over to investigate. I'm able to roll over the flowers the guy in the weird coat warned us about until I'm right in front of the creature. It looks like a massive raccoon with some pink tufts sticking out of the sides of its head. It makes a low purring sound.

I lower myself onto the ground, making sure there aren't any more flowers around, and then start crawling towards it so I don't scare it away. Elizatine is telling me it's not a good idea, but I don't care. I want to see if the creature is all right.

I get a better look at its face. It's incredibly cute. Its face has the usual raccoon coloration and eyes, but the mouth, nose, and ear area look more like an axolotl's. It has four pink ear tufts on each side and big pink, dotted feet. It looks like it's smiling.

"Hi," I say, and I reach out to pet the creature on its side.

"Moron," I hear Rowan say about me. "That thing's going to eat you."

The creature blinks slowly and then looks at me. It seems friendly. I don't think it's going to do me any harm. It opens its mouth to yawn, and its teeth appear to be tiny and soft. Its eyes are big and bright. I think Rowan is wrong.

The creature stands up and looks at me expectantly.

"*Riiiiiide?*" it squeaks. "*Hoolldd meeee?*"

Oh. My. God.

It talks?!

"You're too big for me to carry," I say with a laugh. "I'm so sorry."

"*No,*" the creature squeaks. "*You…riiiide…meeee.*"

The creature walks right up to me and bows down so that its head is in front of mine.

"*Friend,*" the creature says, and I start to cry. Not

because I'm sad, but because I could use a friend right now more than ever.

"That's an Abloosh," a voice says from behind me. "Gentle creatures. Very good judges of character. It likes you."

It's the man who tried to trade his map for my planner.

"I'm headed this way, too," he says. I hope he doesn't ask me for my planner again, because my answer hasn't changed. "I'll give you one more tip. Abloosh don't like loud sounds. They're skittish. No yelling, whooping, that sort of thing. Not unless you want to scare it off."

The man keeps walking past us. He's very big, so his legs carry him far and quickly. I wish I could walk that fast, or really walk at all without feeling like I'm going to pass out.

Anyway, I definitely want to ride this gigantic creature instead of my wheelchair, but I'm not sure how. Do I grip its fur? Won't I get tired from that? What if holding on tight affects my blood pressure? There's so much I don't know, and it's making me feel scared.

Still, this is like a dream come true. I can stop having someone push me around, and I can be the main character of my own story for once. Getting to ride a creature? Amazing! I can't think of anything cooler, and I can't think of a creature more like *me* to ride on: a little mysterious, a little misunderstood, and a little funny-looking. I've always loved raccoons and their sneaky little ways, the way they eat their trash food so delicately. I have a giant stuffed raccoon on my bed at home, and a whole collection of stuffed axolotls on one of my shelves.

I wonder if TQI created this creature just for me to make up for the whole dumb wheelchair situation.

I carefully climb up onto the Abloosh's body. It's silky and smooth, hard to hold on to. I can feel its fur slipping out from between my fingers.

"Here," Elizatine says. She takes out a very long scarf, gently wraps the middle part criss-cross over the Abloosh's chest, crosses it again over the back of its neck, and then hands the loose ends to me. "It's sort of like reins. Might give you a little more stability."

I grab the ends and hold on tight. It does help a little bit. The Abloosh is so large that I don't feel like I'm going to fall off, and I'm not feeling dizzy either.

"What do we do with your chair?" Lana asks.

"Leave it," I say. "I never want to see it again."

"What if something happens?" Tanner asks. "I can bring it with us. It's not a problem. I'd rather you have it in case you need it."

But I refuse, because I can't imagine getting around any other way. If I can't walk, there has to be some other solution. I'm not getting back in the chair. I know wheelchairs help a lot of people and aren't evil, but it's not what I want for myself. That should be my choice to make.

"I'm going to name you…Axocoonia," I whisper into the Abloosh's ear, or at least what I think is its ear.

"Nia for short. Thank you for choosing me, Nia."

"*Nia…friend,*" the creature says, and I choke back more happy tears.

We begin to travel along the path again, me riding on Nia's back. I can even lay down and rest my head on their neck if I need to. I don't know if Nia is a boy or a girl. I should probably ask at some point, because I don't want to assume anything. I look behind me and see that Tanner is still pushing that stupid chair along.

"Leave it!" I nearly shout, frustrated that he ignored me the first time. I'm an adult capable of making my own decisions—it's an extension of my body, so it's *my* decision. "Please!"

"Are you sure?" Tanner asks. He looks like he doesn't trust me, which stings. It's how my mom looks at me, like she knows better than I do about absolutely everything. I can't stand it. It makes me feel like a child.

"Yes," I say again. "I'm *done* with it."

Tanner finally respects my wishes and leaves it off on the side of the path. Rowan shakes his head, Lana shrugs, and Elizatine exchanges a look with Tanner the way my parents used to do when my sister or I did something stupid. I thought being in your twenties meant you were an adult. It seems like the rest of the twenty-year-olds I know don't get treated like this, anyway.

Maybe I'm just too different.

CHAPTER SIX
Elizatine

Surprisingly, the forest proves to be more of the same. Tons of flowers we're not supposed to touch, a thick envelope of trees, and the faint shrieks of mysterious creatures coupled with the vague scent of vanilla. For a forest called the Trembling Forest, I was expecting something more...*threatening*, I suppose, although I'm grateful for the peace and calm we've been graced with so far. I'm still a little shaken up by Amara's encounter with the big raccoon creature and her lack of fucks surrounding it. She didn't give a second thought to crawling over to it, getting right up in its face without knowing what it was capable of. I wanted to grab her by her shoulders and scream at her in that moment. How can you care so little for your own safety? Even though we're in a simulation, we don't *know* that we're safe. We have goals to complete, prizes to glue our eyes on. I'm happy it worked out for her—truly, I am—but what a risk to take.

I can't imagine the pressure of being her parent out in the real world, keeping her impulses in check. I guess the fantasy world is fairly suited for that. Maybe I'll talk to her later about what happened, but in a gentle way. I don't want to have to worry about her.

Eventually, we pass something a little different on the right—a clearing of land in the thickness of trees. Standing in this clearing is a short individual, wielding a sword at a practice target. They seem fairly oblivious to our presence. We stand and watch for a moment, and then the figure leans their sword against the target, stretches, and disappears off into the forest without it.

"That was weird, right?" I ask the group. Amara's new ride lets out a little shrill trill in agreement. "Is this a test, or are we supposed to ignore this and move on?"

Rowan breaks off from the group and heads into the clearing without hesitation.

"What the hell do you think you're doing?" Lana asks.

"I'm taking the sword," Rowan says plainly. "And if any of you had brains, you'd do the same."

I hold my breath as he grabs the sword's hilt and holds it up, pretending like he knows the first thing about how to use it. With a big grin on his face, he runs back up to the group with the sword trailing behind his back.

"What?" Rowan asks, seeing our dumbfounded expression. "We didn't have a single thing to defend ourselves with. Now we do."

"And what happens when that person comes back and chases us down?" I ask. "We don't know who we'd be pissing off or what they're capable of. We could have talked to them, made a deal, plead our case. Dude, go put that thing back."

"Nah, I don't think I will," Rowan says. "Relax. What's the worst that could happen?"

As if on cue, the worst happens. A low growl rumbles through the forest, and the trees begin to tremble.

Oh, *shit*. I guess we're about to find out why this place is called the Trembling Forest.

"What was *that*?" Lana asks as the earth continues to tremble. Beside me, Amara's creature whimpers, retreating behind Tanner as he places a reassuring hand on its head. Suddenly, something begins to stomp through the forest. Something massive.

Something pissed off.

A motherfucking *dragon* emerges slowly and methodically from the clearing, its lips drawn in a ferocious snarl. Its eyes are on the sword. Its skin is green and warted like a frog, but it otherwise looks like a typical, terrifying dragon that's ready to toast a group of idiots down into a crispy snack.

"Rowan, what did you *do*?" I whisper, terrified as the dragon continues to stalk toward us through the clearing.

"I didn't know I'd be pissing off a *dragon*!" Rowan says, as if that excuses his bad decisions. "Here!" he shouts, and he throws the sword on the ground in front of the raging dragon. "Take it! Damn, man!"

But the dragon isn't satisfied by that gesture. In fact, it steps on the sword and dents it slightly as it continues to stalk us down, drawing closer and closer.

The dragon pauses, its eyes trained on Rowan.

Before any of us can react, the dragon swipes out a massive clawed hand and grasps Rowan the way a child might grasp a lizard before squeezing it to death.

"*You…dare…touch…my…treasure?*" the dragon rumbles slowly, raising Rowan up to look at him with one of its massive eyes. Its front fang is as big as Rowan's face.

"Guys, this feels *really* real right now!" Rowan shouts as the dragon flares its nostrils, letting loose a thick trail of hot steam into his face.

As much as I don't love Rowan, I don't want to see his journey cut short. He needs this as much as the rest of us.

"How do we fix things?" I ask, my voice trembling as I address the dragon. It could kill me without a second thought, yet here I am, drawing attention to myself.

"*The…short-ear…must…die,*" the dragon rumbles.

Well, that's not exactly what I wanted to hear. I was hoping it was after something more like an apology.

"What if we traded?" I ask. I don't know much about fantasy lore or dragons, but I do know that they hoard treasure. I'm something of a dragon myself. "His life for…I don't know. I have all kinds of things—"

I start to pull my shiniest pieces of clothing out of my endless bag, and the dragon watches with interest. It holds Rowan perfectly still as it does, still squeezing tight while allowing him to breathe.

"*None…of…those,*" the dragon says. It steps forward and focuses its gaze on me, my hands. "*Zzzsssa…wants…the…ring.*"

I glance down at my hands, which are covered in six fork and spoon rings. I have a sinking feeling about which one the dragon has fixed its gaze on.

The small fork ring on my index finger is the most special of all. I couldn't tell you why since my memory of the real world has faded so severely, but every fiber of my being is protesting the dragon's demand. It's roughly made compared to the others, but it's clear I've worn it for years; there's a deep indentation in my skin beneath it. Tears spring to my eyes even though I have no way of remembering why.

As I look at Rowan, I know I have a simple decision to make.

I take off the ring and set it down on the ground

before me.

"This ring is special to me," I say. "Please take good care of it."

The dragon tosses Rowan to the ground, its eyes squarely on the ring. It shuffles close, so uncomfortably close that I can feel heat radiating from its body against my skin. It examines the ring closely, picking it up with two beastly clawed fingers. Pinching it, the dragon brings my fork ring to its eye, turning it around and examining every detail. Finally, the dragon takes a step backward. From the near distance, Rowan groans on the ground.

"*This…will…do,*" the dragon rumbles. It retreats far enough to gingerly pick up its damaged sword, and then it flaps its massive wings in the clearing, blowing dust on us as it raises itself into the sky. Within a minute, it's flown high in the sky and out of sight into the mountains.

Rowan is still crumpled on the ground, so I go to check on him. He has multiple bleeding cuts and an arm that doesn't look too good, and based on the darkness of his eyes, I have to wonder if he also has a concussion.

"Oh, Rowan," I say with a sigh as he looks at me with a guarded expression. "You sure fucked around and found out, huh?"

"Yeah," he says, his face cracking into a sarcastic smile. "Yeah, I guess I did."

I help him to his feet. He steps forward gingerly.

"We could use that wheelchair right about now,"

Rowan remarks to Amara, limping slightly. "But you didn't think about that, did you? Just about yourself."

"That's unfair, Rowan," I say, but he ignores me.

"Let's just go," Rowan grumbles. "I'll be fine."

My hand feels wrong, naked without the ring. I feel as if I've thrown away a part of a person by giving it up to the dragon. But how could I live with myself if I let Rowan leave the simulation early? We also learned something important here—that we can get hurt and feel deep pain. A bold choice, but humans are wired to avoid pain whenever possible. I can see why we'd need that fear in here with us, keeping us in line.

The group ambles on again, and Amara's creature seems to have recovered from its fright. It strides in the front, happily bouncing from foot to foot as Amara strokes its shiny fur. Lana and Rowan follow behind me, with Tanner trailing in the back. The guy is in great shape, but he still must be tired after pushing the wheelchair for that long before abandoning it.

It strikes me that Rowan hasn't thanked me for what I did. I guess I shouldn't expect anything from him. Rowan answers to no one and does what he wants. Why would he express *gratitude*? Wouldn't that make him look weak? No, he needs to keep posturing—let everyone know that he doesn't give a fuck about what they think and that he doesn't need anyone. It must be a lonely way to live.

Which gets me thinking: now that Felix is gone, I'm feeling a little lonely myself. It wasn't that Felix was my friend; I just appreciated the friendly banter. I've had that to some degree with Tanner, but he's been so busy helping everyone else that I haven't really had a chance to talk to him. Lana is getting increasingly agitated from the lack of booze, Rowan is Rowan, and Amara—well, she won't even look me in the eye anymore. I'm happy that she's bonding with the creature. This is the happiest I remember ever seeing her.

"Take the lead, Amara," I say, and she finally looks at me. There's a spark of something there. "I'm going to fall back for a little bit."

I let Lana and Rowan pass me. They're both in bad moods, so they're bonding by bitching about the dragon. Tanner wipes his face with his hands as he sees me.

"You alright?" I ask Tanner. I try his tactic—putting a hand on his shoulder—but it doesn't seem to have the same effect when I do it.

"Yeah," he says. As if he'd tell me if he *wasn't* doing fine. He's the stoic type; at least, that's what I've noticed since we entered the simulation. I don't remember much about what he, or anyone else in this group, was like before we got here. "Just got some dust in my eyes. I'm good."

Either he's been vigorously rubbing dust out of his eyes or he's been crying, but I'm not going to push him on it.

"You sure you don't want to lead us?" I ask him again, and he chuckles.

"I'm sure I'd do fine," he says, "but you're doing a great job. You certainly have more patience than I do. A good leader has to manage a bunch of personalities at once. Not sure I could do that."

I suppose he's been avoiding Lana in addition to Rowan, which makes sense. He's sober, and she's balls-deep in her party-girl era despite being in her fifties. He has to protect himself. I don't have any barriers up between myself and the other group members. I may not understand all of them, but I feel like I can get along with anyone here—even *Rowan*, if given the chance.

"Thank you," I tell him. "For comforting us. I don't know what it is about you, but your kindness takes the hurt away. I see it, dude, and I appreciate it."

I give him a quick side hug, and he seems a little emotional over the gesture.

"It means a lot to hear you say that," he says. "Thanks."

I feel like I've always liked Tanner. He's one of those people who puts you at ease. Funny, kind, sincere. Always wanting to help. Well, maybe not with Rowan, but that's understandable. Part of me thinks he'll be the next person to leave. He just seems to have himself so pulled together already. What more could he possibly gain by hanging around us?

Then again, I'm almost certain he was crying before I joined him. Maybe he's not doing as well as I thought.

"Hey, Tanner?" I ask, and he perks up. "If you ever want to talk—like, *really* talk, you let me know. You shouldn't have to do this alone."

"I'll keep that in mind, Elizatine," he says, running a hand through his hair. I'm about to say more when Amara's creature trills loudly, startled by something up ahead.

"Oh, thank the fat baby Jesus," Lana says. "Buildings! Sweet, beautiful buildings!"

It seems we've officially made it out of the forest. I was expecting more from it given the name, although it's hard to top meeting a dragon. I'm not sure I want to go through that kind of excitement again. Besides, I'd like to keep the rest of my jewelry.

Like I said, I'm obviously something of a dragon myself.

CHAPTER SEVEN
Lana

I damn near kiss the ground when I see buildings up ahead of us. I'm sweating, seriously sweating. Head pounding. Why on God's green, flat Earth did I not take some booze for the road? Since when have I ever been able to go more than a few hours without it? I could quit if I needed to, though, no problem. It's just more convenient this way, with keeping the headaches and the tremors away. I've got more important problems right now than quitting. Getting off the sauce is low on my list. Maybe that don't make me like Tanner, bless his heart, but I've got a lot going on.

I'm angry. I couldn't tell you why, really, but I think

it has something to do with my husband. Something he did. Whatever it was, it fills my blood with hot liquid rage. I'd wring his neck if he were here, and I don't even remember what that damn man looks like. I think of him, this blank shape of a man, and I just want to deck a bitch. And then drink. I haven't been able to stop thinking about getting a drink since we went through that forest. I'm getting sick of these people already. It's not their fault; I'd be sick of anyone. I just need a quiet moment and a drink and then I'll be back to myself. Back to the old Lana.

Now, I'm not superstitious—just a *little* 'stitious—but some kind of hairy, black frog-thing crosses in front of me and I feel like I've been cursed. You know, like what people say about black cats and walking under ladders. I want to get better, but I feel downright *awful* all the time. Just chasing a little relief over and over, but it never lasts. I look at a girl like Elizatine and feel like life must be so easy. Beautiful, looks great in everything she wears. Seems content enough. I'd say I'm jealous about the attention she gets from the men, but I don't want no man touching me ever again. Maybe a sexy frog-man with all those suckers and shit, but I'd take a ten-foot pole to any human who even tried it on with me. It's not just because I'm married. At least, I think I'm married. Maybe I was and ain't anymore. Who the fuck cares? All I care about right now is getting a drink in me.

I don't even wait to see what everyone else is doing.

I go straight for the building that looks most like a tavern. I don't have many credits left, but I'll get what I can. Wish I had some pain meds for my head to take at the same time. I know you're probably not supposed to do that, mixing drinking and pain pills, but it's what I've done forever—and I'm still here, in all my glory.

I practically run to the bar and slam down a credit.

"Get me as much vodka as this'll buy."

I hate the taste of that shit, but it'll get the job done. Since we don't seem to need water in here, I should probably dump out my water bottle and ration my booze. Stretch it out a ways to keep the headaches away. I won't feel *great*, but I won't get down in the dumps, either. That would be smart, Lana. Ration that shit. Don't you dare drink it all at once. Don't you fuckin' do it, Lana.

Once I get the taste on my lips, I'm drinking more of it than I mean to. I just have that association built up, you know—that when I taste this thing, I'm gonna feel better, so of *course* I want more of it. It's hard to argue with logic like that. Pavlov-ed myself, or whatever they call it.

I go outside and dump my water bottle out, then pour in the pathetic little bit of vodka that's left. It's hardly anything, but it's something. Better than nothing when the sweats hit.

When I get back outside, everyone has gone off to do their own thing. Rowan's skulking around like he does, and Amara is talking to some dude in a cloak.

Me, I'm going to take a walk back in that forest. Try to clear my head. I don't like feeling so angry. I feel like a cauldron about to boil over for no good reason. Over *what*? Who the fuck knows. Leave it to me to be angry over fuckin' *nothing*. Maybe the *air* looked at me funny, I don't know. That's why I have to keep drinking—so I don't turn into the Hulk.

As I walk down the path and look at those weird little flowers we're not supposed to touch, I swear I start hearing little voices. I've heard voices before when I was mixing the wrong meds with my drinks, but I quit doing that shit years ago.

I sit down on the ground and close my eyes, really try to listen.

"*The…fuzz,*" a little voice says fearfully. "*The fuzznado has begun. The fuzznado is on fire.*"

The fuzz-*what* now?

"*It moves down the mountain,*" another voice says, slightly lower than the first. "*We must warn! We must leave!*"

The creatures who said it scurry away, leaving me to try and figure out what in the fresh fuck they're talking about. Whatever it was sounded bad. Fire moving down the mountain? If that's true, we need to get moving.

I jog back into town. The man in the cloak is still there talking to Amara, so I butt into their conversation.

"You ever heard of something called a Fuzznado?"

I ask, and he nods. "Because apparently it's coming down the mountain, and it's on fire."

"Of course," the cloaked man says. "Every year, the Abloosh blow their coats in a shedding ritual. That dry, coarse hair, if whisked up all at once in the air, is called a Fuzznado. They become very large, very powerful. They'll cover whole villages in fur. But I've never heard of a Fuzznado being on fire," he adds, frowning. "Unless, of course…"

He glances up at the mountains, which we have a small view of from where we're standing. It does look like there's a little bit of smoke coming from the trees…

"The Fuzznado may have picked up a creature," he says. "A frantic creature who, in a panic, exhaled fire. A dragon."

Oh, not that motherfuckin' *dragon* again. That was too much the first time. I'm not built for dragons, none of this fantasy D&D shit. And a *Fuzznado*? Who makes up this stuff? TQI, you're on some bullshit right now. Whose benefit is all this for? Not mine. You put me in an old black-and-white movie, a thriller, something like *that* and I'll rise like a damn phoenix. Not this nonsense.

"Well, you got a fire department or what?" I ask. I don't know why I asked, because that's the last thing they'd have around here. Bunch of little frogs or whatever fighting fires? Ha! Like they'd stand a chance.

"Well, no," he says. "When fires break out, we rely on certain humans to use their magic to protect us. It takes a great deal of magic to stop a fire like this one. I hope someone will show up…"

Well, I was able to make that fire roar up in the witch's house. That was really something. I don't think I've ever felt that powerful in my life. Maybe I can make the fire *smaller*. Shit, maybe I can control other elements. We've crossed over a lot of little streams on our way to this town—maybe there's something bigger I could tap into. I could be a water-bender like that girl in that one kid's cartoon, make the water rise up and snuff out the flames. I don't know *how* I'd do it, but I feel weirdly confident that I *can* for some reason. Like something deep inside of me just *knows* how powerful I truly am.

Why not believe it? I'm ready to believe it. Lana, you've got that magic in you.

"Take me to the river," I say. "I think I've got a solution to your problems."

"The river is too far northeast," the man says. "The fire is coming straight down the mountain."

"So I'll move the fire," I say. I don't know why I say that so confidently. I've got no damn idea if I can move the fire or not, but I guess I like the *idea* of being able to move it enough to act like I can.

It's damn stupid, but it's worth a try.

I focus my thinking on what little of the fire I can see, and I try to boss it around a little with my mind. Scootch your ass over. Don't make me come up there and get *la chancla* out. Make yourself a little smaller.

As I do this, I feel that rage coming back. Damn it, not now. I need to focus. That no-good husband of mine can wait a couple of minutes, can't he? Why *now*?

Maybe this is the cost of my magic. Maybe it makes me real mad, brings out that rage. Guess that makes sense; I'm taking the rage out of the fire—it's gotta go somewhere, right?

I don't want all that rage in me, so I don't make the fire go away completely. I just get it to move toward the river. I swear, the Fuzznado has actually changed course and isn't coming straight down the mountain anymore. Against all odds, it's moving up and to the left.

"Well, what do you know?" the man asks, and he sounds impressed. "All right. I'll take you to the river."

Amara follows along with us, even though she wasn't invited. Girl's got shit judgment in my opinion. Not that my judgment's always so hot, but she acts on impulse. She wants to come? Fine. That ain't my problem right now. I don't want to be feeling bad if she gets hurt while I'm trying to solve this thing.

The two of us plus the raccoon thing she's riding jog up a new path toward the river. It only takes a couple minutes to get there. It's a pretty sizable stretch of water. I'd normally be down to take a dip, but I'll probably use every drop of water in this thing if my idea is going to work.

"Move," I think to the water, and a ripple forms on the surface.

So I was right. I can control more than just fire. *Damn*, do I feel like one powerful bitch right now.

I tell the water to move more forcefully, and it sends a bigger ripple through its surface. Lifting water out of the thing is going to be difficult, but it can't be more difficult than dealing with that idiot husband of mine. I get the feeling he's been the biggest struggle of my life.

I nudge the fire over with my mind until it's heading our way. Thank the moldy heavens the Fuzznado lifted off the ground and didn't catch the trees on fire. It's getting lower now, though, so I've only got one shot at making this work—otherwise, it might burn the whole village down because I've lined it up real good with all the buildings.

"Rise!" I shout out loud, giving it my all. Feels like I'm gonna throw my back out or something with how hard I shout it, *will* it with my mind. The water trembles violently, then rises in the air like a fat snake, except it's massive and standing twenty feet above my head. The rage is hot in my head now, boiling over with no-damn-where to go.

The fiery Fuzznado draws closer and closer. I can see the dragon stuck inside, covered in the hair and being thrown around helplessly in a hell of its own making.

Kind of like me, I suppose.

Maybe I wouldn't be like this if I'd never picked up the bottle. Maybe I've been trapped in a fiery Fuzznado of my own for a while now.

"Now!" I scream, willing the water forward. It roars

into the air like a tidal wave and splashes against the blaze of hair, and just like that, the whole thing collapses. An unfathomable, disgusting amount of wet hair splats to the ground just in front of the river bed, coating the ground and trees like nasty snow. The fire is gone, and the dragon is completely covered in hair. Looks more like a yeti than a dragon in its current state. I can't even tell if it's the same dragon that we ran into earlier.

Damn, that was cool.

"Well, that was neat and all, but this is…nasty," I say, gesturing around to the hair all over the place. The man and Amara look at me, and Amara's raccoon creature sneezes daintily. "I'm out of here."

We jog back into town, and when we get there, there's a small crowd of creatures gathered around staring toward the river.

"*Huzzah!*" a tiny frog guy shouts, dancing in the middle of the street. "*We're saved! We're saved! No Weeks of Torturous Cleaning this year!*"

The other creatures let out a cheer, then disperse back to where they came from. Elizatine, Tanner, and Rowan are there, too, and I swear Elizatine's jaw damn near unhinges when I explain what I did to save the town.

"That's incredible," she says, her cheeks glowing. "Lana, you're amazing! How are you feeling?"

It's a good question. With the fire, I felt an indescribable amount of rage, but manipulating the water and seeing it smother the fire—it extinguished my rage, too. I wouldn't say I'm *calm*, because I'm never really calm, but I'd say I'm content. Feeling quite fine in this very moment, like I'm where I need to be.

A creature screams, and a large shadow flashes overhead. It's that damn dragon again. What, is it here to roast us now that I've saved its ass? Why can't the thing just leave us alone? Dumbass Rowan for pissing it off in the first place.

The dragon lands in the center of the town. Creatures are running and hiding, and I'm tempted to do the same. Like I said, I ain't built for dragons and Narnia.

"*You…saved…Zzzsssa,*" the dragon says in its creepy, deep voice.

Technically, I saved the *town*. Saving the dragon was just a side effect, but I don't tell it that.

"*A…gift,*" the dragon continues, "*for…you.*"

A small pile of credits appears at my feet, along with five small bust figurines with a hole in the top of their heads for candles.

"Well, shit," I say, counting the credits. I'm going to be set for a while, I think. "Thank you. Thank you very much."

"*A…candle…placed…and…lit…grants…a gift,*" the dragon says, staring at the figurines specifically. Then, it bows its head curtly at me before flapping its giant-ass wings and leaving us behind in the slightly hairy dust.

"Well, I guess the candle holders are for all of us,"

I say, scooping up the credits and putting them in my pockets. Everyone in the group takes a figurine, the one that looks the most like the each of us. "Elizatine? Lead the way."

Elizatine sheepishly leads us to the town's store, which she already hit up while I was busy saving everyone from the Fuzznado. I find some candles and a lighter, and before we know it, we're gathered around a table at the tavern with our figurines out.

"What are you gonna ask for?" I ask the group. I already know what I want. I want endless booze. It would solve *so* many of my problems right now, and I could save my credits for other stuff instead of blowing through it in the taverns.

"Super strength," Rowan says. I wasn't expecting him to participate. "Let's just say my run-in with the dragon wasn't as…fruitful as yours."

It bums me out real bad that I won't remember what a badass I was after the simulation ends. I commanded fire! I raised water into the sky! Who the fuck else—aside from maybe a firefighter, with their hoses—can claim to have done something like that before? Maybe I'll remember how to do it in my dreams. That would be neat. I'd be like that bald cartoon kid with the arrow on his head.

Feeling that rage, that calm, that power—it was special. More than anything, I felt control. The fire and the water listened to me. It wasn't easy to tell them what to do, but they obeyed. I feel like I didn't get a whole lot of that in real life. Maybe I have kids, then, if I'm thinking of a cartoon show. Would I *really* sign up for a program that would make me forget my kids, though?

Damn. Pretty ruthless if it's true, Lana.

I light up my candle. Part of me knows I could wish for something more magical, but this really will solve a lot of my problems. The headaches will stop. I'll feel in control of myself, like I did when I made the water rise over the blaze.

"I wish for endless alcohol in my water bottle," I say quietly into the candle. "The good shit."

Maybe it's the lighting, but it looks like the eyes of the figurine are glowing a little.

I hear a thunk from my bottle on the table, so I give the lid a turn and take a peek. A whiff of my favorite booze hits me square in the face, and the water bottle is full to the brim. I take a few big swigs, as much as I can stand in one gulp, then look down again.

Still full.

"I need one of these in real life," I say, downing some more of it. I'd save so much money. It feels like liquid relief being poured into my mouth, and not having to worry about how to get more? Lana, you absolute *genius*.

Everyone but Tanner sits around the table to make their wishes; he goes outside. Kind of weird, but that's his business. Elizatine says she saw a silversmith and wants to try using her wish to make us protective jewelry. I think she just wants to show off her skills, but that's fine by me. I could rock a spoon ring. Nice of her to share, anyway. Rowan wants to save his for super strength after getting his shit rocked by the dragon, and Amara whispered her wish too quietly for me to hear.

I don't know what lesson I'm meant to learn in here, but I feel like I'm starting to feel something that I can't put a name to. A realization, or maybe a *want*. I think I want more control in my life. More stability. More peace.

I sure hope I find what's meant for me.

Tanner comes back into the tavern, looking a little spooked.

"The dragon's coming back," he says.

We hurry outside to take a look. There's that damn dragon again, swooping down into the village as creatures scream and dart out of the way. I can't help but notice that Elizatine grabs Tanner's hand as the dragon pulls up toward us, looking pissed as hell.

"What? Back to give us more presents?" I ask, hoping it doesn't pick up on the shakiness of my voice. I want it to think I'm confident, unbreakable. There's dragons, and then there's *Lana*, you big, flappy bitch.

"*Zzzsssa...need...more...help,*" the dragon rumbles, and then that monster does the unthinkable.

It grabs Elizatine and Rowan with its busted old talons and carries them away into the night sky.

CHAPTER EIGHT
Elizatine

The dragon grips me like I'm made of putty as we soar through the sky toward the mountains. I'm screaming my head off. I don't care that this is a simulation—I've never felt something so real and terrifying in my life. Rowan seems to agree; he's yelling and swearing beside me. The vice grip this dragon has me in is no joke; I'm afraid it's going to break my bones, although falling to my death wouldn't be so great either. Finally, the dragon swoops into a high, dark cave and tosses us down onto its massive treasure hoard.

The cave is like something out of Aladdin. The

amount of treasure almost feels comical. Golden coins and resplendent jeweled treasures abound, and also prove to be quite poky and painful as we land directly on top of them.

At least it wasn't a sword.

"Did we land in the Cave of Wonders or something?" Rowan asks, catching the same vibe. "We gonna go rub a magic lamp now?"

"I could use a magic *carpet* right about now," I say, wincing as I survey the damage the dragon and its treasure left on my body. I have a few bleeding cuts. Rowan notices and starts to reach behind him, but he comes up empty-handed.

"Shit," he says. "I left my backpack in the tavern."

I reach into my Sack o'Junk and pull out a dark sock, which I tie around my leg to cover the deepest cut. It's better than nothing, I guess.

Rowan and I cower together as the dragon approaches us, its eyes trained on our bodies. Please tell me this isn't how it ends.

Don't let me be eaten with Rowan on top of a dragon hoard.

I get it, TQI. I own too much shit. I have a problem. There's no need to be so heavy-handed with your commentary.

"*Zzzsssa…need…help…*" the dragon begins, "…organizing."

"You've got to be fucking kidding me," Rowan says as the dragon bows its head and pans around its gigantic lair. Now that I'm looking more closely, I'm noticing that there's been a small attempt at sorting items into piles right near where the dragon seems to sleep, but it's a drop in the bucket compared to all that's in here.

Is this the simulation's equivalent of Hoarders?

"I'm not organizing your shit," Rowan says with a scoff, and the dragon nods.

"*No,*" it says. "You...*get...map.*"

The dragon claws at the pile until a corner of paper sticks up from the treasure. Gingerly, it pinches the paper and pulls it up, revealing an illustration and a map.

"*Zzzsssa's...egg,*" it rumbles, tossing the map to Rowan. "*Stolen.*"

"Yeah? Well, you nearly killed me," Rowan says. "Why should I help you?"

"*Zzzsssa...fry...you...to...crisp.*"

"Ok, well, can't argue with that," Rowan says, defeated. "Where is this egg?"

"*Dalowego,*" the dragon rumbles. "*The...nasty....thief!*"

Rowan picks up the map and studies it.

"So you want me to go after this Dalowego guy and get your egg back, right?" he asks. "How am I supposed to do that? Why don't you just do it yourself?"

The dragon moves to the side, revealing an enormous egg directly behind it.

"*Must...protect,*" the dragon rumbles. "*Cannot...lose...another.*"

This seems to soften something in Rowan, because he hangs his head down for a moment.

"I don't have any supplies," he says. "How am I supposed to steal the egg for you by myself?"

The dragon is silent.

"Great," Rowan remarks. "That's just great."

"And you want me to…sort all of this?" I ask incredulously. This is a warehouse worth of goods. This will take me weeks. "By myself?"

The dragon remains silent.

"Tell you what," I tell Rowan. "Help me sort all of this, and I'll help you find the egg. We'll get out of here and find the others. Deal?"

"Yeah, sure," he says. "Easy peasy."

The dragon has a number of large treasure chests strewn about, so I task us with emptying those out and assigning them a purpose. One for necklaces, one for rings, one for bracelets. The gold coins will have to remain on the floor—there's just too many of them. The bones of the idiots who dared tried to steal the dragon's treasure can go in their own chest too. In a way, this reminds me of the chests I dug through that were full of clothes.

This time, though, it's not fun. It's a total fucking nightmare.

"Here," I say, handing Rowan my cape. "Pick out the jewelry from the pile. Once the cape fills up, take it over to the chests and sort it out. Bones go on the big scarf. We'll line up the bigger, decorative things along the wall. You ready?"

"Ready to kill myself? Sure," Rowan says with a sardonic smile.

"Just start sorting," I say. "It'll be meditative."

Part of me isn't worried because I know we're in a simulation. There's a purpose behind this ridiculous task, surely, and I'll be better off having learned whatever lesson it's supposed to teach me. That said, I'm feeling the loss of the rest of the group. Why only me and Rowan? What is it about us that makes us better suited for this than anyone else?

I'm not a mother—at least, I don't *think* I am—but I feel deeply for the dragon. What a terrible thing to happen, having your egg taken away from you so suddenly. I can't imagine that kind of pain.

Rowan grumbles to himself as he sorts through endless mounds of items. As I predicted, I'm finding it kind of meditative due to its repetitiveness. All the same, I can't help but think that it's just *too much stuff*. I watch as the dragon slips and slides over its hoard to settle up at the top, gold coins scattering everywhere as a small avalanche of goods falls overboard. A gold goblet nearly whacks me in the face on its way down.

"Is this what your place looks like, Elizatine?" Rowan asks with the beginnings of a smirk on his face. "Just clothes and clothes with a side of *more* clothes?"

"Can it, Rowan," I say, although I have no doubt he's right. Based on how I dove into those chests of clothes, I wouldn't expect anything less. Like I said, I see the potential in *things* too clearly. Sometimes, that thing's potential outweighs my own.

"You just don't like it that I'm right," he says, and he's correct—I don't. I don't want to come out of here and live a sad, claustrophobic life like this dragon in its hoard of riches, but how am I supposed to remember that once the simulation ends?

I lug a full coat's worth of jewelry over to the empty chests and sort it out. When I turn around, the demon pile of goods looks exactly the same as it did before; completely overwhelming and beyond the scope of what two little humans can tackle on their own.

"This is insane," I tell myself out loud as I sit down and start another round of sorting. The dragon watches us from afar, no doubt making sure that we aren't pocketing the goods. I wonder if, against all odds, I'll find my precious fork ring in here.

Now *that* would be like looking for a needle in a haystack.

We continue like this for a few hours by torchlight, and then it starts to get freezing cold. The dragon stands up and leads us toward a bare room that's less exposed to the elements.

"*You…sleep…here,*" it says, and then it walks away.

I'm shivering now, so I put on my coat and huddle against one of the walls. Rowan is shivering, too, and I suggest that he wear the cape. We sit across from each other, freezing our asses off. I know what the solution is. I hate it, but I hate the idea of freezing solid even more.

"Time to pool our warmth," I say, gesturing for Rowan to come closer. "Get over here."

"Thought you'd never ask," Rowan says through chattering teeth.

He's taller than I am, so he wraps his body around mine, draping the cape over the both of us. Within a few minutes, I'm feeling a little more comfortable than before—well, aside from Rowan pressing into me, which he's *clearly* into whether he wants to be or not. I try to ignore it. I'm just being a good friend right now, right? This isn't leading him on. This is necessity.

"I know something else that can heat us up," Rowan says half-jokingly.

"*You*, vigorously sobbing after I knee you in the nuts?" I ask sweetly, and that shuts him up.

It's weird to think that after sleeping such a polite distance away from Tanner, I'm now butt-to-crotch with the least-liked member of our little group of nutcases. Maybe we'll learn a little more about each other here, bond a little. I suppose this is one hell of a way to start. Not what I would have chosen, but maybe it's for the greater good.

Most of all, I think about Tanner, Lana, and Amara. How worried they must be. Surely they're going to try to come rescue us. But how? Wouldn't it be better for them to move on and deliver the book instead?

I remember how Tanner took my hand without hesitation when I was scared, and how mine instinctively found his at the first sign of danger. I don't want to forget that. It gives me something to look forward to—that there could be more to explore there if I ever get out of this cave.

"Night, princess," Rowan says as he snuggles closer. The heat feels nice, but his voice in my ear feels gratingly wrong.

"Night, baby girl," I say to him, closing my eyes and hoping beyond hope that I fall asleep soon.

The crash and bang of falling treasure wakes us up just as the sun rises.

"Well, back to the grind," Rowan says, yawning. "Working that simulated 9-5."

We walk back into the dragon's lair—but the sight that meets my eyes isn't at all what I expected.

The dragon finished sorting out the jewelry overnight.

"Did you do this all yourself?" I ask the dragon, eyeing the overflowing chests. It nods. "Well done. It's more than we could have accomplished on our own, so thank you."

The overwhelm of the hoard is still there, but slightly less so now that the jewelry is out of the way. Next are the loose jewels, the goblets, and the crowns, but there's nowhere to put them.

This all feels like some cruel, impossible trick. Even with the dragon's help, it's a massive undertaking. All I want to do is get out of here and get back with the group again.

"Do you have any more chests?" I ask, and the dragon claws around the large pile it sleeps on until a few more chests have been unearthed. Rowan and I dump them out, then line them up against the wall with the others.

"We'll do what we can," I say, "but respectfully, this is insane."

The dragon huffs.

"Can't you just let us go?" Rowan asks. "This isn't about the sword, is it? I'm sorry for stealing your sword."

His words go unacknowledged as the dragon turns, flaps its enormous wings, and flies away.

"We could just…leave," Rowan says, gesturing toward the opening of the cave. "It's not keeping us here right now. Why stay?"

"Because it asked us for help," I say. "Well, demanded. Didn't really give us a choice, but the point is that you and I were asked to do this for a reason. This could be an opportunity to grow."

"By digging through all of this shit? That might be *your* thing, Elizatine, but it sure isn't mine," he says. As he steps forward, he loses his balance and falls right into me, knocking me down on the coat I had laid out behind me. He's on top of me now with his weight on his arms, his face as close to mine as it's ever been. His brown eyes are soft and warm; his whole demeanor changed the second he got close to me.

We stay like that for a few moments in an awkward between-stage until Rowan lifts himself off of me. I'm blushing crimson.

"You can leave, Rowan, but I'm staying," I say, and I sit down and start sorting things again to make my point. "No matter how impossible this feels, I'm not ready to give up."

"Suit yourself, princess," Rowan says. He heads up to the mouth of the cave, and I follow him just to take a look.

"Oh, shit," he says.

The cave opens up on a sharp cliff. There's no getting down unless the dragon takes us down.

"Guess we're stuck with each other a little while longer," I say, and he groans. He's still staring down the side of the cliff, and it takes me a minute to realize he wasn't groaning about what I said—he's petrified of what he's seeing.

He's afraid of heights.

"Hey," I say, moving closer to Rowan. He's frozen in fear. "Let's get you away from this."

I take him by the upper arm and slowly coax him away from the edge of the cliff. He walks backwards, unwilling to turn his back on the death drop just beyond the cave. I can feel his entire body shake.

When we reach the relative darkness of the torch-lit cave, he slides to the floor and begins to hyperventilate.

Right now, I don't see the sassy, rude Rowan I've grown so accustomed to—I see a friend in need of help. I sit down next to him and put my arms around his shoulders.

"Breathe," I say, looking him in the eye as he struggles to make eye contact. "You're ok. You're safe. Just breathe."

I try to set an example for him to follow using the box breathing technique. In for four…hold for four…out for four…pause for four. He joins me after a couple of cycles, looking teary-eyed and bewildered. Above all, he looks utterly embarrassed. I guess we've *both* seen each other at a low point in the simulation now.

I wipe his tears and cup his face with my hands. Even if he's not my favorite person, I hate to see him so scared. I'm certainly not going to make things worse for him.

"You're safe," I repeat.

"And your breath is *kickin'*," he says back to me.

I recoil, and he laughs.

"Kidding," he says, although I can't tell for sure. "I, uh, just wish you hadn't seen that."

"It's fine," I say. "You've seen me at my lowest. Isn't that what all of *this* is for? To be vulnerable with one another? You and I have barely gotten to know one another since this all started. Might as well make up for lost time."

I sit down by my coat and start sorting items again.

"What do you remember about life outside of here?"

"I remember the emotions, but not the details anymore," he says. He joins me and starts sorting nearby. "So much fear. Despair. Numbness. Hatred. Hatred toward *myself*."

"Yeah, I've kind of picked up on that," I say. "It's *incredibly* becoming. Very easy to listen to."

"It's just what I know," he says. "That's life when you're a piece of shit."

"Hey, don't talk about my friend that way," I say, arching an eyebrow. His eyes twinkle a little.

"Friend, eh?" he asks.

"I said what I said."

I do consider him a friend. Maybe not a *great* one yet, but he's out here doing the work with the rest of us. I've decided that counts for something. Plus, he seems to be opening up a little bit more—his posture is more relaxed, and his eyes look less guarded.

"All I know is that I did something that hurt someone," he says. "That it caused a lot of pain to a lot of people. That it was all my fault. The feeling is bad enough in here—I can't imagine what it was like out *there*."

We work in silence for a while until the dragon returns, at which point Rowan stands up and crosses his arms.

"I'm ready to go see Drow...Dalo...what was the guy's name again?"

"Da...lo...we...go," the dragon rumbles slowly, pronouncing it like *dahlowheygo*.

"Yeah. That guy, for the egg."

The dragon looks at me.

"You asked for my help here," I say, "so this is where I'll stay. But I miss my friends. I want to know that they're ok."

The dragon bows its head slightly, then snatches Rowan up unceremoniously and carries him through the sky, swooping down sharply.

Definitely not the route I'd want to take if I had a strong fear of heights.

I climb up the towering dragon hoard in search of more chests. I'm nearly buried by falling treasure several times, but I manage to dig a few chests out from under the pile and drag them off to the side for sorting. It's when I think I've discovered yet another chest that I realize I've uncovered the edge of something else entirely.

A second dragon egg.

I clear the area around it as gently as I can, terrified that the egg will be covered with sparkly shit again if I make a single wrong move. It feels like an excavation, really; like digging for a dinosaur. Finally, I'm able to wriggle the egg free. I hold it firmly as a new slew of treasure comes sliding down, bracing myself as the coins slam against my shoulders and into the back of my head.

I can't climb to the tippy-top of the mound where the other egg rests, so I sit with it in my lap as I continue to sort items. After a few hours of this, I feel like I'm starting to see a little bit of floor space open up. Things don't look quite so jumbled anymore. And most importantly, I solved the case of the missing egg.

So where in the hell is the dragon?

CHAPTER NINE
Rowan

I can't handle these fucking heights.

I don't know what it is about being up high that freaks me out so bad. It makes me feel a thousand things all at once. Panic, sure, that's the first one. It takes over my whole body, makes me shake like a little bitch. Then there's the fear that makes me want to shrink into something two inches tall. Paranoia that I'm going to fall and die, rage that I'm in that situation in the first place, and guilt. All of it together makes me cry. I don't know why there's *guilt* there, exactly, but that's a mystery I'm not jonesing to dive into right now.

Because right now, a fucking *dragon* is carrying me through the sky.

I keep my eyes closed. The sensations are bad enough; the visual would probably kill me where I lay, which is pretty limply at the moment. The dragon is whipping me around like a string cheese in a little kid's hand, ideally minus the tearing and eating part. I just want to get to solid ground below the mountains.

I hate that Elizatine saw me cry.

I don't cry. I mean, I *do*, but not in front of people. Seeing that steep drop and how high up we were, though, that reaction was something I couldn't control. The panic took over and I was gone for a minute, just *gone*. Elizatine was so sweet about it. Most people would've laughed, been uncomfortable, made it worse. She sat there with me through the worst of it, and she was *kind*.

I'm not used to kindness.

When she saved my life by trading that ring to the dragon, something in me broke. I remember why it was important to her—that her baby brother died from Sudden Infant Death syndrome when she was sixteen, and she made that ring from his baby fork and some of his ashes. That her mom killed herself four months later and left Elizatine with a broken-hearted father, who died from early-onset dementia a year before she joined the TQI group.

I could have said something about her past, because I don't think she remembers. There were so many opportunities to hurt her, to make her remember the pain TQI took away. But even *before* she saved me, I kept it to myself. Rare for me to do something like that. I like to stick the knife in first, keep people away. It's not that I enjoy it, but it keeps me safe.

I don't remember what happened that made me this way, but I know I let somebody down in a big way. If I don't get close to anyone, I can't disappoint them. I can't get hurt.

The dragon finally sets me down next to a hovel in the woods, one of those Hobbit-hole looking places like they had at the inn.

This is when it hits me that I've left Elizatine all by herself in the dragon's den.

Damn it, I didn't even think about the situation I'd be leaving her in without anyone to back her up. I was just so ready to get out of there once I knew how high up we were. I mean, I had *some* idea, but seeing it in full color really woke me the fuck up.

What a way to repay her.

I knock on the door of the hovel, and a big man comes out. Wrinkled to hell, pale blue eyes, long stringy, silver-white hair, pointed elf ears, frown lines deeper than the Grand Canyon. Jagged nose. Simply put, the dude hasn't aged well at *all*.

"You're Dalowego, right?" I ask the man, and he nods. "I'm supposed to get a dragon egg from you."

His frown lines sink to Mariana Trench depths now.

"Of course," he says. "But a dragon egg?"

"That you stole," I clarify.

"I did no such thing!" he says, scoffing like I've offended his entire lineage. "What an accusation!"

"Don't shoot the messenger," I say. "That's just what the dragon told me."

"Hmmph," Dalowego says. "That dragon. Always accusing me. I would never set foot in that dragon's den, that's for sure! Bunch of useless junk. And what would I do with a dragon egg, anyway? Eat it? Ha! I'd sooner fly it to the moon."

He looks like he's about to slam the door in my face, so I have to try a different tactic.

"There's a girl in the dragon's den right now, all alone," I say, and that seems to get his attention. He looks concerned.

"A girl? How old?"

"Thirty, I think."

"Son, that's a woman," he says.

I roll my eyes. I can't help it.

"The dragon is making her sort out all of its…treasures," I say. "Losing game, really. It's *packed* in there."

"I wouldn't know," Dalowego says, "because I've never *seen* the damn place!"

Well, shit. I don't know what I was expecting, but it wasn't an old man vehemently denying any wrongdoing. That's usually *my* job.

That dragon's gonna be pissed if I show up empty-handed.

"So what do I do, then?" I ask. "That dragon's expecting an egg, I'm separated from my group, and

Elizatine is trapped up there."

"A group, you say?" he asks, perking up suddenly. "Of weary travelers? Two women and a man?"

"Well, yeah," I say. "Why? You've seen them?"

"Of course!" Dalowego says, beaming. "Come inside!"

I step inside his Hobbit-style house. There's not a whole lot in it; just the bare-bones stuff, like he's living a bachelor life despite being barely alive.

"So, where are they? I should really go find them, get some help," I say.

"Oh, nonsense, boy. They're here!"

The old man opens a door leading down a dark stairwell.

"Here in my basement!"

And with one startlingly strong push, Dalowego shoves me down the stairs and slams the door shut.

CHAPTER TEN
Tanner

*E*arlier...

I never thought it would hurt this bad.

When the witch told me I'd be able to take away someone's pain with a single touch, I was elated. I've always hated seeing people's misery and not being able to do anything about it. It sounded like a dream come true, in a way. I could shoulder their suffering, and I wouldn't have to see them go through it anymore. They could just exist, basking in life and freedom like God intended.

But *damn it*, does it hurt. The enormity of what

these sweet people are carrying with them is more than even *I* can handle.

Elizatine's burning hot embarrassment and shame from the incident in the store.

Amara's confusion and hurt.

Lana's wild, unfathomable rage toward her husband.

But the worst is Rowan. I gave him a friendly smack on the back, and the self-loathing coming off of this guy was just *nuts*. Nearly knocked me over. I don't think I've ever met someone who hates himself as much as he does. It's the kind of self-hatred where you drag yourself through barbed-wire mud because you think you deserve it, that nothing can redeem you but your own, self-inflicted suffering—and even *then*, that's not good enough. Rowan's suffering was almost too much for me, but a miracle came just in time.

When Lana received those wish-granting figurines from the dragon, I knew exactly what I needed to do. I needed a way to let this shit out, keep myself together, so I asked for something that would do just that.

A voiceless scream.

I could turn my back on the group as we walk, scream my fucking head off without anyone hearing it, and keep going like nothing happened. It's already made a huge difference so far. Finally, all that crap has a place to go. It felt like it was going to claw its way out of me, and worst of all, it made me want to go crawling back for a drink.

Whenever I get that itch, I just imagine Elizatine's

hand over mine when we were at the tavern that first night. It was a small gesture, sure, but it stuck with me. Even if I stop caring about letting myself down, I don't want to let *her* down. I want to set a good example for Lana, too, who's right where I was before I finally woke up and heard what the Lord was trying to tell me. That I was a sick fuckin' idiot throwing his life away over nothing. A little temporary relief that only made things worse in the long run.

Quitting alcohol and facing myself was the hardest thing I've ever done. I couldn't even look at myself in the mirror for a while. I was disgusted. I couldn't imagine how I'd fallen so far, becoming a husk of the man I was in my thirties. I don't remember what got me drinking in the first place, but it doesn't matter. I never should have started.

All I've ever wanted to do is be a good person and help people, but I betrayed myself to the fullest. I straight-up abused myself, and couldn't even see it.

I think I feel things too deeply. The hurt of others, their desperation, their venom. It eats at me, and when it gets to be too much, I can't let it out of its cage.

I can only dull it.

But screaming into the void is cathartic. I wouldn't wish this "gift" on anyone else, but I feel like this is my calling. To shoulder the weight of suffering, because someone has to do it. People can't walk alone in their shame, their misery. I'm the person who has the privilege of taking some of that away, giving them a chance to breathe. And even though it hurts, knowing they're doing better allows me to breathe a little, too.

The witch said that talking about my gift would break my ability to use it, so I have to keep quiet. If there was anyone I'd tell, it would be Elizatine. I feel like she'd set me straight.

Damn, am I fascinated by her. She's sweet and hilarious, not to mention stunningly beautiful. I think she's cool with her split-tone hair and spoon rings, her job, her free spirit—everything about her speaks to me even though it shouldn't. I wish I were a little more free like her sometimes. I tend to stick to the conventional, but it would be nice to fly my freak flag a little too. Not that I know what I'm a freak about since I've kept things so strait-laced. Well, aside from the alcohol and a little blow, anyway. I guess I've flown that flag a *little* in my life.

But Elizatine is freshly thirty, and I'm a rusty forty-four. I'm not holding my breath, thinking she's interested. Still, I can admire and appreciate, and try to be respectful about it. The truth isn't as pure and clean as I make it out to be, of course. I got rock hard when we laid down next to each other that first night—I couldn't do a damn thing other than hide it and try not to think about what I'd *like* to be doing with her in that moment. I reminded myself that the Lord above is watching. That killed it pretty quickly.

What I *can* do is take away her pain and try to support her, regardless of how she feels about me. That's all

I want for anyone in this group, is to feel better. And if I can have some small part in meeting that goal, great. I'm fulfilling my purpose.

But *damn*, does she do something to me. And I get the feeling it's been that way for months, that this isn't something new. But it might have been something I was fighting.

Not so much anymore.

We have to accept the things we can't control, right? I gave over my alcoholism to God. I'll give these feelings over, too. I can feel Him in here with me, even now.

I've been through hard things and found the guidance. I just need to shut up and listen.

I'm gonna be ok.

Now, to make sure the same can be said of Elizatine and Rowan.

"We need a plan, *now*," I say, flustered as me, Lana, and Amara just stand around doing nothing. I think we're still in shock that the dragon swooped down and took them. I thought this journey was going to be more linear. That we'd follow a literal path without these insane detours. It doesn't seem ethical, doing scary shit like that. Kidnapping wouldn't fly in real life, so why is it going on in here?

"Yeah, dude, I've got nothing," Lana says, holding her hands out palms-up. "A whole lot of nothing."

"Amara?" I ask.

"Well, this was a *Western* Dragon," she says, "and

those are associated with evil and greed. Not like Eastern Dragons. So she probably took them to her lair. Maybe she thinks they're treasure."

"Great," I mutter.

"But in the east, they're depicted as protectors," she continues, a little too happily. "They control the rain, the water. They're wise and keep people safe."

"Yeah?" I ask, hoping it's not just an info dump and that she has a point.

"It's raining," Amara says.

Well, what do you know? Now that she mentions it, I can feel a few drops hit my cheeks as I look up at the cloudy night sky. This is the first time it's rained since the simulation started. Could be a coincidence, I don't know, but I tend to not believe in coincidences.

I'm not a huge fantasy guy and don't know a lot about dragons, but I do know about St. George slaying a dragon—Satan, essentially—in the book of Revelation. I've never understood dragons to be kind, benevolent creatures, but I also didn't think I'd be having group therapy with a bunch of strangers in a simulation.

And I didn't think I'd be falling for one of them.

"So based on a little rain, we're assuming the dragon is *friendly*?" Lana asks. "Didn't seem so friendly earlier."

"But she gave us gifts," Amara points out.

"It stole our group members!"

"Maybe she needed *help*!"

If there's one thing I hate, it's not being able to do anything to help someone. Short of climbing up the mountain and hoping for a miracle, we have no idea where the dragon's lair could be.

We need information.

"We're going to split up and ask everyone around the village," I say. "Someone has *got* to know something about the dragon, something to get us headed in the right direction."

We split off, and I take a detour around the back of the tavern to do some silent screaming and get my shit together.

I felt how scared Elizatine was, the way she grabbed for my hand thinking I could protect her. And I failed. I couldn't do shit as that massive dragon ripped her away from us, and I couldn't do anything to help Rowan, either. It makes me feel insignificant, weak.

I bang on doors and ask everyone I can find for help. I see all sorts of creatures, some of the weirdest mashups I've seen in my life, but no one seems to have any ideas—that is, until a tall, hooded figure taps me on the shoulder.

"A dragon, you say?" he asks in a low voice. "A mile north from here, there's a broken path that will lead you to the base of the mountains. A man lives there. He is an expert in dragons. He can help you."

"Who are you?" I ask. I don't like that I can't see his face; makes him seem untrustworthy and sneaky, like he's got something to hide.

"I'm hideous," the man says, leaving it at that. He leaves his hood on and stays back in the shadows. "But that's not important. The man's name is Dalowego. Find him, and you will find the dragon."

The man disappears into the darkness before I can ask him any more questions. I don't know what to think at this point. Do I trust some creep from the shadows to lead us down the right path? Do I trust him with Elizatine and Rowan's lives?

I track down the others. Lana is hitting her bottle, and Amara is lying down on her Abloosh. Probably having blood pressure problems from all the stress.

Looks like I'm doing this alone.

"I got a lead," I say, trying to sound more confident than I feel. "But I think I should go alone. You two, stay here. Lana, you're drunk off your ass," I continue, "and Amara, I can tell you don't feel so good. Thank you for telling us about the dragons, though. That gave me some hope."

I expect them to both give me a big argument, but neither has anything negative to say about me going out on my own. Good. I want them to be safe. I wouldn't feel right leading them into something dangerous, which this probably is.

"At least tell us where you're going just in case," Lana says, slurring her words a little bit. The sight of her makes me recoil; not because of her personally, but because I know this is what I must've been like when I was drinking.

I don't want to think about that right now.

"A broken path about a mile up north," I say. "Supposed to lead to the house of a man who can help. Allegedly, anyway. Not sure I believe it, but I guess I'll find out."

I take off without them. The rain continues to fall. Based on how far we are from the foot of the mountains, I suspect I'll be walking all night long just to reach that man's house. That's fine with me. I like my alone time. I can clear my brain, keep my head in check. Brace myself for whatever weird shit I'll find along the way.

Hours pass, and I keep my head empty. No dwelling, no stewing on things I can't control. I'm just a man on a mission, and my job is to walk this path until it runs out. I can't focus on the cold, the loneliness, the guilt. I'll pack that shit away to deal with later.

No, this is my time to be present.

I'm in a flow state now, and it takes a minute to come out of it once I realize I can see the house up in the distance. Sure enough, there's a little cottage there nestled between some trees, situated right before the path opens up into the wide foothills of the mountain range.

At least it's light out now. It stopped raining a while ago, too.

I knock on the door, and an old guy with hair the length of Elizatine's steps forward into the light.

"Yes?" the man asks, and it's as I suspected—the man standing before me was the hooded man who spoke to me in the village.

In a simulation this ridiculous, why wouldn't it be?

"It was you," I say. "But why? Why not just talk to me openly in the village?"

"But why *not*, my friend?" the man asks. "Why *not* invite you into my home, where my maps live? My inventions?"

He gestures for me to step inside. My gut is screaming at me not to do it, but then I think of Elizatine being ripped away from me, and I do it anyway.

His place is minimal. I see one map plastered on a wall, and zero notable inventions.

"What now?" I ask. "Clearly, you tricked me. Well done."

"This isn't the whole house, you presumptuous fool," the man says, annoyed with me. "Come."

He opens the door leading down to a basement. If my guts were screaming *no* before, they're flying a blimp equipped with megaphones now. This is bad news.

I follow Dalowego down the stairwell into the darkness.

CHAPTER ELEVEN
Rowan

"Tanner?"

It's dark down here, but I can make out the outline of Tanner's fur-lined coat. I managed to catch myself on one of the beams leading down the wall, so I didn't get too banged up falling down the stairs.

If this were real life, that asshole could have killed me.

We're in a big, dark, empty room made of grimy gray stones. There's a little bit of light coming in from somewhere, so I'm able to see Tanner's face once he moves into it.

"Rowan?" Tanner asks. "So he got you too, huh? Is

Elizatine with you?"

"Nah, she's still up in the dragon cave. Where are Lana and Amara?" I ask, not because I particularly care right now, but because I feel like I'm *supposed* to want to know.

"I told them to stay put in the village," he says. "So you just left Elizatine there?"

"I'll admit, it wasn't my finest moment," I say, and Tanner glowers. "But she's safe, I think. The dragon is having her sort its treasure. It sent me down here to find a stolen egg."

"This guy doesn't seem to have much of anything," Tanner remarks. "Let alone a dragon egg."

The door clicks open, and Dalowego stands in the entryway with a glowing torch.

"Excellent," he says. "Now that I have you both here, I'll explain everything. The deceptions. I *do* apologize for the deceptions."

He tucks the tall stick of the torch in the crook of his arm and claps his hands together.

"I've been watching the lot of you," he says, "but the smell of self-loathing…oh, the stench coming off of you two! Delicious! It's just what I need, and in order to harvest it, I need to milk the both of you."

I don't know what part of me he thinks he's going to be milking, but good fucking luck with that.

"And by *milk you*," he clarifies, "I mean run you through a gamut—well, of sorts, through which some of your self-loathing can be extracted. Oh, it's so potent and vile! Just what I'm looking for."

"What's in it for *us*?" I ask, and he looks surprised.

"Well, less self-hatred, I suppose," Dalowego says. "This is what most would call a *win-win situation*. Besides," he continues, "you don't have a choice! My basement, my rules!"

He goes up the steps and slams the door shut behind him, leaving us in the dark again. As he does, I notice that the room starts to glow a soft amber color, looking a little more misty and creepy than before.

"Are you seeing this?" I ask Tanner, and he shakes his head. He's staring at the other side of the room, but there's nothing there.

"You see that thing in the mirror, right?" Tanner asks, and it's the only time I've ever heard him sound frightened.

"I don't see anything over there," I say, but then I look over at *my* side of the room and see that the scene has changed.

Where there was once darkness and moldy stones has now been replaced by something I had forgotten all about, and *goddamn* do I wish I could forget about it all over again.

My childhood bedroom.

On the floor is my little brother, still alive. Still playing. I try to scoop him up, but he's just an illusion. He's wearing his little Winnie the Pooh hat.

The one and only time he wore it was on the day that he died.

I know what comes next, and yet I watch.

As if it's happening through my eyes, the view of the scene shifts to the top of the big oak dresser. I had climbed up there, not thinking anything of it. The view changes as I jump off the top of it onto the bed.

I'm all too familiar with what comes next. The crash. The boom as the dresser topples over, heavy as fuck and merciless. The crushing silence beneath it.

The scene zooms out, showing kid me on the bed. It hasn't hit little me yet that my brother is dying under there. I just sit there doing nothing while he suffocates. I'm wide-eyed, worried that I'm going to get in trouble with Mom for jumping around like a *fucking monkey* again.

I've never been the same since that day. I felt it in the way my mother treated me after he died. She helped me, sure, but it felt dry. Forced. Like she did it out of contractual obligation, not because she actually gave a fuck about me. She could barely stand to look at me. I killed her favorite child with my carelessness, after all.

Seeing the moment so clearly again knocks me to the floor. I wish I could go back in time and stop it. My brother was an amazing kid. He deserved to grow up, and I fucked it up—all so I could have a little fun in my room when Mom wasn't looking. I wanted to impress him, make him giggle. I wanted to be the cool big brother who helps get his little brother in trouble.

Beside me, Tanner is locked in a staring match with something.

"What do you see, Tanner?" I ask him. "Because I'm

looking at the worst moment of my life."

"Same," Tanner say quietly, his eyes fixed on something. "It's me. The night I got arrested. I was completely hammered and got into a bar fight. Don't even remember why. I beat a guy up, and then I went in the bathroom to wash his blood off my hands. I didn't even recognize my reflection. I was covered in blood, teeth gnashed, this crazy fucking look in my eye. There was something demonic there, staring back at me. And I'm seeing it again now."

"But that's not who you really are," I say, trying to be helpful. I'm also desperate to distract myself from my own illusion of my dead little brother. "I know I don't know you that well, Tanner, but that's not the guy the rest of us know. When you're sober, you're a solid dude—dare I say kind."

"What are you seeing right now?" Tanner asks, changing the subject. I tell him, and I swear he tears up a little.

"You were just a kid," he tells me. "Not to put the blame on your mom, but that thing should have been secured to the wall. Shitty thing that could've happened to anyone. Could've happened another time without you jumping off it. It wasn't your fault."

"But I'm the one who jumped," I say. "I did this. I got him killed."

"*Bad luck* got him killed," Tanner says. "You can't carry that blame with you. You were just a kid yourself. Your parents are supposed to protect you. It could have been *you*, you know," he adds. His eyes are still on his own illusion. "On a different day, different circumstances. It could have been you."

"I wish it would have been," I mutter.

"But it wasn't," Tanner says. "You're here. You still matter. You're still breathing. You owe it to yourself to let that guilt go. I don't know if you believe in God, Rowan, but you've got to give your pain over to something. You're not meant to carry it alone."

I don't believe in God, but if weird old Dalowego wants to keep my pain for himself? Sure, go right on ahead. I don't fucking want it. I've been living in the shadow of this since I was seven-years-old. I haven't gone a day since without resenting my existence, wishing it had been me instead of my brother.

If Dalowego wants that self-loathing so bad, then fine. I could use the break. I'm in my thirties now, and I'm tired.

"You're not a demon, Tanner," I say, even though I don't think that's what he was trying to tell me. "You were in pain. I know because I've done stuff to dull the pain, too. Stuff that hurts me. Drugs, mostly, but some sex and booze too. You were running from something and took it too far, that's all. Doesn't make you a bad person. Just makes you human like the rest of us. I mean, seriously, you're like some kind of angel the rest of the time. *Everyone's* got a creepy dark side. You're not special."

Tanner chuckles a little at that.

"Ugh. *Demon me* is crawling out of the mirror," Tanner says, stepping backwards. I crawl backwards myself as the dresser begins to move, revealing my brother's reanimated little body lunging toward me angrily.

"You did this to me!" he screams in his sweet little voice. "You killed me! You killed me! Mommy's gonna be *so* mad!"

I scramble backwards as he keeps coming closer, taunting me.

"Don't listen to it, man," Tanner yells from his side of the room. "They're lying to us!"

I put my head in my knees as the apparition gets closer. I can't face him. It's too much.

"Rowan?" a little voice asks, and I take a peek. It's my little brother, looking less terrifying than before. He's just standing there, staring at me in confusion. I reach out to touch him—

—and grab a solid arm.

"Holy shit, Declan," I say, and I pull him in close for a hug. A hug I've needed for so long. "I've missed you, buddy. I'm so sorry I let you down. I should've gotten Mom right away. I never should have jumped off of that dresser."

Declan hugs me back, his little arms and hands squeezing me tightly.

"You were the best big brother ever," Declan says into my chest. "And Mommy still loves you."

"Yeah?" I ask. "How do you know that?"

"Well, she begged you to come *here*, didn't she?" he

points out. "To get better."

Across from me, Tanner is having a heart-to-heart with his own demon. The man is just sobbing now, telling himself how sorry he is for letting him get into that state.

"Mommy never blamed you," Declan says to me, his eyes wide and innocent as ever. "She blamed herself. Hated herself, every day. Both of you did. That makes me sad, Rowan. I don't want either of you to hate yourselves. I want you to be happy."

I pull him in tight again. I know this isn't real, but it might as well be with how realistic this hug feels. I know it's been decades since I've hugged my little brother, but this is exactly how I remember it. His silly, squishy little body with his pinching little fingers and his sweet, soft voice.

Mom *did* beg me to come to TQI, that's true. She thought it could be good for me, being around other people. That I was too glum and morose all the time, and she wanted me to be happy for once. I figured she was sick of seeing me like that, but maybe it was something deeper. Not because my moodiness inconvenienced her, but because she *genuinely* wanted me to be better. See the world, give her grandkids, something like that.

I let go of Declan and look him in the eye.

"You promise you're telling me the truth?" I ask, and Declan nods. "That you guys don't hate me?"

"Mom and I could never hate you," he says. "And I

hope you'll stop hating yourself, because it makes me sad."

"I'll do what I can, buddy," I say, and I mean it this time. "I'll do what I can."

Declan holds out his hands, and it reminds me of the way he'd beg for one of my Charizard Pokémon cards. It was one of the rarer ones, so I never let him hold it. Still, he was always curious and said he just wanted to see it.

I reach into my pocket just for the hell of it, and what do you know—the card is there. Pristine condition. Not that I care anymore because after he died, all I wanted to do was give it to him. We buried him with it.

"Here you go, buddy," I say, placing the card in his outstretched hands. His eyes widen as he giggles gleefully, and then he stares down at the card in wonder, studying the details carefully.

"Thanks, Rowan," he says. "I'll take this with me. I love you."

"Love you too, buddy," I say with tears in my eyes, and then he's gone. The illusion fades, and it's back to the black, dank room with just a sliver of light coming in from a crack in the ceiling.

Next to me, Tanner is sitting on the ground in a stupor. I sit down near him.

"I took his—*my*—drink and gave him water, told him it was going to be okay," Tanner says. "Stupid and simple, I know, but it fixed something in me when I did that."

"I gave my brother a Pokémon card and a hug, so I get it," I say. "But it did something. I—I don't know how to explain it."

"I know exactly what you mean," Tanner says. We sit in silence for a little bit, and then I start to dribble tears down my cheeks. The weight of seeing Declan both in life and in death has been too much. I don't know how to handle it all, so I do what Tanner said. I give it over. To what or to who, I don't know, but I'm letting some of it out. I'm physically incapable of holding these feelings in anymore.

Tanner puts an arm around my shoulder. I think he's tearing up a bit too.

"We're being put through all of these trials for a reason," Tanner says. "We'll be better people for having faced all of this pain head-on, even though it fucking sucks a big one. Hang in there."

Men don't usually touch me—nor do most women, for that matter—and it makes me feel a little calmer for some reason. I guess we all need that human connection every now and then, even if it's from the guy who slept next to your most recent crush the other night.

As we sit there processing everything that just happened, the door creaks open. I guess that's our invitation to leave.

Dalowego stands in his kitchen with a small vial in his hands, looking mighty fucking pleased with himself.

"Delicious. Thank you both," he says, raising the vial

for us to see. Some kind of nearly-clear matter swirls around inside of it. "It was even more potent than I thought!"

"What're you going to use it for?" I ask.

Dalowego smiles.

"Oh, I like to put a little in my tea at night," he says with a slow grin. "Helps me sleep."

He taps a finger against the vial before putting it up on a shelf.

"I have what I need. You're free to go."

"Free to go where?" I ask. "I need to get back to the dragon's lair for Elizatine. How am I supposed to do that?"

"*We*," Tanner says, and I'm annoyed at the thought of him tagging along. I was kind of liking the time alone with Elizatine, even if most of it was spent bickering.

"Won't Lana and Amara worry if you don't come back?" I ask, but Tanner shakes his head.

"Lana and Amara can take care of themselves."

"And what, Elizatine can't?" I ask, which shuts him up good for a second. Yeah, I'm on to you, Tanner. You're not as selfless as you think.

"I have my reasons," Tanner mutters. "We're both going. Maybe she doesn't *need* rescuing, but the fact is that she's out there alone right now. We shouldn't be split up like this."

"That attitude's not very feminist of you," I say, and Tanner shakes his head.

"Yeah? Well, did you stop to consider that *I* might

need to know that she's okay?" he says, which shuts *me* up.

"I kept her warm last night," I say before I can stop myself, because of course I have to stab the knife in whenever I get the chance. "We snuggled up. Big spoon, little spoon. It was her idea, actually."

It doesn't feel as good to say as I thought it would, but I'm used to that. The satisfaction rarely comes—just guilt, followed by doubling down.

"Must've been really cold up there, then," he says.

"Light breeze," I say, but I know he's not buying it. "Balmy, even."

"Enough!" Dalowego's voice bellows from behind us. "Good gracious, how pathetic. Perhaps I ought to milk *that* out of you, too!"

"Easy, old man," I say. "We're not going back in the basement."

"Well, of course not," he says. "Your ride is here!"

I look outside and see the dragon. I'm not looking forward to being flung around again for a fourth time, and I certainly don't want to lose my shit over heights around Tanner.

"Hey, gorgeous," Dalowego says to the dragon, and the dragon blows steam out of its gigantic-ass nostrils in response. "I don't have your egg. You've got to stop blaming me every time something goes missing. I've never been in your lair, and you know it. You won't *let* me in!"

The dragon looks pissed. Before I can react, it grabs

me and Tanner and shoots off into the sky before anyone can get a word in edgewise.

I can't help but scream, and I'm pretty sure Tanner does, too. Since this isn't my first rodeo, I know a little more about what to expect. I just hope she doesn't toss me on a sword in her hoard pile.

Tanner curses from behind me as we tumble down onto a patch of solid ground. Sure enough, we're at the dragon's den, but Elizatine made a huge amount of progress with cleaning it up. There are at least fifty swords lined up along the wall, and a bunch of other shit is sorted out into categories.

And there are two giant-ass dragon eggs on the very top of the hoard.

"The fuck?" I ask.

"Just what I was thinking," Elizatine says, rounding the corner of the hoard. She gives me a shoulder hug. I was hoping for a bigger one, but I'll take it. "Turns out it was buried under the hoard this whole time!"

I chuckle darkly.

"You have no idea what we went through with that Dalowego dude," I say, dusting myself off. "It was—"

"We?" she asks, and that's when she spots Tanner. Unlike with me, she runs toward him and throws her arms around him, the way I wished she'd throw her arms around me.

Like she means it.

"Lana and Amara?" she asks, and Tanner shakes his head.

"Not here. Back in the village."

"Well, as glad as I am to see you guys," she says, "there's no climbing down from here. We're at the mercy of the dragon for that. So unless we can convince her to let us go, we're stuck here."

Elizatine shows Tanner around, and I take a look at her progress on the treasure. I can't believe she was able to do all of this in the time I was gone.

And as I'm taking all of this in, a glowing, floating portal appears.

"The fuck?" I balk.

There's a thin, glowing portal door hovering just above one of the mounds of gold coins. I know better than to go through without telling the others first, so I call Elizatine and Tanner over to look at our new guest.

"Whoa," Elizatine says. "Should I touch it? Maybe we all hold on to each other in case touching it pulls me through. At least we'd all be together."

Not the worst idea, so Tanner and I each put a hand on one of her shoulders as she reaches through the portal with her left hand. Nothing happens, thankfully, so we're just standing here looking like idiots instead.

"It felt warm on the other side," she says. "Not like here. Holy shit, does it get *cold* in here."

"Sounds great to me," I say. "I'm out of here."

"Same," Tanner says. He keeps his hand on Elizatine's arm, but I take mine away. "Looks like we're off to our next adventure. Maybe it'll take us back to Lana and Amara."

"I'm exhausted from sorting all of this shit," Elizatine admits, leaning against Tanner briefly. A surge of jealousy hits me, and it feels gross to even acknowledge it. "Let's go."

Elizatine leads us through the glowing portal. It tickles. It's what I figure walking through TV static would feel like—tons of vibrations and fuzzy sensations all over, with too many colors to name. I close my eyes, and when I open them again, I'm somewhere else.

But Elizatine and Tanner aren't with me.

I take a look around. I'm in a circular room with tall windows, some sort of projector screen that doesn't belong in medieval times, and a bunch of shit like clothes and books thrown around. I head over to one of the windows, thinking I can just climb out.

Nope.

I'm in a tower a hundred feet above the ground.

Well, smack my ass and call me Rapunzel.

CHAPTER TWELVE

Lana

Earlier...

"We're not waiting for Tanner to come back, right?" I ask, bottle in hand as I take another hard-earned swig of my booze. Hits the spot real good. "No way am I sitting here in this tavern doing nothing today. We gotta go explore."

Amara looks at me like I've got five heads. She slept until dawn, that girl, but I've been up all night itching to *do* something.

"But Tanner told us to stay put," she argues from her seat. That Abloosh creature next to her lies down and looks like it wants to take a nap, but I know it's not real—I ain't feeling sorry for it.

"I'm a grown-ass woman," I tell her. "Girl, I can go where I want. Tanner's not God. We just leave him a note, tell him where we went, and when we'll be back. Easy."

I take another swig.

"Let me put it this way. You either come with me, or I'm leaving you here. I don't have the patience to sit around. I need to *do* something."

Amara thinks for a minute. I think I've got her on my side.

"Fine," Amara says. "We'll go with you."

Amara's not the easiest girl to talk to, but that's all right. We don't have to talk. I've got my bottle, my thoughts, and a nice crisp walk through the forest to look forward to.

"Should we walk up the path Tanner told me about, or should we take a peek toward the bog?" I ask Amara once we're outside, because I haven't quite made up my mind either way. Amara ponders it for a moment while I take another swig.

"Why not *that* way?" she asks, pointing to a third path altogether that cuts through some forest behind the tavern. I hadn't noticed that before; it's almost as if it appeared out of thin air. "Maybe there's something interesting over there."

I'm not particular about the destination so much as I am about keeping my ass moving, so I indulge her.

That gets a big smile out of the girl. I get the feeling she gets told *no* a lot. Makes sense. She's not the most responsible, level-headed twenty-something I've ever seen. She's got a lot of growing up to do.

Riding on the Abloosh now, Amara scribbles a note for Tanner and leaves it on a table in the tavern.

"It's *go time*, I guess," Amara says, and the two of us set off. I don't know what to bring up around her. She's sensitive, and certain things get her riled up—like politics. Good God, I will *not* bring up politics.

What did *I* like to do in my twenties? Smoke a fat one, probably. I've never been a good girl. Protesting, singing, doing all kinds of shit. Then there's this big ol' gap in my memory after college. I must've gotten married. Maybe I have kids. I'd like to assume I do, at my age. They'd be, what, Amara's age now, wouldn't they? I hope they have a thicker skin.

"You can ride the Abloosh too, you know," Amara offers, but I ain't sitting on that thing if I can help it. It's cute and all, but the idea of it makes me squirm. I need to move my body, especially with all this booze. I get restless. Some people conk out when they've hit the sauce too hard, but not me. I'm like a great white shark; I'd probably die if I stopped moving.

We walk down a winding path with more of the same tall, dense trees that we saw before. Nothing too interesting, but I'm getting my wiggles out and the Abloosh seems happy enough about it.

And then that damn witch steps out from behind

the trees. If I still had to go pee in this place, I would've pissed my pants.

"Ah," the witch says with that Boston accent again. "You're taking the path less traveled. Nice. I have something for each of you."

She hands us each a key. Mine is a bit spiky-looking, and Amara's looks just like a classic skeleton key.

"There is a test, of sorts," she says, "and the keys will unlock something that you desire. But only one will be deemed worthy, you understand?"

"Then why *two* keys?" I ask, but she snaps her fingers and disappears into thin air with a smile on her face. Bitch, I'd do that too if I could. Just exit an argument in style, get the last word in every time.

As I'm about to ask Amara what she thinks about that whole little encounter, a glowing entity appears in front of us in the path.

"A portal!" Amara exclaims, like it's the most exciting thing she's ever seen. You couldn't pay me *enough* to go through a portal if I don't know what's waiting for me on the other side. Go around, *go around*, Lana!

"We have to go through it," Amara says. "To use these keys."

Well, no *shit*. But do I *want* to? *Hell* no! But still, there's a little part of me that's curious, that wants to poke my face through and take a little peek.

I sigh loud and scrunch up my face. I'm not drunk enough for this.

"Guess I'll see you on the other side, huh?" I tell her,

and then I watch as she dashes through the portal with the Abloosh without even hesitating. Not a pause, not one thought in her head about the dangers that could lie ahead.

I breathe in deep. Align my chakras, all that shit.

I'm going in.

My body tingles all over, like a big orgasm that overstayed its welcome. Or maybe like having cotton balls rubbed all over my body. Maybe both. Whatever it is, it's bizarre. The feeling doesn't last long because I'm suddenly standing somewhere new, and it's not the forest anymore.

It's an arena.

Not just any arena—it's one of those old, enclosed gladiator arenas. Darkly lit except for the very center, where there's a table with a couple of mugs on it being illuminated by a spotlight up above. Maybe it's the sun peeking through a crack since gladiator arenas don't have spotlights. Who the hell knows. I don't know why I'm fixating on the lighting when I've been teleported into a *goddamn arena*.

"Amara?" I call, but I can already tell she and I went two separate places. Plus, I'm hearing footsteps, and she's not exactly a big walker.

"Who's that?" I ask. "The fuck are you doing?"

"It's Tanner," he says from somewhere in the dark. "Lana, that's you, right?"

"Damn *right* it's me," I say, relieved that I have friendly company. "I'll meet you in the light. This is too damn creepy, talking in the shadows like this. Feel like someone's gonna come stab me any second now."

We meet at the lit-up table in the center of the arena. On it are two very full mugs of beer; one for each of us. On the ground around the table are a variety of old-timey weapons; swords, lances, and a spiky chain-ball contraption—of course I can't remember the name of it.

"Cheers?" I ask, picking up one of the beers, but Tanner shakes his head. I take a sip, then spit it out almost as quickly. This is the most vile beer I've ever tasted, and I've tasted some pretty bad booze before.

"Oh, jiggly baby Jesus, you're not missing out on *anything*," I say. "Good gracious *fuck*, that's bad."

From one of the big gated entryways, I suddenly hear low growling.

"Don't tell us we gotta *fight* something," I say with a groan. I'm not built for any of this. Tanner, though, he'd stand a chance. Especially since that man wants to get back to Elizatine. Lust'll make a man crazy, that's for sure. But me? What am I fighting for? What do I have to look forward to? I guess I haven't figured that one out yet. Maybe not wanting to give up and die is reason enough.

I pick up a sword from the ground and hold it in front of me. I don't know what I'm doing, but it's better than standing there and gawking. Tanner picks up the spiked ball and chain contraption and widens his stance.

The growling gets louder.

A gate retracts, and something starts running out of

it. It sounds rabid, *awful*.

Damn it, Tanner, you'd best be saving the both of us because I don't stand a chance on God's flat green Earth against this thing.

The *thing* enters into the light, and it's not a thing. It's two people, almost zombie-like in their movements and looks. They're out of control, spraying spit and screaming and ready to attack.

They're *us*.

I'm looking right at Zombie Lana, and she's looking at me. Well, not really looking. She's too out of control. She's trying to claw at everything in sight. Zombie Tanner is throwing wild, vicious punches and screaming about how he's going to kill us. Some fuckin' scary shit.

Is this what he and I are like when we're drunk?

I stick my sword out, pressing the hilt against my belly. I'll keep her in front of me, and if she gets any closer, she'll have to impale herself.

Tanner is swinging the contraption, and Zombie Tanner is lunging forward like he's ready to kill.

Zombie Lana tries to fuck around and find out, and the sword goes right through her stomach. *Well, that was easy*, I think, and then I quickly realize I was a fool because the wound in her stomach immediately heals itself over like nothing happened at all.

How the hell are we supposed to get out of here if these things are unkillable?

Next to me, Tanner is swinging at his zombie counterpart and taking chunks out of its face—chunks that immediately reappear. Zombie Tanner pulls one over Tanner and clocks him in the face, and real Tanner's face still looks busted; no magic healing for us, I guess.

The two Tanners keep swinging at each other as Zombie Lana keeps trying to come for me, getting stuck on my sword each time.

She's not the brightest, Zombie Lana.

Goddamn. I should probably stop drinking.

We're in a simulation, where everything's a learning experience and a test. If these things can't be defeated, what are we supposed to do? Find a way to escape, or is the solution something more metaphorical? I know those kinds of tests can get clever, make you use your brain. While Tanner's busy throwing punches, I'm looking all around the arena.

Zombie Tanner bumps into the table, and a little bit of the beers splash out of the mugs. In that instant, the zombies seem to freeze. It lasts maybe half a second, and then they're back at it, trying to kill us all over again.

The beers.

"Pour out your beer!" I say. I lunge for mine and hurl it in Zombie Lana's face because I'm pissed at her for existing. For being so weak and embarrassing. I wouldn't want to meet Zombie Tanner, but Zombie *Lana*? She's just pathetic, even for a zombie.

My lesser self disappears.

Tanner follows my lead and hurls his beer at Zombie Tanner, and he too disappears into thin air.

"Holy shit," I say, dropping my sword and sinking to the ground. My heart is pounding like a race horse. "They really went there. Put us up against our drunk-ass selves."

I brace my hands against the floor.

"Goddamn, Tanner. Is that really what you're like when you're drunk? You never struck me as a violent guy."

Tanner looks down at the ground.

"Yeah," he admits. "I don't remember the details, but I'd throw stuff. Scream. Go out looking for a fight."

"But you seem like such an angel," I tell him. "How's there a demon living inside of you like that?"

I probably shouldn't have worded it like that since he's a man of God, but he purses his lips and nods.

"He got in when I drank," he says. "So I just don't drink anymore."

"The demon?" I ask.

"The devil," he corrects. "Demonic forces. I don't know if you believe in that kind of stuff, but I do. Satan got a hold of me, took me over, and I can't let it continue. Not if I want to walk on the right path."

"Well, Amara and I sure picked the wrong one earlier," I say, and I tell him all about Amara and I leaving the village against his instructions. "But we ran into the witch again, and she gave us *this*."

I take the skeleton key out of my pocket and hand it to him.

"Here," I say. "Take it. You didn't drink. I think you

won this round."

As if on cue, a small wooden box appears in front of us on the table where the beers stood. Tanner carefully inserts the key, and the box springs open. Inside is a small spy glass, just big enough to hold in the palm of your hand. It looks like a child's toy.

"Uh...thanks, I guess?" Tanner says, looking around. He peers through it, but nothing happens. "If only this were a magic looking glass. I could say *show me Elizatine* and it would—"

He does a double-take and looks through the glass.

"No fucking way," he says, and then he hands over the spy glass to show me.

I can see Elizatine—not only her, but Amara and the Abloosh. They're walking together through some kind of busy marketplace.

"Well, at least we know they're still well and kicking," I say. "That's something, right? Even if we don't know where *we* are?"

"Yeah, but where's Rowan?" he asks. "Show me Rowan."

We look in the spy glass together, and it looks like Rowan is locked up in a big room. Some kind of tower. He seems like he's given up on trying to get out. He's just pacing around, doing a whole lot of nothing.

"So what do we do?" I ask.

And then we hear a voice—Elizatine's voice—ring out from Tanner's hand.

CHAPTER THIRTEEN
Amara

I didn't know what to expect when I went through the portal, but I didn't care what was on the other side. I've spent my whole life reading and watching fantasy, dreaming of a life where I could go on magical adventures and escape from the real world—from my illnesses—for just a little while. It's hard to be the girl who has to say no all the time because she's sick. Not capable of going out. Lately, I couldn't go out because I needed the wheelchair and Mom couldn't drive me. So to be able to jump through a magic portal on a wonderful talking creature? I *had* to!

I guess I just wasn't expecting to end up at a street

market.

It looks like something out of the Middle East. It's an indoor market with all sorts of vendors and items. I can already see some things I'm interested in, and I have so many questions.

I like to know as much as I can about different things. My interests don't always make sense, but I just get so *invested*. I can tell you all about leopard geckos and their husbandry needs even though I don't own one. I can tell you what supplies to use for repainting a doll head and how different sealants interact with the vinyl over time. I even know an extensive amount about different Crayola crayon releases and theme park accidents. I suppose I find comfort in information and sharing it with other people, although sometimes they aren't as interested in hearing it as I'd hoped they'd be.

To some people, that makes me weird. I'd like to consider myself informed and interesting.

"Amara?" someone asks. I turn around and see Elizatine standing in the bazaar, looking confused. How did she get here? I thought she was stuck with the dragon and that Tanner went to rescue her.

"How did you get here?" I ask her. "I was just with Lana. I don't see her anywhere."

"Did you go through a portal, too?" Elizatine asks. "I was with Tanner and Rowan."

"Airthsept gave us keys," I say before I forget. I hold it up. "She said only one person can earn it. Maybe she was talking about you and me. Maybe there's something waiting for us at the end of this market."

"Maybe," Elizatine says. She looks nervous. I get it. We're in a big shopping district, and that's Elizatine's biggest weakness. I remember how she looked in the clothing store when the bag made her gain a bunch of weight. I know she doesn't want to go through that again.

This should be easy for me. I like shopping, but I'm used to not having a lot of money. I rarely get what I want. Elizatine seems like she buys whatever she wants. It must be nice having that kind of freedom and money. I have so many collections I want to finish, like my shelf of axolotls. I know you can't technically *finish* a collection of something so general, but I want to add to it. Books, an anatomical model, maybe some more plushies. It just feels incomplete the way it is. Most of those were bought *for* me. I didn't get to pick them out. My friends and my mom did.

"Don't buy anything," I tell Elizatine, hoping my reminder helps. "It'll make you gain weight."

Elizatine smiles and nods. Good. I think I've helped her.

We begin walking through the bazaar at separate paces. It's just one big line, stretching as far as the eye can see. I bet our goal is to make it all the way to the end. Easy. I could just close my eyes and let Nia carry me so I don't get distracted.

I squeeze my eyes closed tight and hold tight onto Nia. I'm definitely going to earn that key.

But suddenly, I hear someone shout: *get your leopard geckos! Easy pets! Get your leopard geckos here!*

My eyes fly open. *Easy pets*? Like *hell* they are!

"That's not true," I tell the man who yelled it. He has a bunch of leopard geckos in cups, and he has a tiny ten-gallon tank on display with sand in it. The inside of the tank has mist actively spraying on the walls.

"This is all wrong," I begin. "They need a 40-gallon tank, minimum. They need a mix of reptile-safe soil and play sand, or just paper towels. The mist can give them upper respiratory infections. They need enrichment, not an empty tank with nowhere to hide and nothing to do. Would you like living in an empty, gross little tank your entire life?" I tell the man, and my voice is getting louder the angrier I get. "How *awful* that would be? They're living creatures! No pet is easy! How dare you imply that they need so little?"

The man looks at me, smiles, and then looks past me out into the crowd of creatures in the bazaar.

"Leopard geckos! Come get your leopard geckos! They're great sautéed over a little lemon sauce! Taste great boiled alive! Come get your leopard geckos!"

"No!" I scream in the man's face. "They're not food! They're pets!"

I can feel my face turning red. I'm so angry, I don't know what to do with myself. I know my blood pressure is getting out of control, so I lie down on Nia and wait for it to come down again.

A creature comes over, interested in the man's offer.

It snatches a cup off of the table and inspects the leopard gecko inside.

"Ah, a beauty indeed," the man says. "For cooking or for keeping?"

"I can't decide," the creature says. "It's just too cute!"

"I can fry it up for you right here," the man says, and that jolts me upright again.

"No! Stop!" I shout. I grab the creature's arm. "This isn't right! They have feelings—you can't just cook them alive! They're meant to be pets, or better yet, free in the wild!"

"Well, I don't know about all that," the creature says. "*I* cook leopard geckos alive all the time."

Tears spring to my eyes. This is horrendous and completely unfair.

"I'm not going anywhere until you put that leopard gecko down," I say, crossing my arms. "You need to educate yourself. Pack all of this up and go home. You've got it all wrong. You're torturing these animals."

"Yeah? Well, right now, you're torturing *me*," the man says, giving me an angry look. "Get out of here."

"No," I say, crossing my arms. I'll sit here as long as it takes for him to do the right thing.

Even if it takes me all day.

CHAPTER FOURTEEN
Elizatine

The bazaar is completely overwhelming.

Not in a visual way—I'm quite fascinated, actually—but emotionally, it's devastating. It feels like a personal attack, confronting me with my dream shopping scenario where the goods are cheap and plentiful. Nothing gets me going like a fucking flea market, and this is one on steroids.

I have to keep things in perspective here.

This is a simulation. None of this stuff is real or meaningful—only the members of my group are real. My relationships with *them* are what matters. The stuff is beautiful, but the cost to me is too high.

It's just stuff. It's just stuff.

I chant this in my head as I walk by. I try to keep my head down and not engage with the booth owners, who I'd normally get sucked into conversation and a bargain with right away. I've got to keep my head down, keep my shit together, and get through this bazaar without buying anything. I can do this. Perspective, dammit. Perspective.

An elegant, sequined dress catches my eye whether I want it to or not. It looks to be my size, and it's absolutely stunning. Long, gold and black, incredibly elaborate. Only two credits. I can afford it, I would certainly love it, and I would look amazing in it.

You *can't*, Elizatine. If anything, you should be getting *rid* of things.

That thought gives me an idea.

"Hey, are you buying?" I ask the owner of the booth. I try to avoid eye contact with the dress. "I have something similar to that dress you might like."

I pull out the sequined vest I bought from the trunks on our first night in the simulation, and I feel my midsection shrink a little. The booth owner gives it a good look-over, then makes an offer.

"What about an even trade?"

Damn it. I don't know if I can resist that. The dress is absolutely stunning. This test is breaking my resolve like none other.

But I think of my friends, and I think of Amara's blunt warning before we started walking.

Perspective.

"I just want to sell," I say, holding my head up high. Time to treat the dress like an unobtainable work of art. I can appreciate it without buying it. I have a great outfit already that I can wear all of the time. I don't need to do this to myself.

And above all else, I want to get back to the rest of the group.

Perspective, Elizatine, perspective.

"Sure. Two credits," he says, and my heart leaps in my chest as he takes the vest and hands me two coins.

Holy *shit*. Not only did I avoid buying something, I actually *sold* a piece of my hoard. If I can get through the rest of this bazaar, I'll have left with less than what I started with.

I keep walking. Things keep catching my eye, but I keep the word *perspective* at the tip of my brain; it seems to keep me in line. Eventually, I hear a familiar voice—Amara, who's screaming loudly about something not being fair.

"Amara," I say gently as she sobs into the Abloosh's fur. Next to us, a man is spinning a small lizard on a skewer over an open flame. "Amara, it's ok."

"None of this is ok!" she screams. "He's keeping them in cups, selling them for food! Everything about this is wrong!"

"Amara," I repeat, grabbing her by the shoulders. She looks up at me with tears in her eyes. Her face is puffy from crying, and the man seems to be taking some delight in torturing her. "None of this is real. The man, the geckos, the creatures buying them. None of it is really happening. We're in a simulation. You need to keep some perspective on this, alright? It's cruel, but it's not real. Not in here."

She wipes her tears and nods.

"But it *feels* so real."

"I know, believe me," I say, thinking of the gorgeous dress I passed up. Part of me is hung up on it, but I know leaving it behind was the right thing to do. "But it's not. You, me, the others. We're real. *We're* what matters right now. This is all a test, Amara, nothing more."

"Oh, I'm an idiot," she says, covering her face with her hands. "I got so worked up over nothing."

"It's not *nothing*," I say reassuringly. "You saw an injustice and said something about it. That's brave. You just lost sight of the bigger picture of the simulation, that's all."

I give her a hug.

"Let's get out of here," I say.

We walk together through the rest of the bazaar. I'm able to keep my head together, especially with Amara here—I want to set a good example for her. Things keep popping up to test her resolve—more little geckos being cooked over flames, items from collections she wants to finish, incorrect information being shouted out to the crowd—but I remind her about the bigger picture each time, that none of this is real at the moment. It's difficult for her, but we're able to keep going until at long last, we reach the end of the bazaar. At the very end is a small table with a locked chest on top.

"Can I try it?" Amara asks hopefully. I don't want to hurt her feelings, so I nod. She climbs off of her Abloosh and approaches the table. She sticks the key in and tries to turn it, but the lock won't budge.

"It's *so close*," she says, trying again, but nothing happens.

"I'm sorry, Amara," I say, "but can I give it a try?"

She leaves the key on the table and climbs back on Nia as I stick the key in. This time, the box opens without any issues.

"It's a spy glass," I say, holding it up for her to see. "Maybe even a magic one. Worth a shot. Show me… show me Rowan!"

I say it as a joke, but Rowan really does appear in the glass. I'm so shocked that I nearly drop it.

"Holy shit," I say. "Amara, look at this. I can *see him*."

Rowan is in some kind of tower. From what little I can see of the room, there's no exit. He's pacing around, looking pissed off and bored.

"Well, that would explain where *he* went," I say. "Show me Tanner."

I can hear Tanner talking to someone, but I can't see him. Just darkness. The other voice sounds suspiciously like Lana.

"Tanner?" I say loudly into the glass. I feel like an idiot, but who's to say it's not like a camera phone? There are no rules, no strict magic system to follow in this simulation. We're at TQI's creative whims here. "Tanner, are you there?"

The darkness fades from the glass, and a blur of motion follows. Soon, I can see a close-up of Tanner's eye, followed by a zoomed-out view of his face as he holds the spy glass as far away as possible.

"Can you see me?" he asks, and I nod. My stomach is fluttering at the sight of him.

"Tell Lana that Amara's here with me," I say. "And Rowan's—well, Rowan's in some kind of tower."

"I saw," Tanner says. "We're trying to figure out where to go next, how to get to him. It's clear he needs to be rescued. Damsel-in-distress kind of situation."

We each explain how we got our spy glasses.

"Tanner is a scary drunk, Elizatine," Lana blurts. "Throwing shit, screaming, raging, the works. Like a monster. I'd piss myself if I saw him like that in real life."

"I was going to tell her myself," I hear Tanner mutter quietly.

"Whatever," Lana says, waving him off. "She deserves to know."

Of course I don't like the sound of that, although I can understand Tanner wanting to admit to that on his own terms. I had already suspected as much—the man certainly can't be perfect—but my stomach tightens a little at the thought of an angry, violent Tanner when the Tanner I know is so sweet and mild-mannered.

"I still like you, Tanner, don't worry," I tell him with

a smile. "No judgement here."

Next to me, Amara looks like she's judging quite harshly. That's understandable. If I'm remembering correctly, her father was a bit like that. Drunk, angry, belligerent. I'm sure she doesn't need a reminder of that dynamic.

I can't remember what my parents were like.

"So how do we all get our big, happy family back together again?" Lana asks. "We've been split up every which way for a while."

"Not to mention the *book*," I say. "So many little side-quests—we're nowhere *close* to delivering this thing."

"I have no idea where we are," Tanner admits. "Do you?"

"Not a clue," I say. "It'd be nice if some portals appeared right about now."

I'm hoping that my wishful thinking will pan out like it did with the spy glass, but nothing happens.

"The only thing I see is a red balloon on a very long string in the distance," Tanner says, "and I'm pretty sure that wasn't there a minute ago. What about you?"

I take a spin around and, sure enough, a red balloon on a long string is visible in the distance for us as well. I can see the outline of something red and white; just a sliver, but enough to make sense of what it might be.

A carnival tent.

"You're not going to believe this," I say, "but I can see it, too. It looks like some kind of circus tent."

"Guess we'll see you there, then," Tanner says, looking back over at the balloon. "Can't wait to see what kind of horrors await us. It's going to be clowns, right? Just a shit load of clowns?"

"You afraid of a little old clown, Tanner?" Lana asks teasingly.

"I read *It* too young," he says. "Hell *yeah*, I'm afraid of clowns."

I'm pretty sure I have a small collection of baby doll clowns in real life. I'd better keep that to myself.

"Only one way to find out," I say. Amara is still glowering, probably thinking about her father. "We'll see you there."

I pocket the spy glass and gesture for Amara and Nia to follow me, and we walk toward the mysterious carnival together.

CHAPTER FIFTEEN
Elizatine

Lana and Tanner are already waiting for us when we reach the carnival.

"Hey," Tanner says, and I breathe a sigh of relief. For the second time today, I run over and throw my arms around him, followed by giving Lana a big hug, too. I don't know why I'm such a touchy-feely person, but no one in the group seems to mind aside from maybe Rowan. I find myself wanting to touch Tanner in particular, but I'm not certain he's into it. I don't want to make him uncomfortable.

"So, what do we think *this* is?" I ask as we stare at the huge red and white canopy before us. It's quite tall and looms ominously above our heads. "Some kind of a test, surely."

"I'm tired," Lana says, taking another swig from her bottle. "Can't we knock out for the night and deal with this tomorrow?"

As if on cue, a large banner unfurls from the top of the canopy.

One night only!

"You fuckers just don't quit, do you?" Lana shouts up into the sky, as if TQI is watching us from above. "Let me *sleep*, damn it!"

A second panel unfolds from the previous, larger panel.

A Play Presented by the Timeless Quaint Innertainers.

"T.Q.I.," Amara says, noticing the initials right away.

"Maybe we just sit and watch," I say hopefully. "Maybe it's not as...*involved* as the other tasks have been."

"If I have to fight another Zombie Tanner, I'm gonna lose it," Tanner says.

"What about a *clown* Tanner?" I ask teasingly. He shudders.

"You take that back, Elizatine," Tanner says. "I can't do clowns. I don't even want to *think* about them."

Despite worrying about being too touchy-feely, I can't help but gently hold on to Tanner's arm as we enter the tent. Inside is a large, illuminated stage surrounded by dimly-lit, backless seating. We sit down and wait for something to happen. I leave my hand on his arm because not only does he not seem to mind, but there's a feeling of comfort there.

In fact, I think I'll graduate to putting my arm around his shoulders in case there are any clowns.

"Is this helping?" I ask with my arm around his shoulder. Hopefully I'm not making him uncomfortable and he's just too polite to say anything about it.

"Yeah, it's helping," he says, the beginnings of a smile tugging at the corners of his mouth as he leans in a little closer. "The killer clowns won't stand a chance against me now."

Lana looks over at us and gives me a knowing smirk. She knows what's up, that something is brewing there. I don't know what that is yet, exactly, but I just feel drawn to Tanner. Comfortable. I see him and feel like I'm at peace again. Maybe it's strange considering he's fourteen years older than me, but I don't particularly care. Right now, my burgeoning feelings outweigh the age difference.

I wonder if he feels the same way.

I jump in my seat as circus music begins to blare from above, and Tanner puts his hand on my knee. I expect to see performers start streaming from the wings, but nothing happens. Just an empty stage, looking more sinister now that the music is blaring for a crowd of five. The Abloosh trembles, and Amara frantically strokes her fur to dissuade her from running away.

Finally, a curtain rises and four actors are visible on stage; three women and one man. One woman is darker-skinned with gray hair, the second has split-tone hair just like mine, and the third has brown hair in a low ponytail. The man has tousled, dark-blond hair and a strong build.

They're supposed to be us.

"Ladies and gentlemen," a booming voice announces over the circus music, "the *Timeless Quaint Innertainers* are proud to present…*So Far Away!*"

Three of the players retreat backwards, and the one who looks like Lana steps forward.

"Oh, shit," Lana says. "This is *just* like that cartoon about the bald kid with the arrow on his head."

Tanner and I don't get the reference, but Amara does.

"In the very beginning," the announcer says in a long, drawn-out way, "there was a woman named Lana. Her childhood was a *peaceful* time, full of wonder and love. Her parents had great hopes for her. She even attended *college*—the first of her siblings. The pride and joy of the family!"

The announcer pauses. The player dances across the stage; books and backpack in hand with a wide smile on her face.

"And then she went and fucked…it…all…up," the announcer continues slowly. The player stumbles forward and drops her books on the ground, and a shadowy figure appears before her.

"Lana married young. Lana chose poorly. Lana's husband was vicious, condescending, *controlling*. Lana wilted away like a forgotten row of flowers on the windowsill, rotting from within. Lana drank poison to numb the pain. Lana became a shell of herself. Lana's children bore witness. Lana's children no longer speak with her. Lana is all alone."

The player is curled up on the floor, alone, the shadowy figure having disappeared somewhere along the way.

I grab Lana's shoulder, and she reaches back and holds my hand.

"Along came Tanner," the voice continues. "A strapping young lad with good things ahead of him. But the pain came, and he drank. He started young, outpacing even his father. And the rage! Oh, the *rage*!"

The player representing Tanner begins to scream savagely, throwing cups and plates all along the stage. They shatter and disappear. The real Tanner is tense, not breathing.

"The rage consumed him, brought *more* pain, and he drank once more to numb that pain. He simply… couldn't…*stop*!"

Several shadows appear. The player screams and lunges at the tallest, and they all disappear.

"Rage and pain, rage and pain!" the announcer repeats, almost mockingly. "Now, gaze upon the devil himself!"

Jail cell bars appear before the player, and the player crumples into a ball on the ground before quickly rising and retreating to the darkened background.

"And Elizatine!" the announcer continues, and my own player steps forward. "Sweet Elizatine. Such tragedy. So much loss at such a young age. There was pain, *certainly*, but no rage. Instead, she consumed. Oh, how she *consumed*!"

The player is suddenly surrounded by mountains of clothing and snack foods, and false Elizatine begins stuffing her mouth full in a grotesque fashion, her eyes vacant. Packages drop from the ceiling onto the floor all around her—but still she stares into the void, shoveling food in her mouth without pause.

"Poor Elizatine, all alone in the world. Unlike *Amara*," he says darkly, and the players quickly switch positions. "So many friends, an adoring mother. So ungrateful for all of them."

The player stands tall, then crumples to the ground. A wheelchair shoots out of the background, bumping into her back.

"Ungrateful for the opportunities presented to her."

Amara's player pushes the wheelchair away and lies on the ground.

"Ungrateful for the care shown to her."

A figure representing her mother crosses the stage, blocking a third shadowy figure from reaching Amara.

"Poor me, poor me!" the announcer says in a singsong voice. "Nothing's *my* fault! *I'm* the victim!"

Amara is too far away from me to reach, so Tanner tries to put a hand on her shoulder. She shirks away, opting to pet Nia instead.

"These unfortunate four—so far away from their homes, their realities, their *lives*—are now left to reflect on their monstrous qualities. The things that strip them of their humanity. Do not forget what you have seen here, for these unholy traits live inside you, clawing themselves free at every opportunity. Keep them at bay, and let us never meet to tell you the tale again! A good night to all, and to all a good night!"

The curtains close, and canned laughter and applause plays from overhead. The four of us sit in stunned silence as the circus music resumes, punctuating our brutal roasting. I feel like they went relatively easy on me, but the others—*damn*.

They made us look *pathetic*.

"Are you guys all right?" I ask as the music begins to dim along with the stage lights. "We should go. That was a lot."

I'm trying to remember the loss the announcer mentioned, but it's not coming to me. I don't think I *want* to remember quite yet, if I'm being honest with myself.

"I'm pissed as hell," Lana says. "I need a minute, you guys."

Lana bolts out of the tent. Amara looks teary-eyed and embarrassed, and Tanner looks shaken.

"I think I need a minute, too," Amara says, taking off her glasses briefly to wipe her eyes. She takes off on the Abloosh toward some trees, leaving me and Tanner alone together.

"Do you want to talk about it?" I ask. Honestly, seeing that kind of rage acted out has left me a little shaken, too.

"I don't know," he admits. "It's just…it's hard to face who I became. Who I *am* when I drink. What that looks like under the harsh light of sobriety."

He hangs his head down low.

"You'd think a man dedicated to Christ would do better," he says. "That I'd be a peaceful, enlightened dude all of the time. I'm usually pretty unbothered by things, but there's this current of rage under the surface. When I get drunk, I tap right into it. It's like digging a nail into an exposed nerve. I become this whole other person, this—this *thing*. I'm not even human anymore. I'm gone. I'm an unthinking creature full of resentment, taking it out on everyone and everything. I lose control. It's not who I am, who I want to be. I just want peace."

I give him a hug and hold him for a while, which he seems to appreciate.

"What about you, Elizatine?" he asks. "How are you doing?"

"Trying not to think about the *loss* piece too much," I say, even though I have a gut feeling growing about what the announcer was referring to. "As for the rest of what he said, well, you guys already saw my gluttony in action back at the store. It just stung to see me up there looking so…so detached from reality."

I let him go.

"All of us are dissociating from our pain," Tanner says with a sad smile. "That's what it comes down to. We haven't learned to cope with the weight of living yet. That's why we're here."

He's not wrong. When I go to the thrift store, I *abso-*

lutely dissociate. I get lost in the colors, textures, possibilities—I'm not thinking about real life anymore. I'm somewhere else, somewhere free from suffering.

"Do you think we'll get better?" I ask, and he nods.

"You and I will," he says. "Lana and Amara—well, maybe. Guess we'll see. They have some work to do."

"Does all of this make you want to go and drink?" I ask him. It's not coming from a place of judgement; I'm genuinely curious about his answer.

"Yes and no," he says. "I want to dull the shame, sure, but the desire to never see *devil-me* in the mirror again is stronger. I can't go back to that life. I'd rather die. And if I broke my sobriety, I think I *would* die. I'd either pick a fight with the wrong guy or my liver would give up on me. Either way, it wouldn't be pretty."

He runs his hands through his hair nervously.

"Hopefully that wasn't too off-putting," he says.

It did give me pause, but I still find myself wanting to be around him. Is that wrong of me, to feel that way? Being a person is so complicated. Then again, we're in a simulation. So *what* if I have some feelings for him? I'm not going to remember any of this when I get out of here. I can feel however I want. It won't matter in the long run anyway. I should just allow myself to feel what I feel and move on.

"It just confirms that you'd better not ever fucking drink again," I say, putting a hand on his shoulder. "But you already knew that. We're good, Tanner. I promise."

"Good," he says, relieved by my answer. I hear footsteps; Lana has returned, looking puffy-eyed and angry.

"*Now* can we sleep?" Lana slurs. She must have hit her bottle hard alone out there in the woods. "Because I'm tapped out. I'm done. I can't handle one more fucking thing tonight."

We find a spot nearby so Amara can join us when she's ready. I sleep between Tanner and Lana again, although I've moved a little closer to Tanner this time. Not so close that we're touching, but close enough that we *could* be if we wanted to.

Close enough to whisper to one another and look into each other's eyes under the pale moonlight.

"You're not a gluttonous monster, Elizatine," he whispers to me. "You're cool as fuck."

I giggle a little, and Lana shushes me.

"And you're not the spawn of Satan, Tanner," I say. "You just act like one when you're drunk."

I reach out and bop him on the nose.

"Good night. Don't let the bed clowns bite," I whisper, and he groans.

"If y'all don't *shut the fuck up*," Lana grumbles, and I do everything I can to not make another peep.

Once again, the three of us drift off to sleep beneath the starry sky.

And when we wake up in the morning, Rowan's frantic voice comes echoing from the spy glasses in our pockets.

CHAPTER SIXTEEN
Rowan

I'm trapped up in this boring-ass tower, and I'm losing my mind.

There's nothing to do. Sure, the view is great, but I'm *afraid of heights*, remember? All looking out the window does is make me want to hurl. I want nothing more than to get down to solid ground, but there's no way out. I've looked everywhere, tried lifting every stone. Short of a portal, I don't think anyone is getting in or out of this thing without some serious help.

This is probably some kind of test, isn't it?

I try turning on the projector. Nothing. Try lifting up every object in the room. Nothing. I even try screaming sorry real loud, just in case that satisfies someone. No dice. I'm just stuck here, doing a whole lot of nothing. Waiting for someone to come rescue me. If I weren't so petrified of heights, I'd climb down all by myself. Tie some sheets together and just scale it. It's not like I'd actually die in here if I fell…*right*? I'd probably re-spawn somewhere—worst case scenario, I'd be removed from the simulation. There's no *real* risk, right?

Still, it's too much for me to even consider. Nah, they've got to pick the *one* thing I'm scared of most. If climbing down is the test, I'm going to fail. I know that much. I can't even *look* down from the window without breaking into a cold sweat and nearly having a panic attack. Where did that fear even come from, anyway? Is it because of how my brother died?

Maybe a shrink can help me with that once I get out of here.

I flop down on the bed and lie limp. What else am I supposed to do? I've already checked out everything in the room. If only I could get that stupid projector to work.

I get up and start fiddling with it again, and that's when I notice something that looks like a spy glass taped in front of the projector. Suspicious. I pick it up and look it over. It's pretty ordinary, like what you'd find in a detective kit for kids. Still, the fact that it was taped there makes me think there's something special about it.

"Show me your secrets, you piece of shit," I tell it.

I'm at the end of my rope here. Shockingly, something happens. I start to see something else appear in the glass; darkness.

"Hello?" I ask. "Helloooooo? Is someone there?"

"Did you hear that?" I hear a voice say. It's faint, but it almost sounded like Elizatine.

"Yeah," another voice, male this time, says. Damn it, that would be Tanner.

Suddenly, the light shifts and Elizatine comes into view. I flip the spy glass over and Tanner is visible on the other side.

"The fuck?" I ask, flipping back and forth between the two of them. "How am I seeing you guys right now?"

"Magic spy glass," Elizatine says. "I assume you have one, too?"

"Yeah," I say. "It was taped to a projector in this tower I'm trapped in. You guys wouldn't happen to know where I am, would you?"

"No clue," Tanner says, "but try putting the looking glass back the way it was taped before. Maybe it was there for a reason."

He may have a point. I put the spy glass back and re-secure the tape over it. Nothing happens at first, but then Elizatine is projected on the big screen. As her face appears, a large amount of glare bounces off of the metal sides of the projector screen.

"We see a bright light in the distance," Tanner says. "Can you wave your hand in front of the glass a couple of times?"

I do it, which blocks the light and probably makes it flash like a beacon for everyone else.

"It's him," Tanner says to Elizatine.

"Great," Tanner says loudly to me. "We'll follow the light. You can let down your hair when we get there, Rapunzel."

I roll my eyes.

"But seriously, we'll find a way to get you out of there. Just hang tight. Keep flashing your hand in front of the light so we don't lose sight of you."

I have to listen to everyone yapping away while I wait. Part of me is jealous that I'm not there, that I've been singled out. I didn't like the Rapunzel comment even though I already made that connection myself, plus I *did* talk shit like that about Felix when he was still here. I guess I'm one of those people who can dish it, but can't take it. I still don't know how they're going to get me out of here, though. It seems impossible from where I'm standing.

Many minutes go by. I'm so fucking bored, just sitting here waving my hand over a beam of light that's starting to fade the more the sun rises. I hope they find me before the glare goes away completely.

I can't help but think about Declan. His cute, wide smile and bright, twinkling eyes. How we lost him. There's no escaping it. This is one of the many moments where I wish it had been me. What kind of a life would he be living right now if it weren't for me? I wouldn't even be in this tower in the first place. Maybe he and I would be on a trip somewhere, backpacking across a mountain range. Smiling. Enjoying life. Instead, I'm consumed with guilt and can barely breathe sometimes, it gets so heavy.

I hope I can forgive myself someday. It's true that I was just a kid. I probably didn't know better. I just wanted him to have fun. I didn't kill him on purpose. It was an accident. I was just a kid myself. But how do I *not* blame myself when I'm the one who knocked over the dresser? How can I ever separate myself and my worth from that action? *Everything* hinged on that moment. That exact moment where I jumped off and it came toppling down.

If I could go back in time and undo it, I would. I'd give up my life, anything to change it. It would make my mom so happy, and I wouldn't have to suffer anymore.

"We're here," I hear Elizatine say. I look down from one of the windows, and my stomach clenches as I see them down there. They seem tiny from such a high vantage point.

"Time to get saved," I mutter, sitting down on the floor like the useless sack of crap I am.

CHAPTER SEVENTEEN
Tanner

I don't know how we're going to get Rowan down from this tower.

We've walked all around it a dozen times. Dug around in the ground. Tried yelling commands at it, hoping a door would appear and solve all of our problems. As far as we can tell, it's impenetrable.

Currently, the only way for a human to get in or out is through the windows.

"Call me crazy," I say, "but should we try to find the dragon again and convince it to help us?"

Lana scoffs.

"No more damn dragons," she says. "Gladiator zombie battles, I can handle. Dragons? You can fuck right off with that."

"I mean, think about it," I say as I'm picturing the dragon's massive hoard of treasure. "We've been using these spy glasses to communicate. Who's to say the dragon doesn't have one, too?"

I feel ridiculous as I'm saying all of this, but I'm trying to keep my mind open here. Then it hits me.

The gifts from the witch.

Specifically *Amara's* gift, which I had completely forgotten about because she never uses it. And why would she?

"Amara," I say. "Your wings. I know letting them out hurts you, but would you consider trying to…well, fly up there and help him?

"I don't know how," Amara says. "I haven't tried since I got them. Besides, he's too heavy for me. I wouldn't be able to get him down."

"But maybe you could bring him something," I say. What, though, I don't know. "Anyone else got any ideas?"

Elizatine shakes her head.

"Rowan left his bag back at the tavern," Elizatine says, "so he can't use his figurine, either. We don't even know where the tavern is in relation to here."

That gives *me* an idea.

"I'm sorry to put this on you, Amara," I say, "but if you were able to fly up high enough to look around, you might be able to spot the village. We could go back, get the figurine, fly it up to him. Have him wish for something that can get him down from the tower. It's either that or the dragon," I add, looking at Lana.

"I vote for the figurine," Lana says immediately, raising a hand as she takes a swig. "One hundred percent."

"But I don't know how!" Amara repeats, frustrated.

"I know," I say gently, placing a hand on her shoulder. I draw her panic into my own body, and it's already clawing to get out. Deep breaths, man. "Just try letting them out. One step at a time."

Now that she's a little less panicked, Amara takes a deep breath in before pushing her wings out. She screams as they emerge, and I feel bad for even suggesting it in the first place.

"I'm sorry," I say, touching her on the shoulder again. Apparently my gift only works on mental pain, not physical. "I couldn't think of a better way."

"I'll try flapping," she says, tears in her eyes. I feel like a monster for having suggested this. We all watch as her wings begin to move, awkwardly at first, but more bird-like on her subsequent tries. She's gritting her teeth.

"I can't do this for very long," she says. "It hurts so bad."

She builds up enough speed to start lifting herself off of the ground.

"Try landing before you get too high," I suggest. "So that you learn how to do it now."

She seems to have an instinct for what she's doing,

because she's able to land gently on her feet without any issues. She quickly sinks to the ground, no doubt dizzy from the pain and effort.

"Hang on and I'll try it again," she says, breathing hard. After a few minutes, she grits her teeth again and pushes the wings out, and this time she springs to action immediately. We cheer for her from the ground as she rises up with a confidence I haven't seen from her before. At the same time, I'm terrified for her as she rises above the tree line. If she can't land safely, there's nothing any of us can do to help.

"The village is that way!" she shouts, pointing southwest of our current location. "It's not even that far from us. I think I can make it there!"

"Wait, Amara!" I shout, but it's no use. Once she gets an idea in her head, she runs with it. Amara swoops away in the direction of the village, probably mistaking our shouts for cheers.

Well, *shit*.

"Should've taken one of the spy glasses with her," Lana says, shaking her head. "That girl…"

"She just wants to help," Elizatine says in her defense. "Maybe it wasn't the most responsible choice, but her heart's in the right place. And for *Rowan*, who's been nothing but vicious toward her this entire time."

All we can do is wait and hope she's able to find the backpack and bring it back to us. I'm a little frustrated with her for just taking off like that. If I were her dad—which I very well could be at my age—I'd be pissed, but maybe a little proud of her confidence, whether it's misplaced or not. A lot of people never work up the nerve to do big things, but she's willing to jump right in. Good for her.

Elizatine touches my arm. I love it when she does that, although I don't think she realizes how much it means to me. Men don't get a lot of random physical contact. It makes me feel seen, valued somehow. Like she wants me to stay so badly that she's making sure I haven't disappeared.

Well, maybe it's not *that* dramatic, but a man can dream a little.

"I'm so worried for her," Elizatine says to me quietly. "Imagine falling from that height. How much that would hurt. Do we die in here? What would happen to her then?"

I push my luck a little and put my arm around her, and she moves in closer to me. Not the worst sign.

"She's clever," I say, hoping that I'm not talking out of my ass. "She'll be fine."

A few minutes go by with the three of us standing around with the Abloosh—and Lana giving us some side-eye—until Amara returns. She has a big grin on her teary face and the backpack in her hands. She glides over to the highest window of the tower and passes the backpack through to Rowan, then carefully lowers herself to the ground and collapses, crying but smiling through the pain.

"I did it," she says, as if she can hardly believe it herself. "I did it all by myself."

She's too tired to get up, so her Abloosh lowers itself so that she can climb on and lie down. Maybe she needs a service animal once she gets out of here. An unconditional friend, one who's not going to berate her for anything. I hope that pans out. I think it'd be good for her.

"You did an incredible job, Amara," Elizatine says, crouching down next to her with her hand on Amara's back. "You've saved Rowan. You should be so proud of yourself."

"I *am*," Amara says. "You don't need to tell me to be."

Elizatine winces through her smile, but stays crouched down next to Amara. I congratulate her, and Lana holds back some choice words regarding her irresponsibility.

"I'll be right back, you guys," I say, and I head out into the woods by myself for a moment.

When everyone is out of sight, I scream and scream until I can't scream any more. Silently, of course, thanks to the wish I cashed in on from the dragon.

Amara's pain was getting to be too much on top of my own. I had to let it out before it consumed me.

Now, all that's left is to wait for Rowan to get himself out of there.

CHAPTER EIGHTEEN
Rowan

She did it. Somehow, that girl actually did it—she busted out those excruciating wings, *flew*, and brought me my backpack. All while I could barely even bring myself to look out of the window.

I'm a certified pathetic piece of shit. I already knew that, but seeing the disparity in our actions really solidifies it. I've treated her like crap with all my snarkiness, yet she still went through all that pain just to help me. At the very least, I probably owe her an apology. Not exactly my strong suit, but I can try. I *have* to try.

Just like I have to try to get out of this tower.

I don't want wings. I don't want to scale the outside of this thing. I want solid ground below me the entire time.

I want to bust out of here.

Maybe it's stupid, but I still want super-strength. The ability to tear down the walls. I just *know* there's a staircase down there. There *has* to be. Because I've realized the point of this whole thing wasn't to make me confront my fear of heights.

It was to let other people help me.

People don't help me. I push them away long before they'd ever want to offer a helping hand, and that's by design. Historically, I haven't wanted it. I learned to take care of myself. I even pushed my mom away, although I still don't know if she pushed me away first. Chicken-and-egg kind of situation. So to have to rely on other people to save me—people I haven't treated very well—was difficult.

I don't know if I believed they'd take the time to get me down from here. I figured they'd leave me behind, complete the quest on their own. Maybe come back and get me down when they felt like it. But instead, they made me a priority, and they did it because I'm part of the group. An equal to the rest of them.

That realization was *huge*.

I'm lucky I have the lighter with me. With shaking hands, I open up my backpack and set up the figurine, shoving a candle into its thick head. I set the wick alight and watch as the figurine's eyes glow back at me.

"I wish for super strength," I say, feeling ridiculous saying the words out loud.

The figurine glows white, then cracks in half.

I don't feel any different at first, but as I lift my backpack up back over my shoulders, it feels like nothing. Light as air. I pocket the spy glass in case I need it later, and then I go over to one of the thicker stone walls and really work my fingers into the cracks, then pull. The stone dislodges, tumbling down at my feet.

That one was a test; now, I'm digging into the stones on the floor, prying them up with my suddenly strong fingers. I pull up about eight stones before I start to see what looks like a spiral staircase descending into darkness. I lower myself through the hole onto the steps and start heading down, flicking the lighter on as I get further along. It's claustrophobic and dark, but I can feel the relief settling into my body as I get closer to the ground. When I can't go any further down, I dislodge a few more of the stones until I can see daylight glowing through the hole I've made. Finally, I'm able to climb out.

I'm free.

The group rounds the corner, and Elizatine runs up and hugs me tightly. It catches me off guard, and I hug her back. I feel grounded, both by her embrace and the literal dirt beneath my feet. I can't believe they came back for me, that *Amara* of all people helped me.

And I can't believe I got myself out of there even

though I was completely fucking petrified.

"I'm so glad you're okay, Rowan," Elizatine says over my shoulder. "I was worried about you."

I glance up and see Tanner, who looks a little pained. *Good*, I think to myself, even though I don't really have anything against the guy. There's just a little smugness in me that Elizatine is choosing *me* over *him* in this moment.

"Well, where to from here?" I ask, as if it's all no big deal. "Back to the village?"

"Seems like a good place to start," Tanner says. "If we head southwest, we should come up on it soon."

As we walk, the others fill me in on what I missed—some sort of gladiator-style demon fight, a market, and a circus roast. I can't help but wonder why I wasn't included in that play. Maybe it's because I roast myself enough already. Or maybe the worst is still yet to come for me. Maybe the tower was just a prelude to something even more sinister.

After a while, we hit the village again. It feels like so much has happened between when we were last here and now. Getting snatched up by a dragon, locked in a tower—just the most *bizarre* shit.

I'm not a baby, but I'm ready for a nap.

CHAPTER NINETEEN
Amara

"You're back," a deep voice says from behind me.

I turn around. It's the man in the cloak I was talking to the other day, the one who explained the Fuzznado to me and Lana.

"Hey," I tell him with a small wave. It's just me and him outside in the village right now. Everyone else has gone off to do something else. Lana is at the tavern, Rowan is in a room, Elizatine probably went shopping, and Tanner's out walking one of the paths by himself.

I really liked talking to the man in the cloak yesterday. I got going about some of my interests and he actually *listened*. Not many people will do that for me.

I would have kept talking to him, too, if Lana hadn't come up and interrupted. He even told me he thought I was *smart*. I wish more people would tell me that. I don't like feeling stupid—no one does, right?

"You never told me your name," I say to him.

"It's not important," the man says with a smile. "But you were telling me the most fascinating story about your friends when we were interrupted. Do you remember? Go on, continue!"

I feel happiness taking over my body as he says that. He remembered my story. He listened. What a kind person, to pay attention like that.

"Well, my friends bought tickets to the event," I say, and I start to explain it again. He nods with interest, asking questions and reacting to the crazier parts of the story. I take out my planner to show him the ticket stub, and he studies it like it's something incredible.

I feel a little sad. Why can't my friends and my mom act like this around me? They seem almost disinterested. I wish they cared about my stories and interests as much as this man did.

"How old are you?" I ask him.

"I'm not sure," he says. "But not *that* old."

"I'm twenty-one," I say. "So a three-year-old adult."

He laughs.

"Here," he says, handing the ticket back to me. "That was interesting. What else do you have in that incredible book of yours?"

I flip through the pages again until I find a new

poem I wrote. I offer to read it out loud to him. No one wants to hear my poetry.

"Of course!" he says, and I recite it from memory. It's a poem about losing my independence, how much it hurts to be reliant on my mom for getting around. I want to perform someday at an open mic, but that would involve having my mom drive me there with the wheelchair in the back of the minivan. The irony, right?

"That was well done," the man says with a smile. "I'm sorry you're going through that. It sounds very difficult."

"Not as difficult as getting this big book delivered," I say, and I explain all about the cursed book wrapped in skins because I think he'd like to hear about it. "And we can't even touch it! I feel bad that we have to deliver it. I hope it doesn't curse anyone."

"And you need to deliver it to a…man-frog, you said?" he asks.

"Yes. His name is Glaks," I say, proud of myself for remembering. "Oh, and this is my Abloosh, Nia. I don't think I introduced you."

"Hi, Nia," the man says, and Nia moves away from his hand. I guess she's feeling shy today.

"You know," the man says, "I actually know Glaks, where he lives. If you'd like, I can show you the way."

"That would be amazing!" I say. "Should I go let everyone else know?"

"No, no," he says. "There's no need. It'll be quicker if just you and I and Nia go. You told me about how you flew here and back all on your own, and this is another opportunity to impress your friends with how capable you are! Because really, you're capable of anything, Amara," he says with a big smile. "Absolutely anything you set your mind to. You're incredible."

I feel myself blushing. He's cute—maybe in his thirties, I can't really tell, but cute all the same. Maybe he likes me.

"Thank you," I say. "That's so kind of you to say."

"Bring your books and meet me back here later tonight," he says, putting a hand on my shoulder. "We can go together. We'll be back before anyone would know you'd even left!"

The idea of being the one to deliver the book is exciting. I can just imagine telling all of the others, how proud of me they'd be for doing such a big task all by myself. I want them to be proud of me. *I* want to be proud of me.

"It's a plan," I say, and he tells me he'll see me soon.

Tonight, when everyone is asleep, I'll sneak out and deliver the book.

They're going to be so happy with me.

CHAPTER TWENTY
Elizatine

It's starting to get dark, so I decide to turn in for the night. It's been a long-ass couple of days. I'd bought myself some sterling silver spoons while Lana was off saving the town, and I'm hoping to turn them into jewelry tomorrow as part of my wish.

I'm so proud of everyone. Lana, for that Fuzznado business. That must have felt amazing, to control the elements. I love to see a powerful woman. If she would just stop drinking, she could be unstoppable. Tanner, for confronting his demons. Amara, for pushing through the pain to do something incredible, but resting when she needed to. Rowan, for helping himself get out of the tower despite his fear of heights.

But me? I'm not so sure yet.

The inn in this town isn't quite as charming as the first one we encountered. There are no treehouses here; just a long stretch of hill-side, Hobbit-hole type dwellings that cost four credits a night. I'm a broke bitch, so I get cozy at the foot of a tall tree just to the side of the right-most dwelling; Amara is staying in that one. I pull my cape out from my bag and feel my pants loosen slightly. I take out a coat for Tanner, who I'm not entirely surprised to see out here again. I don't think it's about saving credits anymore—I think he just likes sleeping under the beauty of the stars.

"Well, damn," Tanner remarks. "I'm beat."

"Me too," I say. "The emotional devastation has been off the charts, hasn't it?"

I rub the spot where my fork ring used to be on my finger. It feels like I'm missing an appendage without it.

"That was nice, what you did," Tanner says, glancing down at my hand. "I know how much that ring meant to you."

"Yeah?" I ask, but I quickly realize I should have played along and pretended I knew, too.

"You don't remember?" he remarks, watching my face carefully. "It's not my place to say, then. Just know that what you did was huge."

We lay down under the stars together. Not too close

together, but not so far that we can't talk comfortably.

"You missing Felix yet?" he asks with a smirk. *Felix.* That feels like an eternity ago, after all that's happened.

"I wouldn't say I'm missing *him*," I say. "But we had our charismatic leader, and now he's gone. It changed the dynamic. I feel like an impostor. Plus I'm shit at singing."

"You haven't heard *me*," Tanner says with a grin. "Don't think I've hit a right note in my life."

He frowns slightly.

"I still can't remember much about myself before the simulation," he says. "What about you?"

"I remember how to make spoon rings," I say, "but as far as family goes, life out there? Nothing. It's crazy to consider the possibilities."

We lay in silence for a few moments.

"I think I was lonely out there," Tanner says. "I don't know, I just have a feeling. It's been nice, being here with you guys. Hasn't been easy, obviously, but there's this heaviness that feels like it's lifting a little."

"I know what you mean," I say, because I'm feeling the same way. "It helps to be around people who understand. People with the same kinds of flaws and urges."

I think back to the night at the store, when everyone but Tanner stood and stared at me in my moment of great shame. I could kiss him for that, for covering me up without a second thought.

"Who do you think is leaving the simulation next?" I ask. He thinks for a moment.

"Lana," he says. "She's going to get sloshed off her ass with that never-ending drink wish and have a come-to-Jesus moment. Who do *you* think's going to be next?"

"You," I say, and Tanner looks surprised. "You seem like you have it all together."

He chuckles darkly.

"You'd be surprised, Elizatine. And I hope it's *not* me. I'm not ready to leave—not yet."

"Why? Hoping we run into another dragon?" I ask, but he doesn't elaborate further. He just looks over at me with a sort of wistful expression on his face.

"Good night," he says, closing his eyes slowly. "Don't let the bed-frogs bite."

I reach over, run my fingers down his arm, and give him a light pinch. He smiles softly.

"Oops. Too late," I say, smiling back. "Good night, Tanner."

I watch him for a few minutes. He's a handsome guy. Not as pretty as Felix, but Tanner still has that *je ne sais quoi* about him that makes him unquestionably attractive. Maybe it's all in the squint. It's different to see his expression relaxed now. He looks boyish, more sweet and innocent than usual. He tends to look a little more war-torn and haunted during the day.

Tanner opens one eye a little and smiles.

"Were you…watching me?" he asks.

Whoops. Busted.

"You wish," I say, arching an eyebrow. I flip over lest I get caught again. "See you in the morning."

And this time, I let my thoughts fade and my mind drift off to wild, simulated sleep.

"Good mooooorrrnnningggg!" a voice calls from a foot away from my face—Lana's. I can smell the alcohol from here.

Did she stay up all night drinking?

"Damn, girl," I say, blinking fast as the morning rays hit my face. "Say it, don't spray it."

"You're just…you're just silly, with your silly hair and those silly rings," Lana slurs, gripping her water bottle tightly in her hand. "*Sillytine.*"

"Oh, *Jesus*, Lana," I say, sitting up. I reach out to take the water bottle from her, but she swipes it away just in time. "We're supposed to keep following the path this morning. Are you sure you can even *walk*?"

"Relax," Lana says, stumbling forward just a bit. Tanner sits up as well, and Lana holds out the water bottle. "Want some, T-Bone?"

"Nah," Tanner says, clearly uncomfortable. He's no doubt been in this state before. "Maybe you should give that water bottle to someone else, Lana. Let them hold on to it for you."

"I'm moderating myself just fine, thank you," Lana says, shaking her head. "I can handle myself. I'm a grown-ass woman."

"And I'm a grown-ass man," Tanner says, standing up. "Doesn't mean we don't need a little help sometimes."

"I saved this whole goddamn village," she says. "Don't tell me about needing help. *You* need help."

Tanner looks like he wants to say something, but I put my hand on his back—his *very* muscular back—and shake my head. I leave my hand there and lead him away as Lana continues to verbally poke at our sore spots. She's an intense drunk, that's for sure, and the wish she made was certainly something of a curse for the rest of us.

"Like you said, rock bottom," I remind Tanner, rubbing his back lightly. "She'll get there all on her own. She's not going to listen to us, and especially not to *you*—the guy who has it figured out."

"You're right," he says. "It just hurts to see it, knowing I've been there myself. I wish I could save her from herself."

"The only one who can save Lana is *Lana*," I say, and he nods. "We have to remember that, no matter how painful it gets. We can only do so much."

Rowan walks past us.

"So, what are you two *lovebirds* up to today?" Rowan says, noticing my hand on Tanner's back. I quickly pull it away, even though it's none of his business.

I can feel that my cheeks are flushed from Rowan's *lovebird* comment. Why did that embarrass me? That's something I'd usually be able to laugh right off, no problem.

"*Not* lovebirds," I correct. "And we're lamenting… well, that."

I gesture over to Lana, who's drunkenly monologuing to the tree we slept under last night.

"Jesus Christ," Rowan says, watching Lana. "I say we take that bottle and chuck it. Give it to the dragon."

"Imagine *you* against a drunk dragon, Rowan," I say with a smirk. "Given your new Hulk powers, though, maybe you'd actually stand a chance."

"Amara?" I ask, knocking hard on her door. She's the only one who hasn't come out yet. There's no answer or sounds of stirring, so I try the door handle. To my surprise, the door opens, revealing an empty room and bed.

"Have you seen Amara?" I ask Rowan, and he shakes his head. It's a no from Lana as well, which has me worried. Amara is impulsive—she could have gotten an idea in her head and taken off without talking to the rest of us, thinking she had everything under control.

Shit. The book.

I run back to her room to look for the cursed book, but it's gone as well. Wherever she went, she took the book and the Abloosh with her.

She could have gone anywhere.

"This might be a stupid idea," I tell the remainder of the group, "but I think we should split up. Two of us search the town, two of us check the path ahead. I saw flares in the shop—we could send up a green flare if we find her, an orange flare if we're coming back clueless, and both at the same time if we found her and need help. She could be literally anywhere," I say, a tinge of rage biting at my insides, "and we have shit to do. Let's find her and get back on track, shall we?"

I pair myself with Rowan, and Tanner with Lana. I trust that Tanner won't partake in Lana's endless drink trough, plus I'm secretly hoping they'll have a little heart-to-heart moment that nudges her even closer to her rock bottom. She deserves the growth, to not suffer like this anymore. I never want her to get this drunk ever again. I want her to live a fulfilling, happy life.

"Alright, Rowan," I say. As revenge—and to show him who's boss—I intertwine my fingers with his and wrap my right hand around his darkly-clad bicep. "Off we go. Two lovebirds."

What I don't expect is for him to genuinely smile. Just for a moment; it's fleeting, but it's there.

"Whatever you say, princess," he tells me with a wink.

Lana cackles, and Tanner looks away.

"I'll get the flares," Lana says, patting her pockets full of riches. "You guys keep doing whatever...*this* is."

I let go of Rowan and sit in my discomfort a minute while Lana gets us some flares. Rowan and Tanner don't say a word to me or to each other.

What have I *done*?

Lana returns with the flares and distributes them between us. I'm suddenly regretting my group distributions. Then again, could I *really* trust Rowan and Lana to stay on track together? They'd probably go get drunk and forget that we're looking for Amara.

"Let's go find Amara," I say. "Tanner, Lana, you guys check the town. We're going to check out the major pathways. We'll meet back here in a couple of hours if we don't find anything."

The group splits off, and I'm stuck with Rowan. Rowan, who might have taken a genuine liking to me at some point in this journey. Was it when I saved his life and he never even thanked me for it?

"Well, where should we start?" Rowan asks, looking to me. Great Leader and all that.

"Maybe she went ahead of us, trying to scout things out and be helpful. We could start there, look for footprints or signs that she's been around."

We head up the path in relative silence.

"So you and Tanner, huh?" Rowan asks after a few minutes. "Isn't he, what, a hundred?"

"Forty-four," I say, rolling my eyes. "And there's no *me and Tanner*. There's no me and *anyone*. I'm just trying to get through this thing. Why do you care?"

"But you're like thirty, right?" he asks. "That's a fourteen year difference. He was fourteen when you were *born*."

"Rowan," I say. "Dude. For the last time. Drop it."

"I'm just saying," Rowan grumbles, but he thankfully shuts up about it. It's strange to have him care about something, *anything*, other than himself. I just wish it wasn't about this.

I'm not ready to think about Tanner or Rowan right now. We need to focus on getting Amara back before something bad happens.

The path is similar to what came before it, except the purple flowers we were warned not to touch are even more densely packed than before. I wonder if we'll ever find out what they do. Paralysis? Death? Hallucinations? It must be something atrocious.

"Wait a second," I say, stopping dead in my tracks as I hear something faintly in the distance. It almost sounded like laughter. "Do you hear that?"

"Hear what?" he asks, and I gesture for him to stop walking. He pauses and listens.

"Yeah, that's creepy," he says. "It sounds like someone's...giggling?"

The more we walk, the clearer the laughter gets. It doesn't sound like genuine laughter. It sounds like the kind of laughter you'd get if you *told* someone to laugh while also holding them at gunpoint—forced, strained, uncomfortable.

It's eerie, but most importantly, it sounds like Amara.

"Amara?" I shout into the void of trees and flowers. There's a louder bout of laughter, and then it dies down to a forced chuckle.

I start to smell smoke.

"This way," I say, spotting a faint trail of smoke in the air. We carefully step over the flowers as we go off-path, and we eventually reach a small clearing. There's a little house there, and in front of it is Amara, her torso tied to a chair built into the ground. In front of her is a burning bonfire, and above the bonfire dangles the cursed book, which is slowly slipping out of its protective skins.

Amara bursts into nervous laughter as soon as she sees us. The front door opens, and a cloaked man steps out.

"*You*," Rowan says. "You're from the village. I saw you talking to Amara a couple of days ago."

"You are correct," he says. He removes the hood of his cloak, exposing a somewhat familiar face.

"You're the guy who wanted to trade Amara's planner for the map," I say. "With the big coat. Why are you doing this?"

"For the…what did you call it? The planner? For the *planner*," he says. "Its construction is spell-binding, and I simply *must* have it. But I gave your friend here a choice. She can save your cursed book from falling into the fire and get her planner back, or she can let it fall into the fire. Your quest will be over, but she will remain un-cursed, and the planner will be mine."

All of this diabolical shit over a *planner*? Make it make sense. This cannot be happening.

"This is insane," Rowan says, articulating what we're both thinking. "Why do you need this planner so badly? Amara, why don't you just give it to him and be done with this?"

"I can't!" she shouts between involuntary laughs. "It's...too...special!"

"And why is she laughing like this?" I ask.

"Oh, that?" the man asks, as if he hadn't noticed until I brought it up. "She touched the Laughing Flowers. Grazed them with her ankle, wasn't paying attention."

So *that's* what the flowers do. I thought it would be something far worse. Then again, everything about her forced laughter is creepy. It's certainly setting an ambiance.

As we talk, the book continues to slip forward toward the fire. I don't know what letting it burn would mean for our quest, for this journey we're supposed to be on. It feels too important, like no single person's issues should trump the completion of our task.

Amara looks between the book and the planner, clearly unsure which one she should save.

"The planner isn't real, Amara, but this quest is," I tell her pleadingly. "It's supposed to help all of us. Remember the bigger picture? Keeping perspective? This is one of those times. We need to get the book down."

Just as I'm about to grab the book from the very top where the skins are still attached, the book starts to fall. There's no thinking, no time to do anything but act.

I catch the cursed book with my bare hands.

Instantly, I start to feel numb. My body, real or not, feels like it's shutting down. I drop the book on the ground beside me and look helplessly at Rowan, the only one who can deal with this situation now.

"Help me," I whisper, but it feels like a big ask. What's he supposed to do? Wave a magic wand and fix me? No. I chose to do this, to step in and save Amara from the consequences of her actions. Now I'm fading fast, unable to do anything to help anyone.

The man tosses the planner at Amara's feet, waves the flames away with his hands, and removes her restraints.

"Until next time," he says. "You know where to find me."

He goes inside his cottage and slams the door shut, leaving the three of us together with the cursed book loose.

"Shit, shit, *shit*," Rowan says to himself. He takes down the hanging animal skins and uses them to grab the book, gingerly re-wrapping it until none of the cover is visible.

"Here," he says, angrily shoving the book back into Amara's backpack. He thrusts the backpack into her arms, the planner still on the ground. From behind her, Amara's Abloosh timidly emerges from the woods. "Take it. Good fucking job."

My vision is starting to blur, and my hearing isn't so good, either. Still, I can very clearly hear Rowan scream two single words.

"NOW GO!"

The Abloosh freezes, then bolts away in fear; faster than I've ever seen it move before. Nia zips through the trees and far out of sight, leaving Amara completely on her own.

"I…" I start to say, but I'm fading out. It feels like going under sedation. I'm trying to fight it, but at a certain point, the scale tips and there's no winning anymore.

I'm losing that fight.

CHAPTER TWENTY-ONE
Rowan

Good golly fuck. What do I do?

When I've imagined Elizatine sleeping next to me, this really isn't what I had in mind. I thought I'd win her over somehow. Show her I'm not a total asshole. Get her to soften toward me, give a guy like me a chance. I know I'm not winning any prizes out here for being likable. Still, I imagined she'd see past the pain, past the bullshit I put up and break me down like a crumbling wall.

And then she held my hand.

I swear, my Grinch heart grew three sizes in that moment. All the hurt and longing came to the surface, and for what felt like the first time in a long time, I felt seen. Comfortable, even though I knew she was joking. For a split second, it just felt real. Attainable.

I get the feeling I never had a good dating life. I can't imagine how that would have worked, anyway. How could I find love when I push everyone away? I'd be a nightmare. Hot and cold, toying with their emotions like a cat with a dying mouse. No, I probably scared people off and then resented them for leaving. Classic Rowan. I'd no doubt do the same to Elizatine, whether I wanted to or not.

And I see the way she looks at Tanner. That comfort I felt—I think she feels that around *him*. Where it's simple, calm, like everything in the world is all right. And that's my own damn fault. I wouldn't want to be around me. I know I'm insufferable, and still, I just can't stop myself. It's like a compulsion. I push and I push, and then I resent being alone. It's sick.

"*You*," I shout, glaring at Amara. "*You* did this!"

I dig the flares out of Elizatine's backpack and set them off, tossing them in her direction.

"I can't even look at you," I mutter, and she starts to cry. Good. What she did was so utterly stupid. I don't know how Amara's even alive right now with all the moronic decisions she makes. "You can get back to the village all on your own."

With a whimper and more annoying giggles that she can't control, Amara limps off into the forest away from us. I don't know how she's going to get back to the village when she can only walk short distances without passing out, but I don't particularly care right now.

Good fuckin' riddance.

The strength I wished for up in the tower is still there, so I scoop up Elizatine with one arm under her legs and one under her upper back, the way you'd carry a kid. She's dead weight, but manageable. I try not to stare down at her chest as I carry her forward, step by step, hoping and pleading with something unseen that she's going to be okay.

I hate that she won't remember this—that I cared so much. That I saved her all by myself. She probably just sees me as an asshole, which makes sense because that's all I've been since I got here.

I'll never forgive Amara. That...that *child* thinks she can do whatever she wants, *whenever* she wants. Look at the consequence. Look at what it's done to Elizatine, who had to step in and save her ass.

Elizatine just saves anyone from their poor decisions, huh?

Even me.

It takes a while, but I make it back to the village before dark. Tanner and Lana passed me on the trail to go find Amara, and I refused to talk about what happened. Told them to ask Amara what she'd done. Tanner rushed forward and tried to take Elizatine from my arms, but I refused. I carried her this far. He's not getting a single drop of the credit. I'm staying with her until she wakes up.

If she ever wakes up.

I take her around to the back of one of the buildings. I want some privacy. She doesn't need people staring at her, and neither do I. Tanner and Lana go off and try to get advice from the townsfolk, and Amara holes herself up in her room to mope.

It's kind of cold out here, so I hold Elizatine against my chest, her body against mine. I hope she won't hate this when she wakes up. I haven't exactly been nice to her. I wish I had been. When she gained all that weight right in front of me, it broke my brain. It was too absurd. I couldn't feel empathy—just disgust. But that's quickly shifted. I can't believe how quickly, actually. Maybe it's been there all along, back in our group sessions before the simulation. I don't know what else would explain it, but you'd never guess it based on how I've acted. I wish it was different. I wish *I* were different.

The way she held me, though, that changed everything. That made it real.

That gave me hope.

We were told it would take an enormous amount of magic to undo contact with the book. I think I know what that means.

I'm pretty sure Lana and Tanner won't find out anything helpful from the villagers. From the very first second she fell unconscious, I knew what needed to be done.

Nope, this one's all on me.

CHAPTER TWENTY-TWO
Elizatine

As I'm thrust back into consciousness, the first thing I feel is the heat of someone's body against my back. I open my eyes expecting to see Tanner holding me, but it's Rowan.

And he's stroking my hair.

"Did I miss something?" I ask, glancing down at my hair. He has me cradled against his chest, and as shocked as I am to say this, I don't mind it. There's a softness in his eyes now that I'm not used to, but that I appreciate.

"It worked," Rowan says, breathing a sigh of relief. He holds me tighter, and I'm torn between laughing nervously or drinking it in. "Thank fuck, it worked."

"*What* worked?" I ask, looking up at his face. There's fear there accompanying the softness; more vulnerability than I think I've ever seen from him before.

"Remember how the witch took me and Tanner aside to give us our gifts?" he asks, and I nod. "Well, mine was a doozy."

He pauses.

"I know this is kind of crazy, but can I kiss you?"

My brain feels broken. I nod, mainly out of curiosity. He leans forward and kisses me deeply, his fingers grasping my hair. My heart is beating like crazy, and there are butterflies in my stomach moshing around. The kiss feels hot, a little unhinged—*dangerous*, in a way.

"Was that part of saving me?" I ask after he pulls away.

"Nah, I just wanted to kiss you," he admits, and I squint my eyes at him judgmentally.

"I don't understand," I say, climbing out of his lap to give myself a little more space. The kiss is still burning at my lips. "I thought you could barely stand me. Now you're all over me. What happened? Did you hit your head?"

"Could *barely stand you*? Elizatine, I—wow, I fucked up," he says darkly. "I'm sorry. That's just my dickish personality shining through. The truth is that I admired you. I admired your strength, all the spoon stuff you do, your confidence. I don't have that. Maybe I've been jealous, in a way. But I can definitely stand you."

He looks down at the ground.

"Thank you for saving my life," he said. "I know it came at a price. Saving yours came at a price, too, but it's one I'm happy to pay. You…you deserve it. You've been very kind to me."

He breathes in deep.

"The witch told me I could save anyone, but it'd be at the cost of staying in the simulation. That it'd be over after that, at least for me. I didn't think I'd actually use that magic, but here we are. You deserve to get better. I'm giving that to you. I'll see you on the other side of this, Elizatine. I hope you find some peace."

He squeezes my hand.

"Thank you," he says, smiling a little.

And just like that, he vanishes. The pressure from his hand releases, and the man I was just talking to has disappeared into thin air.

"Rowan?" I ask weakly, even though I know damn well what happened.

He gave up his spot in the simulation to bring me back.

Panic bubbles in my chest as I rise to my feet, grabbing my bag and his. Where are the other group members? I'm on the precipice of my first Menty-B since we arrived in the simulation. My breathing is getting ragged, and I feel like I'm hyperventilating. Am

I crying? What do I do? How the fuck did this happen? I can't even remember how I *got* here. One minute I was reaching out to protect Amara, and now—

"Elizatine?" Tanner asks. I round the corner and see Tanner, looking concerned as Lana trails behind him.

I don't think twice—I drop the bags, run up to Tanner, and bury my face in his chest as I sob uncontrollably. He holds me tight, not asking questions, just keeping me together with brute force alone. I can't even get the words out to ask if Amara is safe. I'm too overwhelmed. I just want to melt down into the ground, become the dirt, anything to escape the crushing feeling of human emotion in this moment.

Tanner puts a comforting hand on my shoulder, and the world suddenly feels right again. I melt into him, and we sink down to the ground, our backs against the same building where Rowan held me just a minute ago.

"He's gone," I manage to choke out. "He sacrificed himself to bring me back."

"We know," Lana says. "He told us. Did you know that he left Amara and the book there, in the forest? All by herself with the flares lit? He only brought *you* back."

Nothing about that surprises me, but it does make me feel more embarrassed for having let him kiss me—not to mention running into Tanner's arms immediately afterward. I wonder what Tanner would think if he knew. To be fair, though, I thought the kiss was some kind of Sleeping Beauty situation required for saving my ass.

"Where is she now?" I ask.

"Back in one of the rooms at the inn," Tanner says. His voice vibrates through his chest and into mine. "We walked her back. Took a lot of breaks. She's devastated about the Abloosh running off. She has no way to get around now."

"What about the wings?" I ask.

"She says it hurts too much," he says. "But if she's desperate enough, she just might try it again."

I don't know if I can face her yet. I'm angry. Angry because despite Rowan's callousness, he deserved a chance at getting better. He had to give it up for *me*—all because she decided to listen to a stranger and keep secrets from the rest of us.

I look up at Tanner, who seems a little misty-eyed himself.

"Maybe it's selfish," Tanner says, pulling me closer, "but I'm glad you're still here."

"Mmm," Lana says, a knowing look in her eyes. "I can see why Rowan called you two *lovebirds*. Sweet baby Jesus, get yourselves a room."

She walks off, leaving Tanner and I alone together. We break our embrace and stand around awkwardly, although it's a comfortable sort of awkwardness.

"Now that Rowan's gone, it's three against one," I say. "How's it feel, being the only guy left?"

He smiles guiltily.

"Well, it's a learning opportunity," he admits. "I'll just shut up and listen."

"Is Lana right?" I ask after a moment. "*Do* we need to get ourselves a room?"

He chuckles.

"You know I'm too cheap for that," he jokes, but he doesn't seem to want to entertain the notion any further. I can't tell if it's a rejection or if he's just feeling put on the spot, so I leave it at that. Still, I can't help but imagine what such an arrangement would look like—us tangled up in the bedsheets, me running my hands over his chest, trailing down a little lower…

"I'd better go talk to Amara," I say, because the tension has suddenly become unbearable. "See what she has to say about all of this. I'll, uh, leave you to simmer for a while."

Leave you to simmer? What the fuck does that even *mean*?

My feelings have jumped from guy to guy to guy in here. Is that a normal part of group therapy? Am I *supposed* to catch a little bit of feelings for everyone?

What a mess. I need to get a grip.

I find Amara in her original room, minus the Abloosh. She's sitting on the edge of the bed leafing through a handful of stickers, her cheeks red from crying.

"Hey," I say, sitting down next to her. She tucks the stickers away and frowns.

"Are you here to yell at me, too?" she asks, staring down at the floor.

"No," I say, although I do have a decent amount of rage bubbling up in me all the same. "I just want to understand. Why did you leave without telling us?"

"He was just *so* convincing," she says. "He told me that you guys wouldn't understand, that you're not sensitive enough. He seemed like such a nice, helpful person. I thought you guys would be proud of me for taking care of it all by myself."

"But the whole point of this book delivery quest is that it's a *team* effort," I say, placing my hand on hers. "We all need to pitch in. It's not a contest, and it's not something we need to speed through. The quest is taking time for a *reason*. We all have lessons we need to learn along the way."

"And Rowan?" she asks, sniffling. "Where's he?"

"He's gone," I say. "He sacrificed his spot in the simulation to bring me back."

"Oh," Amara says simply. She's probably relieved, and I wouldn't blame her. Rowan certainly didn't treat her well. Maybe she reminded him too much of himself; impulsive, self-centered.

"I'm sorry about Nia," I say, and Amara sniffles again. "It's hard to lose a friend. I'm sure she's safe out there somewhere, though."

"It's Rowan's fault that she's gone," she mutters. "If he hadn't yelled and scared her off, she'd still be here."

I don't bother to correct her—that if *she* hadn't run

off in the first place with a stranger, none of this would have happened.

"We'll go back for your wheelchair tonight," I say. "It'll take about four hours round-trip."

"No," Amara says stubbornly. "Just leave me here. Deliver the book without me. I'd probably just mess everything up anyway."

Sometimes her way of thinking can be so childish and black-and-white. I can't let myself take it personally. She's not acting this way on purpose; it's just how her mind operates.

"This is a team effort, and you're a part of the team," I say. "We're going back for your wheelchair. No matter what, you need to be able to get around safely. I know none of this is fair, and I'm sorry. We're all just doing the best we can—you included."

But there's one thing I need to do first—I need to cash in on my wish.

There's a silversmith in town that agreed to let me use some of their workspace for one credit, and they have all of the tools I need—a jeweler's saw, a torch, a stepped ring mandrel, and a rawhide mallet. I picked up a bunch of beautiful silver spoons and forks in town, and I want to make magic-infused jewelry for everyone. I suppose each remaining person will get more magic than they would have with the whole gang here.

I still don't know what to expect out of the Beasteous Bog, so we might as well go in prepared. Heaven help me if we run into the dragon again on bad terms. One of us would finally get turned into a Rice Krispy.

I take my utensils to the silversmith and get set up. Of *course* they happen to have all of the specialized tools I need; I suppose it's one of the perks of being in a tailored simulation.

I carefully measure the lengths I want to cut, then mark them and use a jeweler's saw to hack the rest of the utensil away. I file each piece down, leaving no sharp edges.

Time for the torch now. I blast the silver until it's red hot. Once everything has cooled down, the silver is much more pliable, and I'm able to wrap the lengths around the mandrel and re-shape each piece into a ring with some heavy thwacks of the rawhide mallet. The fork ring that the dragon took was the first piece I'd ever made—I didn't know better, so I used a regular hammer and dented the shit out of it. I've refined my materials and my technique over the years to avoid this, and thankfully, each of the pieces I'm making today turn out smooth and polished.

For me, I made a four-tined fork ring to replace the one I traded for Rowan. When each of us leave the simulation, a tine will break off—at least, that's what I'm *intending* to happen. That way, there's no uncertainty if someone ascends when separated from the rest of the group. We won't have to wonder; we'll just know.

Lana's is my way of telling her that she's got a problem: a spoon ring that glows hot when she's twice over the legal alcohol limit. I figured her drinking is more of a threat to her wellbeing than any of the creatures in here, plus she can chuck the ring into the bog for all I care. Amara's ring is very ornate, and my hope is for her to see her problems from the perspective of another person. I feel like that's one of her big issues; she takes a self-centered approach to everything and doesn't stop to consider how it affects everyone else. Maybe this will prove to be insightful.

Tanner's ring takes me the longest because I want it to be perfect—in general, of course, but also perfect for him. Finally, I settle on a relatively simple design using the end of a fork with a banded design. His ring will burn hot when he needs to talk to someone for the sake of his sanity.

Fuck, maybe *I* should become a therapist and work for TQI. I could have given everyone cool powers and shit—but here I am, trying to protect us from ourselves instead. But to be fair, our own flaws are what landed us here. The creatures and the bog aren't the real threat—it's us and our broken-ass brains.

Once the rings have cooled down enough, I go around to each person and explain what their new adornment does. Lana huffs in my face, but puts the ring on anyway; Amara looks crestfallen and embarrassed despite my gentle explanation, and Tanner puts his ring on and winces, as it's no doubt glowing hot on his hand right now.

He and I will have a little talk later.

I slide my own ring on. I engraved the first letter of each of our names onto the four fork tines. Funnily enough, it spells LATE from top to bottom. Is that what we are, late? Are we taking too much time in here? It's only been four or five days.

Then again, they warned us it could take *years*.

The day passed quickly and it's dark out now, so our plan is to rest for the night before going back for Amara's wheelchair in the morning. It's just me and Tanner under the stars again tonight.

As we settle into a pile of leaves with our coats and capes pulled snug, I reach over and feel his hand.

"You're burning up, T-Bone," I say, tapping my finger against his ring. "Talk."

"I can't," he says. "I want to, believe me, but I literally can't. Not about this."

"Why not?" I ask.

"I can't tell you *that* either," he says. "But think about Rowan's gift, how he received it, and you might figure it out in a roundabout way. I shouldn't say more than that."

I know he and Rowan visited the witch privately, so that must be it. Whatever his power is, it's taking a big toll and he's not allowed to talk about it—maybe at the expense of the power itself.

"Ok, I think I've got it," I say. "I'm sorry. That's a lot to hold on to by yourself. Maybe it's not worth it if it's hurting you so badly, man."

"Oh, it's worth it," he says, although it sounds like

he's saying it more to convince himself than to convince me. "Just trust me on that."

"I can't think of many things that would be worth that kind of suffering," I say, glancing at his ring. It's no doubt burning him, so I do what I should have done earlier—I grab his hand and take the ring off. "And you don't have to torture yourself wearing this."

"I like that you made it," he says, looking over at me with a bashful smile. "And it didn't hurt *that* bad."

The burned patch of skin on his finger begs to differ, but I don't say anything otherwise.

"You didn't answer me earlier, by the way," I say, feeling a little bold. "About needing to get a room. Is there something there, or am I just imagining things?"

Tanner looks up at the stars.

"Yeah, there's something there," he admits, and I smile. "But we don't have to rush it, you know? We don't want to forget why we're here. If it's meant to be, we'll know. We'll kiss. We'll take it further—if you want to, of course. I don't want to assume anything."

He's assuming correctly, of course. Part of me wants to jump him right here and now in the moonlight regardless of who—or what—is watching.

"Tell you what," I say, glancing down at my new ring. "If T and E are ever the only prongs left on this thing, we're making out like there's no tomorrow. Deal?"

"Deal," he says quickly, stifling a laugh. "I'd do it right now, Elizatine, believe me, but I'm trying not to lose sight of why we're here in the first place."

"Can I at least move a little closer?" I ask. We're still in that awkward spacing stage where we're giving each other room, but not so much that we can't have a conversation. "You feel too far away."

"Yeah. Get over here," he says, and I take the opportunity to snuggle up right next to him, my head on his upper chest and arm. He wraps his other arm around me and breathes in deep.

"Better?" he asks, his breathing a little ragged.

"Better," I say, draping my free arm over his arms and willing it not to wander.

For the first time since the simulation started, I feel completely safe. Content. Like I'm where I need to be. He's right, of course, about not losing sight of the bigger picture, but how can I ignore how good this feels?

"Don't let the bed-frogs bite," he whispers to me before we drift off to sleep once again under a sea of stars.

And as I sleep, a single tine on my newly-forged ring snaps.

CHAPTER TWENTY-THREE
Amara

I have to fix this.

If I thought everyone in the group hated me before, they *definitely* hate me now. I trusted a stranger, I lost Nia, I nearly got Elizatine killed, and Rowan—I suppose they blame me for Rowan, too. I don't want to be blamed for anything else.

The witch gave me these wings for a reason, and I've been too scared to use them. They hurt a lot. I don't like being in pain. I've been through too much pain—why would I want to go through *more*? But maybe it's time to bring them out again, just like I did when I brought Rowan's figurine to the tower. I need to prove them wrong about me, that I don't need their help. That I don't need the wheelchair. That I can get around just fine on my own, protect myself.

I'll be back before they even knew I was gone.

I watch Tanner and Elizatine from my window. They're cuddled up and laughing, and it makes me feel jealous. Not of either of them, specifically, because neither are really my type and they're too old for me anyway. Jealous that they have something that I want. I feel like relationships never work out for me. They don't stick around, and I'm left alone over and over again. Why is that? What did I do to deserve everyone leaving me all the time? The only person I'm glad has left beside my dad is Rowan, although I don't like that I'm being blamed for it. He made that decision, not me. He could have stayed.

He and Elizatine didn't have to help me. That shouldn't be my fault.

Once Elizatine and Tanner seem to have fallen asleep together, I take my planner and tuck it into my waistband, cinching my belt tight around it. I don't want to leave it behind. It's like a friend to me. I sneak out of my room and around to the back of a couple of buildings. I have to sit down within a minute because I'm getting so dizzy, but at least I made it to somewhere private first. I think I'll be ok once I start flying as long as my body is horizontal while I do it.

I will my wings out with my mind and try not to wail as the giant, black appendages shoot out of my shoulder blades. It feels just like one of those charlie horses I get at night from not drinking enough water. I hate the feeling and can barely tolerate it, but being blamed for everything is somehow worse.

I tell my wings to flap, and they do. I start to rise into the air like a drunk baby bird. I still don't know exactly what to do, but I try to use my imagination. What would a bird do? It takes some experimenting, but soon I'm about ten feet in the air with my wings flapping and burning. I don't feel dizzy yet even though I'm vertical. I still don't know if the pain is worth it, but I guess I'm about to find out.

I start commanding my wings to move toward the path we haven't traveled yet, over by the Beasteous Bog. If I can scout it out ahead of time, I can be useful. I can draw a map for everyone up here in the sky and take notes. They'll be less mad at me if I can help them somehow. I expect they'll want me to make things up to them, and this is a way I can do that.

I keep flying forward. It's tolerable at first, but the further I fly, the more and more it burns. Soon, the pain is so searing that I have to stop. I feel like I'm dying. I can't control it; I land hard on the path, and my wings retract back into my body.

It hurts *so fucking bad*.

I lie there on the ground for a few minutes, completely out of breath. My whole back hurts. I wish I hadn't left. I wasn't planning to land yet. I was just going to fly ahead a *little*, take some notes, and fly back without losing sight of the village. Maybe I shouldn't have done this. Why do I keep doing things that get me in trouble with everyone else?

I look around. Up ahead off of the path is a small house glowing with light. Someone must be home.

Maybe they can help me. I don't know if I can fly back.

I start to fidget with the ring Elizatine gave me. I was tempted to throw it away, but it's too beautiful to get rid of. It hurt my feelings that she thinks I can't consider other people's perspectives. I know that the group is mad at me for making bad decisions. That's all I *need* to know, really.

But as I start to trudge forward toward the cottage, I start thinking about my mom. How I'd feel if I had to put *her* in a wheelchair. If she was having that much trouble getting around and was in danger of falling and hurting herself, I'd feel better knowing she was safe. She'd also be able to do more on her own; not everything, but more than she could do while being worried about hitting her head and dying. I'd be happy to help drive her around if it meant she was safe. It would be a small price to pay. She wouldn't be able to do *everything* she used to do, but she could do *some things*.

After a couple of breaks, I finally make it to the little cottage and knock on the door. The door creaks open, but no one is standing there.

"Come in!" a voice says, and I enter the cottage. It's a tiny little place, sparsely decorated, except for a big shelf filled with unusual books.

Uh-oh.

A frog-hand reaches out toward me, and I scream as the man's face comes into view. It's the same man who's been stalking me and my planner from the very beginning.

The man we're supposed to deliver the cursed book to for our quest.

"You've come to deliver your…planner?" he asks. His frog feet are making gross squishing sounds against the floor. "You have changed your mind, come to your senses?"

I wrap my arms around my chest protectively.

"I came here for help," I say. "Please, leave me and my planner alone. It's all I have left."

"You are more than your book, child," the frog-man says to me angrily. "So much more! Why do you feel you are one and the same with an inanimate object?"

"Because it's a part of me!" I exclaim. "It has all of my notes, my stickers, my *life* in it!"

"Does your *mind* not contain your life?" the frog-man counters. "Your memories? Why risk your life and the lives of others to save this book? I am a *lover* of books, and even I do not understand. I have offered you the finest rewards, the things that would help you most on your quest—and *still* you refuse. You are a foolish human."

I pull the planner out of my waistband and look at it. I can't imagine giving it up. I know I have my memories right now, sort of, but my memories might not always be there. This will be. This is the closest thing to a friend that I have. I can tell my planner anything—my worries, my hyper-fixations, my crushes—and have it be kept a secret. My real-life friends weren't much good for that.

But then I think of Elizatine and her fork ring, the one she used to get Rowan back. I remember the story of why she made it, what it's made from. How she was so willing to give it up to save a complete jerk. Why was it so easy for her? Doesn't she miss it?

This is my fault.

If I look at all of this from Elizatine's perspective, I *chose* to leave my wheelchair behind with no backup plan. I *chose* to keep my planner instead of a map that could get us closer to our goal. I *chose* to run off with—and trust—a stranger. I *chose* to fly off in the middle of the night after my previous choices led to some really bad things happening, including Rowan leaving the simulation.

When I think about it that way, it makes me look really fucking bad.

Fuck it.

I give my planner a kiss, then throw it at the creature's feet.

"Fine! You want it so bad, you can *have it!*" I shout. "Just help us! Give us the map, take the cursed book back, and take me back to the village!"

The creature picks up my planner and smiles.

"Well, well. What made you change your mind?" he asks, stroking the cover with his weird frog fingers.

"Because I *fucked up*, ok!" I shout. "I've been fucking up ever since I got here!"

"Go on," the creature says, which makes me even angrier.

"I made bad choices!" I shout. "Is that what you want to hear? I didn't want to be in that stupid chair, and I couldn't wait to get rid of it! I just wanted to get around without anyone helping me!"

"And…?" the creature says.

"But I *need* the help," I say, and then I break down crying. I'm on the floor now, dizzy and sobbing. "Whether I want it or not, I need the help. And people are happy to give it to me. And I keep pushing them away because I'm…"

I press my hands against the ground.

"Because I don't want it to be true. I don't want this to be my life. To rely on people pushing me, driving me, doing stuff for me. I want to be an adult."

"Both things can be true at the same time," the creature muses. "Do you think life is easy for me, with the head of a human and the body of a frog? How my fingers stick to the pages of my beloved books, ripping them apart? Yet still, I persevere. And I ask my wife for help."

I continue to cry on the floor.

"You feel like a child because you behave like one," the creature continues. "You do not feel like an adult because you do not think like one. The chair, the help, it is irrelevant. You do not take responsibility for your poor choices. Instead, you blame others."

I lie down on the floor. I hate that the creature is right. He has to be, right? Is this why I still feel like a child? Am I a child in an adult's body? I do blame other people a lot. He's not wrong about that. I blame the chair, I blame my mom, I blame my friends. When I do put the blame on myself, it's more of a pity-blame. *I fucked up, everyone's mad at me for being a fuck-up*, stuff like that. But I suppose I never *own* it. Never apologize, not really. I keep pushing the problem away from me, because it *can't* be me. I don't know how to live if it's *me* who's to blame. Because how do you get past that shame?

How do you peel yourself out of that swamp once you're in it?

"Ah," the creature says, looking me in the eye. "You see it now, don't you?"

"Just please, help us," I say. "Help…help *me*."

"I will deliver the map to your friends," he says, patting my planner. "And you have just helped yourself. Goodbye, Amara."

At first, I think he means *he's* leaving the cottage to go deliver the map, but I quickly realize he's talking about *me*. I feel tingly, like something's happening to my body beyond the usual POTS bullshit.

I'm sorry, everyone. I'm sorry, Nia.

I'm sorry, Mom.

The lights begin to dim. My senses are fading. I'm leaving the simulation behind.

CHAPTER TWENTY-FOUR
Elizatine

I wake up with my arm still strewn over Tanner's chest. Lana stares down at us with a wide, triumphant smirk on her face.

"See, what did I *tell* you?" she asks. "I don't understand why you two don't just get a room already. You're both young, but you're not getting any younger!"

I don't know what to say to that, so I just laugh. She's not wrong, but neither was Tanner. It's tempting to start focusing on the wrong things in here, but the truth is that we're here for individual healing. I don't know if relationships are meant to be a part of that.

I glance down at my rings to make sure Tanner's is

still on my thumb, which it is—but the broken tine on my new index finger ring is what gets my attention.

"Shit," I say, raising up my finger. "Amara's gone."

"Gone, like, not in her room?" Lana asks, but I think she knows the truth based on the look on my face.

"Gone from the simulation," I say. "She left while we were sleeping. We didn't even get to say goodbye."

I scramble to my feet, waking Tanner up in the process. I show him my ring, and it's all he needs in order to understand what happened. Sure enough, her room is empty and her planner is gone—and so is the cursed book.

"She must have gone somewhere," I say, taking note of the missing planner. "Maybe she met up with that stranger again. Gave him the planner. Maybe it was some sort of redemption. She could have used her wings out of guilt."

As I leave her room, I hear a familiar booming voice.

"Your map and your book."

The frog-man holds out a thick cardboard tube and the tightly-wrapped book.

"And Amara?" I ask.

"She's in a better place now," the creature says. He doesn't say it in a sinister way—it sounds genuine, encompassing more than her just leaving the simulation. That she's somewhere better mentally.

"Any chance you'll take the book now?" I ask, gesturing down at it. It's clear that the large coat, gloves, and shoes he wore during our previous encounter were to hide the fact that he's the book's intended recipient—the mysterious brother with the human head and frog body.

"Not a chance," the creature says. "I will see you in my home past the Beasteous Bog."

As the creature departs, I bring the map and book into Amara's abandoned room. I feel bad that I didn't even get to say goodbye—that she left so abruptly while most of us weren't feeling so kindly about her decisions.

"Alright," I say, spreading the map over a table along the wall in the room. "Let's see what we've got."

I laugh the moment I open the map because although there *are* notes scribbled in the margins like the creature said, they're unreadable—scribbled in what looks to be another language, or maybe it's just gibberish. Fair enough. The actual map is in tact, although the village names are similarly illegible.

"That must be the Beasteous Bog," Tanner says, pointing to a murky-looking area of the map that's not too far from our current village. There's a drawing of tall rubber boots next to it, so maybe we each need to pick up a pair. "Man. Look at those."

Depicted in the bog are three hideous creatures. It's difficult to make them out clearly, but one appears to be a large worm attached to a human-like figure's head, another human-like creature with an anteater snout, and a third that's fully a creature, complete with sharp-looking tentacles. Of course, there are no legible notes about these abominations on the map. We're going to have to figure out how to get past them ourselves.

"We should probably pick up some weapons, too," I say, eyeing the tentacled creature in particular. "We might need to cut off a few appendages."

We travel to the shop together, which I'm getting to know very well at this point. I pick up a long knife, Tanner gets a spear, and Lana opts for a small dagger. I wrap the knife's holder around my thigh, hoping it stays put. It looks kind of silly next to my tall rubber boots.

"Are we doing this?" I ask. We've been in this village for a couple of days now, and so much has happened even in that short amount of time. "Are we heading into the bog?"

"Why not?" Lana asks with a shrug. "It's not like we have anything better to do."

With that, we load the cursed book into Amara's freshly-emptied backpack and head down the unexplored path to our right. It's quiet. I suddenly miss Rowan's sassy quips from the back of the pack.

I walk close to Tanner, willing myself to not make it weird. Don't walk too close, don't try to breathe him in, don't try to slyly hold his hand. Don't think about him *that* way. Still, it's hard not to remember how good it felt to sleep in his arms, how good he smells despite us being in a simulation.

How close we are to our deal.

Not that I *want* Lana to exit the simulation before she's ready—but *damn*, what I would do for some alone time with Tanner…

Eventually, the air chills as the path leads to the Beasteous Bog. It's fearsomely quiet here. The trees are dead, the air is still; no scurrying around from little creatures in fallen leaves. Just a whole lot of eerie *nothing*.

I take the first step into the bog. The muck rises up to my calf, letting out a wet squelching sound as if I'd stepped on a decaying body. I shudder. Nasty. Tanner and Lana follow close behind, the three of us making the most God-awful sounds as we wade through the bog. It's a sea of pale-green moss and sludge that's difficult, but not impossible, to walk through. Up ahead and all around us is a thick fog; great for concealing the terrifying creatures we saw on the map, which is now jutting out of Tanner's backpack.

"This is revolting," I say as the fog thickens. My voice feels so loud in comparison to the absolute stillness around us, even with the sloshing of our feet in the mucky water. I can barely see in front of me, and it's getting harder to breathe.

"I dnn knw hw t—"

I can't talk.

There's something long emerging from my face, something taking over my lips and nose. I try to scream, but it sounds garbled. Whatever the thing is, it keeps growing longer and longer, lengthening until it stops just short of the bog water. Behind me, Lana shrieks as something slaps the water all around her, and Tanner yells as a shlurping sound envelops the air around him.

The fog clears, and we're left with sudden, horrifying clarity about the illustrations on the map.

The creatures don't live in the bog.

The creatures are us.

Tanner has an enormous worm protruding from the back of his neck, which reaches over the back of his head with its enormous maw clamped over the top of Tanner's skull. Blood dribbles down the sides of his face as the worm wiggles, its eyes human-like and wide as it consumes more of Tanner's face. Lana's arms and legs have turned into wet, slapping tentacles with barbed edges she can't seem to control, and her skin is turning purple. The barbed ends strike her all over her body, leaving bloody marks at every turn.

And then there's me.

At first, I think it's an elephant trunk that's protruding from my face and leaving me speechless, but it's too thin and rigid. It's as if my whole face has been brought forward, my eyes moved to the sides over my snout.

Like an anteater.

Leave it to TQI to turn me into a living vacuum; a creature that licks up as many bugs as it can all at once—just like me with the clothing.

A glutton.

"Mmm!" I shout, but it's useless. My mouth is contorted into a long snout, and it's impossible for me to form words. Tanner tries to pry the giant worm from his head, but it keeps wriggling down centimeter by centimeter. It's getting close to his eyes now.

"Mmm!" I shriek as one of Lana's barbed tentacles hits me. She's looking less human, her head becoming more gelatinous and blobby by the second.

I point forward urgently. We have to keep going. It's tempting to turn around, but there's no way this is going to last forever.

The only way out is through.

Using one eye and the rope Tanner keeps tied to the back of his backpack, I form a lasso of sorts and tie it around Lana's midsection. She strikes me with her tentacles again, and if my anteater face could cry, it damn well would. I hold on to the end of the rope with one hand, and I grab Tanner's arm with the other as the worm devours his eyes.

You're useless, a voice says.

The voice sounds disembodied and genderless, and I don't try to respond. It sounds like the kind of taunting that's used to break someone's resolve, get them to doubt everything. I don't believe the words right now. I'm literally leading my two friends through a bog as we suffer horrifying, beastial transformations. That's about as useful as I *could* be right now.

You couldn't save them.

I don't know exactly what this one means, but it pulls at something inside of me. Something tender, something that feels like a massive gut punch to the stomach. Still, I wade on, pulling Tanner and Lana behind me as they thrash against their own demons.

You'll never be loved.

I think about the way Tanner held me last night, the way Rowan sacrificed himself to keep me in the simulation, and I know that it's a lie. I'm a good person—or at least, I *try* to be. Being thicker than a Snicker hasn't stopped me yet, and it doesn't seem to be now either. I'm capable and competent.

Fuck *you*, disembodied bog voice.

For each taunt that it throws out, I have a valid counter. It's all I can do to keep going, leading my friends through the suffocating fog as the voice plays out every self-doubt I've probably thrust upon myself in this lifetime.

It's when I'm about to collapse from exhaustion—mental and physical—that the fog lifts.

We've made it to the other side.

I step out of the bog, and my long snout immediately begins to retract. Tanner steps next to me, and the worm begins to slide back up his face, exposing his mouth as he gasps for air. Within seconds, the beastly additions to our bodies have slithered away into nothingness.

"We made it," I gasp, holding Tanner tightly. He's standing completely still, looking at the space directly behind us where Lana should be. "Holy shit, we made it."

But Lana isn't behind us anymore.

CHAPTER TWENTY-FIVE

Lana

You're useless.

A hideous voice starts talking to me out here in the bog, and I can't help but listen. I'm barely in control. All these damn legs are thrashing about, hitting me, tearing up my skin like a dog shredding carpet. Poor Elizatine is trying to pull me through the fog, but I'm slipping out of the rope she tied around me as my body contorts into something I don't even recognize. Some kind of octopus, jellyfish, who the fuck knows what.

I *am* feeling pretty damn useless right now.

I can't talk. I don't even feel human. I feel completely out of control now, like I'm going to tear myself apart. Just writhing, choking, and clawing at the air when I don't even have any nails anymore. I want to grab, stand, do *something* to stop moving, but I'm like a slick pad of soap on the shower floor—one slippery motherfucker. There's no stopping me. I'm flailing like a tantruming child.

You always fuck up.

Well, now, *that's* a mean one. I didn't fuck up when I joined this program, did I? Except now that I'm turning into a creature, I'm starting to second-guess myself. I feel like someone must have told me this a lot because the sting is old, familiar; a wound that never quite healed.

You're a drunk.

So *what* if I am? I manage myself. I moderate. I drink just enough to keep the headaches and the shakes at bay. If I had the time and the resources, I'd quit, but it's just not in the cards for me right now. I have to keep going. In the meantime, I've got it under control.

You're a drunk.

Oh, *shut the fuck up*. If I was a drunk, I'd be stumbling around, flailing like an old weirdo on a street corner and yelling bullshit to the birds. You don't see me doing that.

You're an alcoholic.

I sputter in the bog as my body shortens into something squishy and slimy. I'm flailing even more now with nothing to grab hold of—the rope Elizatine wrapped around me slips over my dumb head, and I'm left in the middle of the bog with nothing. No support, no words, just pain.

Just reality.

My legs keep flailing even though I tell those slimy fuckers to cut it out. They have a mind of their own. I'm powerless against them.

I've never liked the term *alcoholic*. Reminds me too much of hooligan, with the "hol" and all. I knew plenty of alcoholics before, that much I can tell. I don't see how I can be one of them when I'm responsible with my drinking. Sure, I do think about drinking a lot, but it's *because* I'm responsible. I ain't getting shitfaced for no good reason. It's just to keep me stable until I quit, and I'll quit. I *know* I can quit.

You don't want to quit.

I feel like I'm drowning in a pool of mucus. My body's getting heavier, sinking below the surface of the bog. I'm gasping for air, desperate to grab hold of something, but my body keeps getting lower and lower under the mossy water.

The hell you *mean*, I don't *want* to quit? Of course, I want to quit. You think I like living like this, planning my whole life around when I can get a drink? It consumes me. It's all I think about sometimes. Of *course,* I want my life back.

Except I don't know what that would even look like.

A tentacle starts listening to me. I can move it where I want, so I push it down against the ground to keep myself from sinking any further.

It's hard to imagine my life without drinking. There's a certain comfort to the routine, to the sensations. What would I feel like without it? How would I deal with pain? Life's full of such exquisite pain. Ain't nothing else that dulls it quite like a stiff drink.

Keep going.

Another tentacle starts cooperating, and I put that one under me as well. The other arms and legs are still thrashing about, but at least I'm not getting any lower into this nasty-ass water. I can still breathe. I can't see Elizatine and Tanner anymore. I'm all alone out here now.

I've gotta save myself.

You're scared.

Well, no *shit*, Sherlock. Of course, I'm scared! I'm living life one step ahead of myself at all times, trying to balance this shit and manage my symptoms before they get real bad. It's a never-ending cycle. But a life without drinking, well, I can't imagine that either. Because what would I have left then?

You're going to die a drunk.

No, no. That's not right at all. How many times do I gotta say that I'm just treating the symptoms! I'm no frat boy. I'm just a human trying to numb their pain a little, take the edge off, keep things from getting worse. Bare minimum dosage.

You're going to die alone.

This one really strikes a nerve, chaotic and distressing like a thunderbolt hitting a school bus. In this moment, I really do feel like I'm going to die alone out here. Elizatine and Tanner can't save me. Shit, I'm not even sure I can save *myself*.

Is this whole thing some kind of metaphor, me sinking into the bog all alone? Is this what I've been doing to myself all along?

The bog water hits my mouth, and it tastes like alcohol. It keeps getting in my mouth because my tentacles are all flailing every which way again, and even though I don't want it, it's seeping in through every pore, filling me up like a balloon.

Is this how I die? Don't let this be how you die, Lana. This is terrible.

I close my eyes and let myself sink to the bottom of the bog. My tentacles go limp, and I hit the bottom like a big, useless sack of shit in an abyss of darkness.

I'm accepting my reality.

This has gotten way bigger than I can handle alone.

If I don't stop doing this shit, I'm going to die.

And I'm probably going to die alone.

My limp body rises back up in the water, and the water starts to move, pushing me forward a little. I don't fight it at all; I just let it take me forward. It pushes me all the way to the end of the bog where Elizatine and Tanner are standing, and then it disappears, leaving me to take my first step back onto solid ground.

I push my tentacles forward and step back on the path. The suckers and all the slippery, slimy stuff coming out of me starts to wiggle, writhe, and shrink until it's all gone, leaving me a weepy mess. Elizatine and Tanner run up and hug me together.

Just us three, a big happy family of broken addicts.

"It got me," I say. "It got *through* to me."

I'm too tired to say much else. The three of us keep walking in silence until we find the next little village. It looks about the same as the second one, except it's got those treehouses again. More importantly, there's a tavern.

Except I don't know if I even want to go in there.

"Elizatine, can you spare your boyfriend for a few minutes?" I ask. I like teasing them. Gives me something to do. "I wanna have a little heart-to-heart with him. Fellow alcoholic and all."

Elizatine doesn't smirk like I figure she would; she comes up and hugs me instead.

"We're losing people left and right," she says. "If we're about to lose you, too, I at least want to say goodbye."

She waves at me as I take off with Tanner, leading him by his arm to the tavern.

"A beer," I ask the sort-of human-looking bartender, and I slide him a credit. "Nothing for him."

I look Tanner in the eye, and he's watching me real concerned-like. He's handsome, all right. I can see why Elizatine likes him, although I think fourteen years might be a bit much. At least they're both adults.

"How'd you do it?" I ask him.

"Do what? Stop drinking?" he asks.

"Get sober."

He thinks for a minute.

"I can't really remember the specifics," Tanner says, "but I do remember hitting rock bottom. Something so bad that I couldn't lie to myself about what drinking was doing to me anymore. The *shame*, Lana—the shame hit like a tidal wave. When the detox ended and I had to face what I'd done, it almost took me out. But you learn to face it, to live with it. I can look at myself in mirrors again. Couldn't do that for a long time. The temptation to drink is still there," he continues, "but I'm strong enough to fight it now. To remember how fucking *bad* it got, how I never want to end up there again. In here, I've got you guys. I've got Elizatine. And I don't ever want her to see me like that, not even in a simulation. I told myself it can't happen again, and it won't. It *can't*."

I take a few long sips of my drink, which I'm suspecting might be my last.

"Well, Tanner," I say with a smile. "I'm Lana. I'm an alcoholic, and I need help."

My body starts to tingle, and it's not from the alcohol. I guess I finally hit rock bottom.

"You two—be good to each other," I say. "And goddamn, son, go *fuck that woman* already!"

I close my eyes as every fiber in me starts to lift, feeling fuzzy and light.

Consider me an enlightened woman.

CHAPTER TWENTY-SIX
Tanner

Elizatine comes into the bar and sees me sitting in silence, a half-consumed beer sitting across from me on the table.

Lana's gone.

"She finally admitted she's an alcoholic and needs help," I say.

"About damn time," Elizatine says, sighing with relief. "She must have gone through hell in the bog. Speaking of which, are we going to talk about that experience, or just pretend it never happened?"

I run my fingers over the area where the giant worm first latched on to my head. That hurt so fucking bad, having that thing clamping down and swallowing me whole. Couldn't see, couldn't breathe—an absolute nightmare of an existence.

God felt very far away in that moment.

"You looked hot as an aardvark," I joke. "Not that I could see you for very long."

"Anteater," she corrects. "And yeah, that was horrifying. Seeing that thing eat you, drain you like that."

"Just like my drinking," I admit.

Elizatine moves Lana's drink to a nearby table and sits down across from me.

"Well, look what we have here," she says, holding up her index finger. "Just T & E left. We made a deal, remember? Looks like it's meant to be."

"Even after seeing me get eaten by a worm?" I ask, because I'm still somewhat embarrassed about her seeing me that way.

"We've seen each other through our lowests, whether we remember them or not," she says. "I'm just glad you're okay."

We rise from the table at the same time.

"I want to tell you about something," I say, and I can feel the nerves bubbling up in my chest. I never thought I'd shed myself of the gift the witch gave me, but it's becoming too much. I need to finally tell Elizatine the truth. "Can we take a walk?"

"Of course," she says, putting a hand around my upper arm. "Let's do it."

We step outside and start walking through the village toward the path leading to the bog. We'll stop short of it, I'm sure. I'm not dying to go back in it again.

"The witch gave me a…power, I guess you could call it," I begin, and Elizatine nods. "If I talk about it, it goes away. I thought I was doing something important by using it, but really…it's killing me. It's too much for a single person to handle. I guess that's the lesson I was supposed to learn. Took me a while to learn it, but the bog really solidified it. I've been doing everyone a disservice."

I put my hand on her shoulder and draw her turmoil away for the last time. Her shoulders loosen, and the worry in her eyes softens. I'll miss being able to take that hard edge off of people, let them breathe a little.

But it's not my responsibility.

"I've been calming you guys down with a touch," I admit. "A hand on the shoulder, slap on the back, whatever it took. But the pain has to go somewhere, and all of it went into me."

Elizatine stops walking and grabs my hands when she realizes the enormity of what I've just admitted.

"So all those times that everything felt better all of a sudden—that was *you*," she says. "It was you in the clothing store. After Rowan. Shit, Tanner, how many times have you done this?"

"A lot," I admit. "More than I should have. I just hated to see you guys suffer. I thought I could handle the pain, that I was strong enough for it. And for a while,

I was, but—"

Elizatine looks surprisingly angry.

"Tanner, those feelings are important. It's fine that they're negative. It's the shitty spice of life! You stole from me," she says admonishingly, "even if it *was* garbage. That shouldn't have been your call. I needed to work through that stuff and feel the pain, and you gave me the easy way out instead."

Her face softens.

"But I understand. It's hard to see other people in pain. I wish I could take yours away like that. I tried once," she says, and her cheeks redden. "Didn't work. But the temptation was there, so I get it."

She squeezes my hands.

"How did you deal with our pain?"

"Well, remember those figurines Lana got from the dragon?" I ask. "I, uh, may have used mine to give myself the ability to silently scream. I needed a way to get the hurt out of me, and that seemed like the quickest way. You know, short of breaking my sobriety and drinking to dull the pain."

"When were you doing this screaming?" Elizatine asks, looking crestfallen.

"I'd trail behind you guys, turn around so no one could see. Go walk off by myself. Little moments."

"Well, I'm glad you're done with that," she says. She lets go of one of my hands, and we keep walking. The hand that's still holding mine feels cold. "You're right. That's too much for anyone to bear, even you."

"I kept praying," I say. "Praying the pain away, to be able to keep doing this. I should have listened sooner. I shouldn't have waited until now to stop. Now that it's just you and me, I want to be here for you without taking anything away. It's not my right. I just did it because I can't stand to see people suffer, but that doesn't make me a good person."

I feel tears well up in my eyes.

"I just want to be a good person."

Elizatine wraps me in her arms and lets me fall apart, my face buried in her neck and hair. The tears are dripping, unstoppable; they've been building up for days now after taking hit after hit emotionally. I start to sob, harder than I did when confronted with the demon in the mirror at Dalowego's. I fucked up in a big way, stealing people's emotions just to spare my own. It didn't even work out that way, anyway. I'm still in searing pain from the enormity of it, the crushing weight of everyone's suffering.

And this time, Elizatine is the one saving me from the worst of it.

"Tanner," she says, and I lift my head. She wipes my tears away and smiles. "It's the beauty after the storm. You made it through. Now comes the fun part."

She runs a hand through my hair, and my breath catches as she draws closer. Her lips are inches away from mine, but she hovers there, like she's waiting for something.

Waiting for *me*.

I tuck her long, white hair behind her ear and gently touch her chin, angling her face just a little higher so our lips are almost touching.

Be brave, T-Bone.

I bridge the distance and kiss her.

If kisses came with a fireworks show, this one would. I swear, my whole damn brain lights up as our lips meet. I'm alive again, with synapses firing that haven't fired in a long time. I can't fully convey what I'm feeling, although I'm certainly going to try. I kiss her deeply, with one hand on her lower back and the other in her hair. It's like we can't get close enough, no matter how hard we try.

Any desire to act like a gentleman is fading. My brain is taking a back seat, and the more primal urges are clawing their way to the forefront. I'm imagining me and her in bed, clothes coming off, her soft body under mine as I push deeper in a way that goes beyond kissing.

Whew.

"I guess it's time to finally get a room," I tell her with a wink.

CHAPTER TWENTY-SEVEN
Elizatine

We pause outside of the inn, taking each other in under the moonlight. Everything is about to change. Our whole dynamic.

Tanner steps closer to me.

"You ever wonder who's watching us at TQI?" he asks, reaching forward to stroke my hair. "What they'll see?"

"I hope they'll be discreet about it," I say, cringing a little at the thought. Oh, well. I'm sure it's nothing they haven't seen before.

For the first time since the simulation started, we both enter the front office of the inn to book a room.

Conveniently, there's only one room left with a single bed in it.

Oh, jeez. What a bummer.

I thought I would feel a little more nervous being left here with Tanner, but I just feel at peace. Like this is where I need to be. Maybe it's the pain of my real life getting some much-needed respite. Knowing how much pain Tanner has been carrying, too, it doesn't surprise me that we're the last ones here.

We're meant to do this together.

We go check out the room. It has pale stone walls, aged wood floors and ceiling beams, and beautiful double-arched windows. There's a large four-post bed with cozy white linens in the middle of the room.

Tanner pulls me close. I'm expecting to be ravaged imminently, but he pauses.

"You want to go touch some Laughing Flowers on purpose?" he asks with a boyish grin.

As much as I want to kiss him, I'd be lying if I said I wasn't nervous to take things further. Our dynamic has been so pure and sweet so far; part of me is scared to see it change.

"You bet," I say. He takes my hand, and we make our way back to the edge of the forest.

"Cheers," we say, clinking fingers together before reaching down to touch the forbidden purple flowers. Within seconds, I feel involuntary giggles starting to well up in my chest. They quickly become genuine when I see Tanner choking and sputtering over his own cackling, which only makes him laugh harder. It goes on and on like this as we walk back to the inn, laughing hysterically at each other and the fact that we're completely helpless to stop it.

"How long," I ask between giggles, "does this shit last?"

"Guess we'll find—" Tanner says, doubling over in laughter as the flowers overtake his speech. It's hilarious, overwhelming, and endearing all at the same time. If I weren't laughing so hard with tears streaming down my face, I'd kiss him. God, I've needed this. Something so fun and ridiculous that I forget about everything else for a while. Forget about the losses, the pain, the fear of what comes next.

For a moment, I can just bask in the best of it.

We collapse shoulder to shoulder in the hallway of the inn. I can hardly breathe, I'm laughing so hard. I lean my head against Tanner's shoulder, tears dripping down onto his sleeve. He glances up at the ceiling and wipes at his own eyes.

And then, he tilts my head toward his and kisses me.

Of course, it's hard to kiss him back when I'm giggling like an absolute fool. But I return the kiss eagerly, one hand wandering to his chest and the other to the back of his neck. We have to keep pausing to let the giggles out, but we seem to have our timing together. Kissing, laughing, kissing, laughing. Just pure magic.

If one of us ascends right now, I'm going to be

pissed.

I take Tanner's hand and lead him to our room. We're two cackling fiends, clinging to each other as we stumble to the bed. I push him down on the mattress and climb on top, careful not to put too much weight on him. This causes me to laugh again, and he uses the opportunity to roll me onto the bed and climb on top of *me*, pinning my wrists above my head. Why this is so fucking hilarious, I don't know, but the two of us can't stop laughing enough to escalate things further.

"I'm sorry…I can't," he says between laughs, doubling over again. "I can't stay hard like this. We've just gotta…laugh this out."

In the spirit of keeping things innocent a little longer, we climb into bed together and hold hands as the giggle fits consume us. Eventually, the lights dim, and we start to drift off as the laughter subsides.

Something tells me we're going to have a wild morning.

"Mornin', sunshine," Tanner says.

I squint up at him through the sunlight. Fuck, he's a vision. He took his shirt and pants off at some point last night, and I'm seeing his physique in full force for the first time.

I want him all over me—and *in* me—immediately.

"We're not laughing anymore," I remark. I can't help myself; I let my hands trail all over his bare, smooth chest.

"No, we are not," Tanner says, and then he climbs on top of me.

I thought our first time was going to be passionate love-making, but it's not. It's primal, headboard-splitting sex. The kind that's pure fun. There's no gentle introduction to each other's bodies, no tender kisses as we explore—no, we're just straight-up *fucking*. It's raw, desperate, eager. Overwhelming, but in the best way. Neither of us can get enough, so we go harder and faster until everything ends in its inevitable body-shaking, mind-melting conclusion.

There was way too much tension built up between us. We never stood a chance.

"Holy shit," I say, laying back in bed beside him. My legs are still shaking, and I feel like a sweaty mess. "Did that really just happen?"

"I hope so," he says, grinning from ear to ear as he props himself up on his elbow to watch me. "But I hate that we won't remember this. How good this was."

He has a point, one that I hadn't considered very thoroughly yet. We could have the grandest love story known to man in here, but the second the simulation ends—we're done for. There's no telling if our real selves would recognize our bond or even choose to pursue it.

"Then consider you and I real," I say, "and the end of the simulation our deaths."

I'm not ready to move on from Tanner. We've only just gotten started. I wish we could share more about ourselves, from our pasts; I don't want our experience to feel incomplete. Even still, I like it for what it is.

"We could just…*not* deliver the book," I suggest, biting my lower lip playfully. "Get a house. Live a life together. You heard what they said—that it could take *years* in here to learn our lessons. Maybe that's what we're supposed to do. Just live a happy life. Maybe we haven't had that yet in the real world."

"*Years* without a *phone*?" Tanner says jokingly, and it occurs to me how strange a life like that would be. "How would we *survive*?"

"Well, it's a simulation tailored to making us better," I say, "so there's no real danger here aside from our own minds. We'd figure it out."

"I don't know, Elizatine," he says, looking me up and down through the thin sheet that's only partially covering my body. "You're pretty dangerous, looking like that."

"You gonna do something about it?"

He groans.

"I'm forty-four," he reminds me teasingly. "I need at least an hour to recover."

"Great. Only fifty more minutes to go," I say, eyeing the anachronistic clock on the wall.

Without the rest of the group here, things feel more relaxed. There's no one to answer to. We could stay in this room all day if we felt like it. Why bother returning that book at all at this point? I feel so at peace with him, more warmth and joy than I think I've ever felt in my whole life. I'm not ready to get back to reality yet. I need to soak this all in, imprint it into my DNA; make it an experience that post-simulation Elizatine can't possibly forget.

"Oh, get over here," I say, giggling as I pull him toward me for another kiss. Our bodies press together, and I wrap my leg around his hip. "We have so much to catch up on."

We make out for a while, trading soft kisses for more in-depth ones as Tanner comes back to life. This time, the sex is how I imagined it—a slow, sensual climb up the ladder as our emotions stack together, overlapping one another. The gratitude for knowing one another; the relief in each other's company; the thrill of feeling each other's bodies melt like putty in the other's hands. It's more sensations than I know what to do with, so I channel them through my body and into his. We pass this energy back and forth, letting it grow until it consumes us—or maybe *we* consume *it*, but the end result is the same.

I got spectacularly fucked twice in a row, and I feel like a brand new woman.

"What's next?" I ask, and he groans.

"Elizatine. Please," he begs jokingly. "You're going to kill me."

"Not in *here*," I say with a snort. "Out *there*. The quest. Are we still going to deliver the book? I just...

I'm not ready for this to end," I continue, "and we don't know what happens once the quest is completed. If that would be the end for us."

He thinks for a moment.

"I say we still deliver the book," he says, "but we try to make the most of every minute. TQI could pull us out of here for anything, really, so let's just enjoy it for what it is. And for what it's worth, I hope it lasts a long time. I just can't get enough of you."

I giggle and give him a kiss. I know things are still early on based on our time in the simulation, but I knew him for *months* before this started—four days a week, six hours a day. Surely that counts for something.

Surely my subconscious is having a say in all of this.

With Lana's leftover credits, we technically have enough money to stay more nights—but as hard as it is, we decide to keep going. If we're going to potentially spend a long time in this simulation, it would be nice to be rid of this cursed book once and for all.

Now that we've passed all of the ominous obstacles on the map, we're met with the sight of the most beautiful meadow. It literally takes my breath away with how gorgeous it is. It's sun drenched and glowing, with smatterings of delicate flowers everywhere along the small path leading to a round, medieval-style cottage in the very center of a hill. A vast, looming mountain range is the mind-blowing backdrop for this scene, coupled with a dazzling blue sky and the fluffiest of clouds.

It looks like a painting.

I have no doubt this is where the man-frog creature lives. With Amara's backpack in hand, I knock on the front door. Sure enough, the no-good brother of the creature who tasked us with this mission answers the door. He seems pleased to see us.

"Thank you for coming all this way," he says. "Unfortunately, I must refuse delivery of the book."

"Why?" I ask, my heart sinking.

"Because I don't want it," he says. "It's a cursed book! Who would want *that*? Not even I, and I collect a great deal of things!"

He clicks his frog-fingers together.

"But I have a better deal for you. In exchange for keeping and guarding this book yourselves, you may have my home. It's far too sunny. I prefer to live elsewhere, closer to the bog."

"Are you implying we're going to be here for a while?" I ask, barely able to conceal the hopefulness from my voice. "In the simulation? Long enough to need a house?"

He clicks his fingers together again.

"That is entirely up to you."

Tanner and I glance at each other. I can't hold back my smile.

"This doesn't seem like a fair trade," I admit, "but thank you. We'll take good care of it."

"I am a simulation, after all," the creature says. This

might be the first time any of the creatures have acknowledged their artificial roles in our journey. "The book, the house, this entire world—it's all for you."

The creature hands me a set of thick keys and hops away from the doorway.

"You will not see me again. My job here is done, but you may see my sister. Keep her away from the book… lest she want it back."

The creature bids us farewell and hops away toward the mountains, disappearing from view. We step inside the cottage and are met with an incredible house—far too clean, tidy, and airy for the time period, but the kind of house I'd love to live in if I were back in real life. Everything is cozy. There are plush chairs, blankets, and pillows scattered around. The bedroom is very similar to the room at the inn; the same four-post bed with soft linen sheets. The kitchen—not that we need one—is stone-floored with wooden cabinetry and a large, arched entryway.

It's perfect.

"So we just live here now, huh?" Tanner says, a smile creeping over his handsome face.

"First thing's first," I say, and I take my Bag o'Junk and dump its entire contents out on the floor. As I do, I can feel my body shrink significantly; it makes my back feel so much better. "I won't need this thing again any time soon."

I change out of my usual attire and into a long, white linen dress. It feels fitting for the meadow. I want to traipse around like a little fairy, dancing through the grass with my storybook prince in the sun.

I take Tanner's hand and lead him outside. We explore all around the grounds together. It's not just a house the creature left us with; there's a small river cutting through the property that we're absolutely going to skinny-dip in later, tree swings, a set of iron rocking chairs facing the mountains, and an empty cave just a short hike up one of the mountains.

Most of all, it's so peaceful here. There's no one trying to get a hold of us, no one depending on us—it's just me and him, drinking it all in.

We collapse down in the thick meadow, feeling the dewy grass on our skin. They really spared no expense for the details. It's exquisite; in some ways, it's better than reality. The details are so crisp and vivid, it's nearly overwhelming.

"I'm not ready for real life just yet," I tell Tanner, snuggling up close to him. "I don't think it can top this."

"Neither am I," he admits. "I just…I can't imagine a life without this kind of peace. It's kind of like heaven, isn't it?"

I stroke his hair and face and watch as his expression melts. He's like putty in my hands now, this man.

"Our little piece of heaven," I say as I gaze into his beautiful blue eyes.

And then, the simulation ends.

CHAPTER TWENTY-EIGHT
Tanner

Beep! *Beep! Beep!*

I swat at my phone until the alarm turns off. Fuckin' annoying. I feel like I've been slapped over the head with a brick. Did I do it again? Did I get drunk off my ass last night in my boxers watching sports again?

Yeah, I sure did. I'm on my couch in my little studio apartment, ass half out as the TV blares an obnoxious commercial. Alone as ever. Beer cans everywhere, all over the floor, piled up by the recycling, plus a couple of fresh boxes by the door to get me through the weekend.

I have to go to work in an hour, but I feel the need to

clean this shit up before I head out. It's not like I'll have anyone over anytime soon, but this is pathetic.

Even I can see that.

I grab a trash bag out of the kitchen and start crushing cans with my foot. Ten, twenty, thirty—I lose count somewhere around there and just keep going. How do I have any muscles left, drinking like this? I've gotten a little fat. I should probably do something about that.

I haven't felt right in a while. It feels like something's missing, something huge. If I remembered this *thing*, I'd wake the fuck up and never be the same again. It's hitting me hard. Grief is weird, especially when you don't remember *what* you're grieving. Still, it's there, gnawing at me like a rat on a cord. This weird, quiet devastation that I just can't explain.

I finish picking up the beer cans and collapsing the cardboard boxes, and it leaves my apartment looking a whole lot better. I'd better mop; I've made the floor sticky with all this spilling and stomping. Do I even own a mop? Shit, I don't think I do. I grab some paper towels instead and get to work.

Speaking of work, that's where I'm headed next. My '9-5' as a 911 dispatcher. I work fucky hours. It's 5:00 p.m. now, and my shift starts at 6:00. I'm a call taker, and most of it is benign; Karens ratting out homeless people, follow-ups from police interactions, damaged infrastructure. Rarely is it the big stuff, the car crashes and the rapes and the murders, but *boy* do those fuck you up when they happen. I'm on "breaks" after that, where I pull calls from people needing to get up and take a piss or whatever. After that comes the graveyard hours, which are mercifully slow. When 6:00 a.m. hits, so do the calls about the old people who dropped dead in their sleep, the accidents on the way to work, all that shit. But by then, I'm long out of there. Off to go home, process any trauma I picked up along the way, and spend the day alone watching TV.

This isn't the life I want to be living. I had something better once, I'm sure of it. Something that mattered to me more than anything in the world. No matter how hard I try, I just can't remember.

But those calls where I can make a difference? Magic. That's the shit I live for. People I can talk away from a ledge, help staunch a wound, deliver an entire *baby*. Not many people can say they've done that. Until a couple of years ago, neither could I. I don't remember what got me into this line of work, but I do love it. It just takes a toll on me at the same time.

Work goes fine today, but I still have an old call on my mind. The one where I heard two teenagers gurgle to death on their own blood. I had to sit there and listen, trying to keep them calm while there was absolutely nothing I could do to save them. They haunt me. I can't even listen to the garbage disposal run now because a little bit of that timbre is there in the descent. It's in my head again tonight, and I'm fucking dying to crack open a cold one.

Well, a lukewarm one. I forgot to put them in the

fridge.

I sit down on the couch and turn on the TV, my one comfort. I should go to the gym instead. I've got a paunch going on from all this beer, plus all the hard stuff I've got in my barebones kitchen cabinets.

Instead, I get up and bring over a twelve-pack. This is the life. Just sitting here drinking, consuming, numbing the day away. A nice, big *fuck-you* to my liver. I've been meaning to get blood work done, but I don't know if I can face the music yet. Some days, I swear I'm looking a bit yellow in the eyes. I don't want to know how bad it's gotten.

So instead, I drink.

I crack one open out of habit, but I pause as it reaches my lips. Do I really want to do this, or has it become a compulsion? A punishment born of habit? There's no reason I can't set this down and go to the complex's gym instead. I'm not bound by law to drink this just because I've opened it, right? I can change my mind. I can do better. I can choose to do something that doesn't actively kill me.

I look at the piles of trash bags I cleared earlier. It scares me that all those beers went through my body. An average day is twelve, and a bad day is twenty-four. I'm no quitter; my completionist-ass will finish the whole damn pack every time.

I take a look at the beer in my hand. The crap on TV. Then I check my PTO on my phone, pack a bag, and dump the opened beer down the bathroom sink.

I don't know what's gotten in me today, but something's different. I don't want to live like this anymore, because this ain't living. This is stasis.

I might as well be dead.

I get in the car and follow my GPS to the closest rehab that will take me.

CHAPTER TWENTY-NINE
Elizatine

It's Father's Day.

Specifically, it's the first Father's Day since my dad died.

I thought I'd be okay. Really, I did. I saw the advertisements, the pictures showing daughters and fathers posing with big, cheerful smiles. Happy families. I took it in stride. I didn't click the "unsubscribe to Father's Day emails" option whenever I got an email about special deals.

But today, as the social media posts roll in, I feel numb.

I have the coupon on my phone. Twenty bucks off a

purchase of fifty or more at the local thrift chain. This is the day to go. I can get my hands on some clothes, take in the sights, get out of my head for a while. If there's anywhere that takes the pain away, it's the thrift store, where the possibilities are endless. You never know what you'll find. The landscape can change even while you're *in* the store as new items get put out. I found a Longchamp bag that way; it appeared like magic in the purse section on my second walk-through. Add an ice cream cone or a milkshake to the drive back and you've got yourself the perfect self-date.

No brother, no mother, no father. No boyfriend. Busy friends. I would reach out, but—surprise, surprise—they're with their fathers or their father-in-laws. Not me. I'm as single as a shower chair, no father figure in sight. Sitting in my apartment banging on spoons can only do so much. Once the creative thrill wears off, I feel the need to consume.

And I prefer to consume sick deals at the thrift store.

I get in my car and blast some music as I drive there. It's one part excitement, one part pit-in-my-stomach as I drive. I know I have enough stuff already, but at the same time, I can't get enough of the high. It's like the little click of a dog clicker—I'm trained to salivate and go searching for that little treat. I'm not into drugs and alcohol so much, but give me a store and I'll go on a bender. Even better if they sell vintage spoons. All bets are off.

Never mind that I have hundreds, maybe even

thousands of utensils in my apartment just waiting to be turned into jewelry—the thrill of the hunt trumps all.

I throw my purse over my shoulder and stride into the thrift store. The familiar stale smell comforts me, invites me in. This is my safe place. In here, I don't have to think about my dad dying from early-onset dementia. I don't have to think about losing my mom and baby brother in high school.

I can be free.

I browse the racks, taking in the sea of fabrics and textures. I hit every aisle, carefully examining all of the possibilities.

For some reason, nothing's sticking.

Don't get me wrong, it's still soothing. But nothing is ending up in my arms. It's a bizarre feeling, to have found nothing to buy despite liking plenty of what I've seen. Wrong, almost. I walk around a second time. As I do, there's something gnawing in the pit of my stomach, something other than the sense of dread I get about knowing I'm about to binge.

I feel full.

Not full in the sense of having a full stomach—I'm actually fairly hungry—but satiated of *stuff*. I'm realizing that the stuff I normally would have bought, I put back. The temptation wasn't there. Why is that?

Puzzled but proud of myself, I leave the thrift store.

It occurs to me that I haven't hit the library in a while, so I drive over there and browse around. I find a couple of romance novels I've been meaning to read, and I borrow them. Reading—that'll be good for me, eat up some of my free time. I've been meaning to catch up on my yearly reading goal anyway.

Looks like I start today.

CHAPTER THIRTY
Tanner

"Holy shit."

Beside me, Elizatine pats her body all over as the familiar landscape of the simulation returns.

"We were gone, weren't we?" I ask. Elizatine looks bewildered. "I was just in my apartment. I left for rehab—"

"I ditched thrift shopping to go to a library," she blurts. "Sorry, rehab?"

"Yeah," I say. "That wasn't how my rehab stint really happened, I don't think, but maybe what we just went through was some sort of test. Guess we're not quite done with the simulation yet, though. Not like the others."

"One hundred percent a test," she says. "It was the first Father's Day after my dad died. I—"

She pauses.

"Fuck. My dad died. They all died."

She hadn't remembered that before, and the realization must be hitting her like a sucker punch to the gut.

"I know," I say gently. "I remembered."

I hold her tight as she shrinks down a little, blindsided by the memories. I've remembered her backstory since the simulation began. I'm not sure why those memories remained when so many of my own are missing, but I never wanted her to know the truth. That's the kind of pain a person needs a break from once in a while. It felt like a kindness to keep it to myself, to spare her the needless suffering. She deserves a beautiful life, and keeping that shit to myself was a small way to give her some peace.

"Thank you for not telling me," she says. "I'm so glad I didn't know, at least for a little while. The weight of it is crushing."

"Of course," I say. "And apparently, I'm a 911 operator. I got a bit fucked up, too, from being on the other side of that—the emergencies. I'm sorry, Elizatine. I wish it didn't have to be this way."

We hold each other out there in the field for a while, stunned by our abrupt exits and returns from the simulation. Weirdly enough, this feels more like real life than the apartment and work simulation did. Maybe it's because I feel more alive here in general. The group brought that spark out of me, and Elizatine has kept it glowing.

There was nothing appealing about that life. I'm not at all eager to go back, yet maybe there's a way to rebuild. The willingness is there, at least. That's a start.

"We're so lucky," I say after a moment. "To have found one another. To feel this way. To be so happy, even if it ends up being short-lived. What you and I have will live on," I add tearfully, "even after this ends. We'll be a little glimmer of hope in each other's subconscious minds, a reminder of how incredible life can be. We'll never be apart. Isn't that beautiful?"

She nods. I wipe my tears and kiss her, because kissing Elizatine makes everything better in my opinion. We sink to the ground, kissing and holding one another, hoping TQI doesn't snatch us away again for another little side quest. What they've made here is akin to heaven. You're damn right I don't want to leave it behind.

"I'm not ready for this to end," she says, holding back a sob. "I've never been so happy in my life, Tanner. I know we're very different people, but it's like our souls understand each other. I don't want to lose that. Real life, or the illusion of it, felt so empty before this."

"Real life will be different," I say. "I think we'll recognize it in each other. How could we go through all of this and not feel it afterwards? I pray to God that we find each other out there, Elizatine, but in the meantime, this is us. This is our one guaranteed life together. No matter how short it is, let's make the most of it."

And we did.

We built a whole life together.

It's crazy to say that, knowing we've been living in a simulation and none of this is technically real. But to us, it's everything. It's an absurd sort of perfection, a peace too pure for words. The kind of life you pray for, yearn for, would give up everything to have. And in a way, we *did* give everything up. We gave up our memories, our pasts, pieces of who we were in exchange for what we might become.

I worried we might be lonely as the only two humans in this world, but TQI didn't leave us hanging. More creatures came. First, they only flitted around in the background, living their own lives. After a while, they started asking us for favors and making small talk. Their backstories were surprisingly rich and human, with goals, desires, and some hilarious long-held grudges.

You would think it'd be easy to ignore the creatures, knowing they aren't real. But when a tiny dachshund-frog rolls up to your door with a pleading look in its eyes because the roof of its house is falling apart, you go over and you fix the damn roof. You have them over, have conversations about the goings-on around the village, and let them teach you things.

One of the Groakes started painting rocks with Elizatine, and it's turned into a whole thing around the village. Every Friday, we all get together in the center of the village and make art together. Elizatine has really taken to painting in general over the last few years, so our once-bare house is colorful and alive now. There are painted rocks all along the ground outside of our house, her paintings hang up all along the walls, and gifts from the creatures decorate our flat surfaces. She even painted the dragon along the back wall of our house, and she made sure to include little cartoon drawings of her and Rowan being snatched up in the dragon's fists.

Seeing all of the things she's made over the years makes me smile. As for me, I'm always down to do favors. I've helped rebuild countless houses and buildings. The deer-frogs in particular have a hard time assembling things, and I'm always happy to help. They chat about their friends, things they've seen in the forest, and I tell them about our four friends that left the simulation. Once a month, we have some of the creatures over to our house. We spread blankets out in the field, and the creatures tell us new stories that we haven't heard before. No doubt generated by some kind of AI, but entertaining all the same. They tell their stories with such humanity and sincerity, it's hard *not* to believe it's real.

And when they started having babies, well, that got Elizatine and me thinking.

Unfortunately, that's the one thing the simulation didn't provide—a mechanism for having kids, but maybe it's just as well that we got to focus solely on ourselves and on each other. Still, the idea of a little baby that's half her, half me didn't sound terrible.

I think I was meant to be a dad.

It's never lonely here. Elizatine and I keep busy, not relying on the other to entertain us at all times. Elizatine still makes her silverware jewelry; I would say it's become her job over the past five years. The creatures bring her spoons and commission her, and she jumps for joy every single time they do. It makes my heart melt, her unwavering enthusiasm. She locks in when she's making her rings, and she does such a precise, beautiful job. She's known far and wide for her abilities, and her spoon rings have reached the villages past the bog and the Trembling Forest. We traveled there, once, through the bog with bags and bags of them. We weren't transformed into creatures this time, and her spoon rings sold well. We've never had to worry about money much.

Elizatine buys things every now and then, but she prefers to be home working or spending time together with me; shopping faded away into the background a long time ago.

I love that she gets to do the thing she loves—*me*—

and also make her jewelry.

In all seriousness, we've built a lovely life together. It's cozy, calm, full of love. None of the negative shit that plagues the outside world. No booze, no scrambling to pay for rent, no long hours. The negative temptations are far and few between. Sitting outside our house, taking in the stunning view together with our cups of coffee and the distant sounds of creatures singing and playing lutes together—you can't tell me this place isn't heaven.

Today, we're out in the field. We try to come out here as much as possible and lay down in the grass, talk about our week so far. The weather is always perfect. The grass is always green, and it rarely rains. Today is one of those rare rainy days, so I take Elizatine by the hand and lead her back to our house, passing through the kitchen and straight to the bedroom. We jump into the bed and continue our very important work of kissing and groping one another until, just as things are really starting to heat up, there's a loud knock at the door.

Elizatine and I look at each other worriedly. I pull up my pants, and she slips on a dress before we walk hand-in-hand to the door.

This could be it. This could be the end already, the arrival of our digital deaths.

I brace myself and open the door.

"Congratulations," Lana says. Rowan, Amara, and Felix stand behind her. "It looks like you two finally fucked."

I stand in the doorway, mouth agape as the group piles into our kitchen, looking around at all of our decorations. It's just like old times, except so much has changed since we last saw them.

I'm not sure they understand that.

"What are you guys doing here?" Elizatine ask after a moment. I flee the room to go put a shirt on. "I thought you left the simulation."

"You tell me," I hear Rowan say from the kitchen. "One minute, I was saving your ass. Next minute, I'm seeing…this."

"Wow. You've been living here a while," Lana says, probably looking around at our decorations. "It's cute."

"I'm sorry I went off without telling you guys," Amara says. "I didn't even get to say goodbye."

"Hey, I had to leave here looking at *his* ugly mug," Lana says, referring to me. "No offense, Elizatine."

I'm back in the room by this point, and I take Elizatine's hand.

"Yeah, I'm confused," Felix says. "Can you guys catch me up on everything, or…?"

Recounting all of the events that happened after Felix left takes a while, but we hammer him with the details until he begs for mercy.

"I didn't get the girl," Felix jokes, looking at Elizatine. "Damn."

Damn *right*, he didn't get the girl.

"You know, there are two other girls here as well,"

Amara says.

"Too old for *you*, and too old for *me*," Felix says with a shrug, gesturing at Lana. "Goldilocks kind of situation, I guess."

I stand in stunned silence for a moment as everyone keeps talking around me. I wasn't expecting this today—or at all. I never thought I'd see the other group members again; at least, not within the simulation.

"So that guy who kidnapped Amara just…gave you a house?" Rowan asks. "Wow. Must be nice."

I clear my throat.

"I know we don't look any older," I say, "but you guys haven't asked how long we've been here."

"A month," Lana guesses.

"Ten minutes," Rowan mutters.

"A year?" Amara offers.

"Ten *years*," Elizatine and I say in unison, and the room falls silent.

"Ten…years? Child, that sounds like a *nightmare*," Lana says, throwing her hands up. "Ten years of little creatures and dragons and shit? That *bog*?! Hell. No."

Rowan has a look of defeat on his face, which I feel a little bad about. We weren't the closest, but we did bond a little back then. I know he's been through a lot, and he had a thing for Elizatine, too.

But he's just not the right guy. To him, it's been a week at most of getting to know Elizatine—for me, it's been a week and *ten years*. Ten years of discussions about hopes and dreams, of laughter, of tough conversations, of getting to know one another in the closest ways possible.

There's no competing with that.

"Do you guys have kids?" Amara asks. Asking the important questions.

"No," Elizatine says. "I would have liked to, but it doesn't seem possible here. We do have a pet, though!" she adds, and I grin as she goes out back to let our dear friend back in. From outside runs Amara's old Abloosh, who nearly tackles her from her chair onto the ground.

"Nia!" Amara screams, and Elizatine and I exchange a gleeful look. We never thought we'd see them reunited; we thought taking Nia in six years ago was the closest we'd ever get. Nia has been the best pet we could ask for. Very clean and intelligent; we even ride her around sometimes if we're feeling particularly lazy.

I didn't take the creatures very seriously at first, but I've come to appreciate them and their quirks. Their designs crack me up sometimes, but they have big hearts and even bigger personalities. Nia is no exception. She's skittish, sure, but an absolute sweetheart. I can see why Amara grew so attached to her in the short amount of time they had together.

Nia lowers her body and Amara climbs on, and the pair dash out the back door and into the field behind us. I watch them frolic into the distance like old times, Amara giggling all the way.

"Whoa," Felix says. "A giant raccoon-axolotl…

thing. Nice."

"You missed a lot, Felix," Elizatine says. "Basically everything."

"I'm just *that* mentally healthy, you guys," Felix says. "Minimal intervention for *this* guy!"

Of course, the biggest question about this whole situation is still lingering in the air.

"So why are you all here, then?" I ask, and Felix shrugs.

"No idea. We just sort of…appeared. At your door. Literally seconds before this, I was hitting on Elizatine."

Lana slaps the table and laughs.

"You know what I just thought of?" she says. "This simulation's gotta be almost over, and you two've been together for ten years. I've done wedding vows before. You two should get married before this ends—before we all, you know, expire. Look, she's got the white dress on and everything."

I'm wearing a black long-sleeved shirt, and Elizatine looks radiant as always in her favorite white dress. It's not the craziest suggestion I've ever heard, and Elizatine doesn't look horrified by it either.

I would love to call her my wife.

"What, right now?" Elizatine asks with an eager grin.

"Yes, right now!" Lana says. Rowan walks out of the front door. "We could be yanked out of here any damn second! There's no time to waste!"

Lana ushers us out to our beautiful meadow, where

Amara and Nia are admiring the golden-hour sunlight glittering across the trees.

"Stand here, you two," she says, centering us so that the sun shines between us like an explosion. "Damn it, no ring. Oh well, we'll make do without."

"*Yes*, ring," Rowan says behind us. He holds out something—a sparkling ring that looks like it came straight from a dragon hoard. "This, and a couple other things, got stuck in my boots in the dragon's lair when we were sorting shit. I *swear* I didn't steal it!" he adds, and for some reason I believe him. "But I've had it ever since, and I figured I might as well hang on to it. Seems like you guys need it more than I do."

He hands the ring to me and gives me a nod, like he's not going to hold it against me that I'm marrying his crush.

Lana tells us to hold hands.

"Elizatine, do you take Tanner to be your lawfully... *ish* wedded husband, to love, honor, cherish, and have lots of sex with?"

"I do," she says with a snort of laughter.

"Tanner, do you take Elizatine to be your pseudo-lawfully wedded wife, to love, honor, cherish, and rub her feet whenever she asks?"

"I do," I say, staring into Elizatine's eyes—the most beautiful eyes—unable to focus on anything else.

"Well, good," Lana says. "Because by the power I'm vesting in my *own* damn self, I now pronounce you husband and wife! Kiss! *Kiss!*"

I slide the slightly-too-big ring on Elizatine's finger and pull her in for a kiss. We've kissed hundreds, maybe thousands of times at this point, but it's just as magical and pulse-pounding as ever. I'm grateful that our love was witnessed by others, and I pray that it stays in their hearts. That what we had here lives on in reality, even when our simulated time is up.

And I do fear it's finally up.

"We never delivered the book," I admit to the group. "The frog-man refused it, told us to keep it away from his sister. It's been in a drawer in the kitchen ever since."

"Well, why didn't you give it back?" Felix asks with a shrug.

"We were worried the simulation would end when we did," Elizatine says, "and we weren't ready for it to end."

"But are you ready *now*?" Rowan asks.

"Hell no," I say, grabbing for my wife. My *wife*. She giggles. "But with all of you here, well, maybe it's time. Maybe this is how it's meant to end. The six of us, finally seeing this thing through."

I hate the idea of our world ending, but I can't deny that it would be an appropriate conclusion. I could just see a TQI employee looking very pleased with themselves for having thought it up. One last hurrah, one last quest.

"Now that we've got you two married," Lana says, "it's time to accept the fact that we're all probably about to die."

Elizatine and I have had many discussions about this before. How leaving here will mark our deaths, how our lives together in the simulation were real and have meaning. But I've never been ready for that day to arrive. I could do this damn near forever. Like I said, this is the closest thing to heaven that I could ever imagine.

"So let's have a funeral," I say, and I'm not joking. "Eulogize ourselves. Give all of this some meaning before it's taken away."

"Damn, you guys really *have* been in here a long time," Felix says. "I'm just ready to go get some McDonald's when this is all over."

"To Felix," Elizatine says jokingly. "To quitting his family band and eating McDonald's!"

"To Felix!" a few of us repeat. Rowan looks skeptical, and Amara is distracted by Nia.

"Amara," I say, and she turns and looks at us. "You were brave, trusting, and gave everything your all. I hope you're proud of yourself. What do you want to do when you get out of here?"

Amara thinks for a moment.

"Hug my mom and tell her I'm sorry," she says. "I've been…difficult. I think I took out my resentments about the chair on her, even though she's just trying to help. I don't want to resent people for helping me anymore. It's not fair to them."

"Lana," Elizatine says. "You're a bad-ass bitch, you know that? You cracked me up. You have so much fire and spunk in you. Never lose that, ok? I'm so proud of you for saving the village, for moving literal fire and water to stop that Fuzznado."

"If I stopped drinking, I'd be damn near unstoppable," she says. "That's my dream for out there. I want to clean myself up like you did, Tanner, and go live a good life. The circus people said I have kids. I'd like to see them again, too."

"Rowan," I say, and he won't look me in the eye. "We've been through some shit, man. I haven't forgotten. It's as fresh as if it happened yesterday. The pain you've been through, the blame you've placed on yourself—you don't deserve it. You really stepped up here, grew, learned about yourself."

"Without your sacrifice, none of this would have been possible," Elizatine says, looking a little misty-eyed. "I can't thank you enough. You allowed me to live a beautiful life here. You're capable of so much good, Rowan, because you're a good person. Never forget that."

"Thanks, guys," Rowan says, still looking down but definitely receiving the message. He purses his lips.

"You're not the worst yourself, Tanner," Rowan says. "You're a good guy, through and through. You pulled yourself together when things started slipping, and still found a way to help out the rest of us."

"You guys had no way of knowing this," Elizatine says, "but the power he got from the witch at the beginning of the simulation? He could take away our suffering by touching us. So if you ever got a pat on the back from him and suddenly felt better, well, that's why. He took our pain into his own body and felt all of it for us. That power's gone now, don't worry," she says as Rowan jokingly extends his hand toward me. "Telling me about his power got rid of it. He wasn't allowed to talk about it. But what he did allowed us all to focus on getting better, and I think we owe him a big thanks for that."

"Yeah, that explains some things," Rowan says, and Lana nods. "Too bad you can't be bottled up and sold as an antidepressant, Tanner. I'd be on you for sure."

Rowan clears his throat.

"Elizatine," Rowan says. "I don't know how to put it into words, exactly, but thank you. Thank you for making me feel seen, for being there for me. There's something about you that's comforting, where you helped me feel like I belong."

"Agreed," Amara says. She's sitting on the floor, stroking Nia's fur. "I thought you didn't like me at first, but I was wrong. You're very kind. You got me through the bazaar, and you saved me from the book. You're a helper."

"With some sick-ass hair," Lana interjects.

"And you saved me," Rowan says. "That was pretty cool."

"Elizatine," I say, and she looks at me lovingly. My *wife*. I know it's not in any official capacity, but it just feels right. Boyfriend and girlfriend never felt like adequate words for us anyway; it felt too childish, too simplistic for what we've become. "No matter what happens next, know that I have loved you as deeply as I could ever love another person. You're the light of my life. When I first saw you, I knew you were a good person. I just didn't know I'd have the privilege to discover just how good a person you are. To see your creativity, your kindness, your compassion come through each and every day. Every moment of this has felt real with you. Thank you. Something tells me I will never, ever forget you."

Elizatine smiles tearfully. The rest of the group is watching us in silence.

"Tanner," she says, and my heart skips a beat just hearing her say my name. "My dear husband. My partner in crime, my best friend. I can't imagine a life without you. Thankfully, we've lived one—a short one, maybe, but a good one—together for the last ten years. Our time together will live on, buried deep within us. Keep us company in the dark moments, get us through whatever real life throws at us.

"May we become food for the worms of our subconscious minds. We'll seek out the very best for ourselves because we've set the bar so high in here. How can anything else compete, really? The last ten years have been magical, Tanner, and I can't thank you enough for being my person. My rock. My calm. You're an incredible man. Kind, vulnerable, handsome as hell. I couldn't ask for anything more, and I wouldn't settle for anything less."

"Jesus, Lizza," Lana says. "Save some of these glowing eulogy words for the rest of us."

"We all kicked ass in here," Elizatine says, and I nod my head. "It's hard to put into words, but I think you all know that we're leaving here as different people than when we came in."

"So, if you guys are ready," I say, "let's go walk this book to our deaths."

To prepare for the journey, we get everyone some wading shoes before leading them into the Beasteous Bog. Elizatine and I haven't been here in ages. Going back the way we came still doesn't turn us into monsters, thankfully, so we're just left to wade through the muck and the fog as regular humans. The village beyond that, the one we spent a couple of days in earlier in our journey, is bustling with activity. Elizatine and I don't make it out here very often, but some of the creatures excitedly come over and talk to us, and we introduce them to our long-lost friends. Past that village is the Trembling Forest, when we're careful to avoid the flowers. Finally, we're back in the town where it all began, where Elizatine and I first laid under the stars together.

"Let's go to the tavern," I suggest, holding up the backpack with the book emphatically. "I get the feeling we'll find the sister there."

We pile around a free table just like old times, except Lana doesn't try to order anything. We just sit and wait, hoping that the sister with the human body and frog face will come and take back her cursed book once and for all.

But that's not what I want, not really. I want to stay here with Elizatine. I know we have to die eventually, but I always held out hope that we would get more time. I don't know if *any* amount of time would feel long enough, frankly, especially since we're not getting any older. We could continue this indefinitely, her and I, just appreciating each other and living a good life.

But it's time.

"Did you deliver the book?" a deep voice says. Sure enough, it's the creature who tasked us with delivering the book in the first place. "You have been very difficult to find."

"Your brother refused the delivery," I say. "We were…busy. Haven't been out this way in a while to give it back to you."

"You've kept me waiting a very long time," the creature says. "Why is that, do you think?"

"We were living our lives," Elizatine admits. "Beautifully, I might add. We didn't want it to end."

"And why would returning the book end it, do you think?" the creature asks.

"Well, it brings the quest full circle," I say. "Seems like it would be a fitting end."

"So do it, then," the creature says. "Give me the book."

I take the book out of my backpack and look at

Elizatine. She looks petrified, and I know I don't look much better. This can't be how it ends. Here, in a tavern miles and miles from home. I hoped it would happen while we slept or were out in the meadow. Peaceful, serene, not under duress.

I take my wife's hand and squeeze tightly as I hand the creature the cursed book. It takes the book in its hands and gulps.

"I should have let you keep it," the creature says with a sigh. "I don't want this dreadful thing."

The creature pauses, then looks at us expectantly.

"I have an offer for you. My brother, who lives past the Trembling Forest and the Beasteous Bog, is an avid collector of books. If you could deliver this book to him…"

"Fuck *no*," Lana says with a laugh, and the rest of us laugh along with her at the absurdity of the request. The creature smiles and sets the book down on the table.

"Then your time here is over. Well done, you six. Well done."

The creature bows, picks up the book again, and leaves the tavern as the lights begin to dim.

I pull Elizatine close as my body starts to tingle all over.

This is it. The moment we've been dreading has finally arrived.

"I love you," I tell her, tucking her hair behind her ear for the very last time. It's something I've done at least once a day since we got together. She says it makes her feel calm, loved. I'd do it all day if she asked me to.

"I love you, too," she tells me, running her hand along the side of my face. I'm going to miss this. I don't know if I'll ever find a love like ours again. "Goodbye, Tanner."

And as we kiss one final time, the world around us turns to noise, sensation beyond sensation, blurring into nothingness as we lovingly leave it behind.

CHAPTER THIRTY-ONE
Elizatine

"Elizatine?" a voice asks.

I open my eyes. I'm in the simulation room, still hooked up to all the nodes and needles. I look down at my body and notice my right hand is extended off of the bed, like I'm reaching for something. Similarly, Tanner's left hand is hanging from the side of his bed, like he's reaching for me.

I couldn't tell you why.

I swipe under my eyes as tears start to drip out. I'm not sure why I'm crying, but I clearly went through something intense in that simulation.

"You both started crying at the same time," Amara

says. She's sitting up, and a nurse is beginning to detach her from her equipment. "And moving your hands. You were the last two of us to wake up."

From the far end of the room, I catch our therapist studying me carefully. Maybe she's worried I'll remember something, but she has nothing to worry about. I feel the exact same as I did going into the simulation.

Well, *almost* the same.

There's a fullness there now that I can't explain. It's almost like I feel content, satiated. It's a foreign feeling for me, hard to put a finger on, but that's the best way I can think of to describe it.

Tanner opens his eyes and, like me, wipes tears away from his eyes.

"What, I'm the last one?" he asks as the rest of us stare at him. "Damn. I must have needed a lot of work done on me, then."

All of us are sitting up now, getting unhooked as the therapist comes around and checks on each of us. When it's my turn, I explain how I'm feeling—like myself, but full. She smiles and writes something down on her clipboard, then walks over to Tanner.

It's hard to imagine not seeing any of these people again. I've been in a room with them almost daily for two months, and I've enjoyed their company more than I'd ever expected for a group of strangers.

Once everyone is unhooked, they gather us in a room for one last hurrah before we're dismissed for good from the program. We take our seats in the usual

U-shape of chairs facing a whiteboard, with the therapist sitting at her corner desk in a rolling chair.

"How are we all feeling?" our therapist asks.

"Ashamed," Lana says, raising her hand after she speaks. It's a strange sight to see. She was always so quiet in the group sessions. She usually showed up to the sessions drunk, and you could barely get a word out of her. From what she *did* share, I know that Lana's husband was incredibly abusive and tore her down, but she kept drinking even after his death in order to cope with the pain. Her confidence never returned—at least, not until now. "Like I'm ready to turn my whole damn life around."

I hope my jaw isn't visibly dropping. She sounds so spirited and sure of herself. Like a whole new woman.

Tanner clears his throat.

"I, uh, I feel lighter," he says. "Like the shame isn't crushing me down so much anymore. Freer."

"Me too," Rowan says. "Less angry with myself. Calmer."

"I don't know how I feel," Amara says, clutching at her planner. She sets it down on the table beside her. "Maybe a little less frustrated. It's hard to say."

"I feel relieved," Felix says. "Like a big weight's off my shoulders. I think I know what I need to do next."

Everyone turns to look at me.

"I feel like an emptiness inside of me has been filled," I say. "That hollow space where I'd stuff clothes, food. It usually gnaws at me all of the time, but I don't feel it right now."

"Excellent," our therapist says. "It sounds like you all made incredible progress through the simulation. I wish I could share the details with you, but please know that I am so, so proud of each and every one of you. All of you had at least one major breakthrough. You would be surprised what you're capable of when you put your mind to it. Your teamwork really came through. No one was ever left behind."

"Did anyone hook up?" Felix asks, and I laugh. Of course he'd ask that.

"You *know* I'm not answering that one," our therapist says, but her cheeks redden just enough to betray her. I think about how my hand was reaching for Tanner's and wonder if it was us, which makes my own pale cheeks go absolutely crimson. I glance over at him, and he also happens to be looking over at me.

It *can't* be. There's no fucking way.

"You are all caring, competent, deserving people who are going to do great out there in the real world," our therapist continues, and the redness begins to dissipate. "Seriously. So proud. I gave you challenges, big ones, and you smashed them."

"Did anyone stay in there a long time?" Rowan asks.

"Well…yes, a couple of you spent a long time in there," she says, which was probably a mistake on her part. The last two of us to wake up in the procedure room were me and Tanner, so she's probably talking about us. Did we live a life together? Is that why we were crying and reaching for each other? "But the rest of you were done within a few days. And by days, of course, I mean minutes in real life. The whole procedure took about seven minutes for the entire group."

"Did I keep drinking, or did I quit?" Lana asks.

"I can't answer that," our therapist says, but again, her cheeks betray her slightly. "But you did great, Lana. I think you're on the right track now, darlin'."

Our therapist scoops up our folders full of past worksheets and notes and hands them out.

"For you guys to take home," she says. "Keep them. They're useful."

I clutch at mine and resist the urge to look over at Tanner. I can't explain it, but I feel like there's something nagging at me in my brain, something to do with him. Maybe we have some kind of bond from spending all that time in the simulation together, even if we're not meant to remember it.

Our therapist continues to praise us and wrap things up, but I'm distracted, too busy speculating in my mind to pay much attention. Finally, she claps her hands and smiles.

"Bye, everyone. I know you're going to live big, beautiful lives. Email me if you have any questions about anything we've covered these last couple of months."

With that, everyone stands up and starts getting ready to leave. We're talking to each other, making sure to say our goodbyes before we part ways forever. It's a strange feeling, knowing I won't see any of these people again. We've spent so much time together, we almost feel like family.

"Hey, Felix," I say as he strides over to me for a hug. We embrace briefly. "You ready to get back out there?"

"I think I'm going to quit the band," he says, which comes as no shock to me. It seemed like the obvious answer from the beginning. "Do my own thing. My fam's going to be pissed, but they'll understand. I just can't do it anymore, you know?"

"I have some idea of what you mean, yeah," I say, patting him on the shoulder. "I'll look you up on YouTube, Felix, when you're doing your solo shows. Proud of you."

Next comes Amara, who wheels herself over sheepishly.

"I don't know why, but I feel guilty," she says. "I must have done something in the simulation that hurt you. Whatever it is, I'm sorry."

"Oh, don't be," I say. I reach down and hug her. "I'm just glad to see you. Everything's going to be all right, Amara. You've got this."

She smiles and nods her head.

"Thank you, Elizatine."

Lana gives me a quick shoulder hug and grins.

"This must be weird for you guys, huh? Seeing me like this? It feels even weirder for *me*," she says. "Like old Lana just woke up after a deep sleep or something. I missed me. I hope you guys are where you want to be, too."

I walk over to Rowan, who's not talking to anyone else.

"Hey," I say. He's never been my favorite person in this group, but I feel like something's softened in both of us since the simulation. I'm actually a little sad to see him go. "You take care of yourself, Rowan."

He looks like he wants to ask me something, but he reaches out a hand instead. We shake hands awkwardly.

"You sure you don't want a hug?" I ask, chuckling a little.

"Yeah, I'll take a hug," he says.

I hug him tightly because I think he needs it. He seems to relax in my arms a bit, which is reassuring. Maybe some of his rough edges got worn down in there, made him a kinder person.

"Bye, Rowan," I say, and he waves as he leaves the room.

As everyone starts filing out, it's just me, Tanner, and the therapist left in the room.

"I'll be right back," the therapist says, cheeks red again as she excuses herself. She just confirmed my suspicions, and based on the expression on Tanner's face, he's probably thinking the same thing.

"Do you think you and I…?" I ask, pointing back and forth between the two of us.

"Yeah," he says, blushing. "The way her face keeps turning red, how I had you on my mind when I first woke up. Yeah, I'd say there was something there."

We stare at and study each other, as if seeing the other in a new light.

"I know this is kind of crazy," I say, "but should we exchange phone numbers?"

He looks at me for a long time, then reaches forward and hugs me.

"I don't think that would be a good idea," he says, patting me on the shoulder after he lets go. And it makes sense, really—I know how badly he wants to get back to his estranged wife and his two young daughters. "But thank you for everything. I'll always remember you."

"Likewise," I say, patting him back. My eyes water a little, even though I can't consciously understand why.

"Goodbye, Elizatine," he says, waving as he steps through the door.

"Goodbye, Tanner," I say, and I find myself standing in the room all by myself.

And then there's Elizatine. Death follows me closely, it seems. Dead baby brother from SIDS, dead mother from suicide, dead father from early onset dementia. I visited him every day in the memory care home toward the end, when I finally had to move him in there. I was still in my twenties, trying to juggle the struggles of my own life with managing all of his needs. It got to be too much.

I felt like I was drowning beneath the weight of it all. Each day was a crushing struggle, a rinse and repeat of the same actions. I had no life, no future. I felt guilty when my dad's death brought a taste of freedom along with it. I used that freedom to really ramp up the shopping as a coping mechanism, and that obviously worked out *great* after my boyfriend left. I've never blamed him for that. I'd leave too if I were in his shoes. Strangely enough, though, I don't feel the urge to get into a new relationship as strongly as I did before the simulation. There's a feeling of contentment there, like I found something fulfilling that can't be easily matched.

Tanner and I must have had a hell of a time in there. It's weird to imagine, but the more I think about it, the more I understand the appeal. He was a chill guy, at least while sober. Attentive. Good listener. Kind. All qualities that I like in a guy, although I didn't make that a priority in my last relationship.

Being alone has been hard, but it's probably good for me. It's more time to focus on my goals and dreams. I want to vend at some of the larger art festivals in the country, and in order to do that, I need to build up a huge inventory. This jewelry doesn't make itself. I have to hunch over it with my bad, bad posture and mold it into being, scorching it under a hot fire to make it bend to my will. I don't want to lose sight of my dream in the pursuit of comfort.

Somehow, I'd like them to become one and the same.

I walk out to my car, feeling numb but oddly at peace about things. I sit in the driver's seat and watch from my window as Amara stands up, hugs her mom, and gets in the car while her mom wrangles the wheelchair into the back of their van. I see Lana sitting in the car next to me, staring at her reflection in the mirror on the back of her sunshade. Felix, standing outside with a vape pen in his mouth waiting for his cousin to come pick him up. Rowan, crying in his car while he thinks no one could possibly be looking.

And then there's Tanner, staring at me through his window as he drives away in front of me.

If Tanner's meant to be, he'll find me. He knows the name of my jewelry business, my first and last name; I'm not worried about that. I don't know what we had together in the simulation, but something tells me it's not going to happen in the real world. He's got his family—the family he's been *so* desperate to reunite with since he got here. An amazing, patient wife who's supported him through their separation. Two sweet young daughters. I don't even know if I *want* to have kids. What I *do* want is to make my jewelry, travel the country, to be free. I know relatively little about his values, his political leanings. What if we were on opposite sides of that spectrum? Different views on social issues would be a no-go, I know that much. Despite knowing each other for several months, the vulnerability we all showed each other was forced and manufactured to achieve a goal.

No, there's probably no future there. And that's fine, because I've got a bright future of my own to look forward to—and I couldn't *be* more freakin' stoked about it.

I put the car in reverse and pull out of the parking lot. Chances are that I'll never be back here at TQI again, and leaving it behind feels bittersweet. My plan was to hit the thrift store after this to celebrate, but as I drive past it, the temptation is low—nearly zero—and I decide to skip it. That was the whole point of this experience; to get to a point where I could control myself, to say *no*.

And I just did.

And as I drive off into the sunset toward my apartment, I know deep in my silly little heart that I'm going to be okay.

ACKNOWLEDGEMENTS

I have a lot of people to thank for supporting me through publishing So Far Away!

Editing: Hannah of English Proper Editing, Kate of Bitch'n Books Editorial (first chapter)

Beta Readers: Rosemary of Heartfelt Editing, Melissa of Lthatswhatsheread

Developmental: Kenneth of Red Line Editing, Casie Bazay

Proofreading: Charlotte Ross, Rosemary of Heartfelt Editing

Cherished Supporters (Instagram handles): @cocobearcustom, @jwrose_author, @dame_rho, @akaywrites, @_rhitheartist_, @mmellon12, @amber.maren.writes, @caitlinrose.writes, @heartfeltediting, @englishpropereditingservices, @chapter_and_a_cup, @author_deepika.k.m, @rmstalderauthor, @justbookishchaos, @lthatswhatsheread, @mybookishdelight_, @tashiescorner, @workinonmybookness, @charlierose1416, @bookishbrunetti, @dumbluckco_vintage, @tracyavery.books, @books.with.s.a.m, @bluesaturn.art, @poemsfromaloudmind, @maventhoria, @evelynnewt.author (among many others!)

• The Enchanted Grounds location in Highlands Ranch, Colorado, where I'd park myself for 4-5 hours at a time to write

• My family for putting up with my long writing sessions

• And finally, to the brave individuals I attended group therapy with—I'm so proud of you all!

THE ARTISTS

By @bluesaturn.art

By @winter_illusts

By @justbookishchaos

By Kat Mellon

By @dominiique.art

By Kat Mellon

By @justbookishchaos

By Red's Digital Designs

By Kat Mellon

ABOUT THE AUTHOR

My name is Kat, and I earned a Bachelor's Degree in English from the University of New Mexico in 2012 and self-published several works as a teenager. Like the characters in my novel, I too face struggles relating to chronic illnesses, anxiety, and depression—and I've attended group therapy! When I'm not writing, I design book covers for independently-published authors, sing to myself in the grocery store, and enjoy collecting purses and dolls.

www.ingramcontent.com/pod-product-compliance
Ingram Content Group UK Ltd.
Pitfield, Milton Keynes, MK11 3LW, UK
UKHW041945230426
12048UKWH00008B/153